THE PUSHERMAN

PINTER P.I. SERIES
BOOK 3

LISA BOYLE

The Pusherman

Copyright © 2025 by Lisa Boyle. All rights reserved.

This novel is a work of fiction. Any references to historical events, real people, or real places are used fictitiously. Unless otherwise mentioned in the Author's Note, names, characters, and events are products of the author's imagination, and any resemblance to actual events, places, or persons, living or dead, is entirely coincidental. This book was written in its entirety by a human and has no AI content. No part of this book may be reproduced in any form or by any electronic or mechanical means, including information storage and retrieval systems, without written permission from the author, except for the use of brief quotations in a book review.

ISBN: 979-8-9916169-0-4 (Ebook)

ISBN: 979-8-9916169-1-1 (Paperback)

Copy Editor/Proofreader: Constance Renfrow

Cover Designer: Rafael Andres

[1]

ROBIN

Sweat dripped down Robin's temple as she drew her knees into her chest. This was worse than before.

She watched the ceiling fan wobble as it went around and around on the highest setting. The windows were open, too, and it was only the first week of June, but still she felt no relief from the heat. It pressed on her from all sides, and yet, her body shivered.

She tried to breathe in through her nose and out through her mouth like she'd been taught playing high school basketball. But the pain was becoming unbearable. Like a knife through her stomach, twisting and turning her insides. She let out a sob.

Robin thought about calling an ambulance and then about how useless that would be. Just last week at the rodeo, Sam Sutherland had been tossed from a bull. Knocked out cold and stepped on twice. The reservation hospital's ambulance showed up two hours late, after Sam's father had already driven him to the hospital.

Sam's had been a life-threatening injury and Robin's

wasn't. Or maybe it was. How was she supposed to know? She tried to tell herself that it felt like the pain from last time. That maybe it was the same thing and, like the hospital had said, not that serious. But it *wasn't* like the pain from last time. This was different. Fear washed over her as she gritted her teeth and watched her little boy stack blocks on the carpet next to her. She needed to do *something*.

She should call her husband, Russel. Maybe he could leave work and take her to the hospital. It would take a long time, but at least she knew he would come.

Her little boy looked up and smiled at her. Robin bit her lip and tried to smile back. Maybe he was too young to understand that she was in pain and afraid. She hoped so.

The last time Robin had felt this much pain was when she'd given birth to him. She thought of that pain then—searing through her body as if it were about to rip her open—and she thought of the relief then, too. Oh, the relief.

The peyote. There was more of it, somewhere. Where had she put it? She closed her eyes. The jar. The jar in the cabinet second from the refrigerator. She craned her neck as she gazed at the kitchen. At the phone in there.

Would Russel even be able to leave work? Could they afford for him to? Would he be angry? Would his boss be angry?

Robin swiveled her legs around so they hung off the side of the couch. She wrapped one arm around her midsection, and with the other, she tried to gingerly push herself into a sitting position.

Black spots danced in front of her eyes and she blinked a few times to try to make them go away. Her stomach roiled but she didn't vomit. If she could just get to the kitchen. To the phone. Another sob escaped her lips.

This time, her son looked at her with his little eyebrows knitted together. "Amá?"

Breathe in, Robin told herself. *Breathe out.* She smiled at him. "Amá is okay," she said.

She looked to the kitchen. Maybe six steps away. She could do this. She stood slowly, took one step at a time. When she got to the counter, she steadied herself. Closed her eyes for a moment. She opened the cabinet and tried to focus on the jar and not on how the room seemed to spin. She unscrewed the lid with shaky hands, popped a sliver of peyote button into her mouth, and chewed. The relief would come soon. She breathed.

[2]

JAMES

WHEN JAMES PINTER was a younger man—in love and engaged—he had tried to save up for the big wedding his bride-to-be wanted. A fancy cake. A ballroom. Flowers and a band and lots of alcohol. But that wedding never happened. When James was home from his Vietnam tours, the last thing he wanted to do was listen to wedding bands. Dorothy grew tired of waiting and James never became a husband. Until now.

This wedding was nothing like the one he had braced himself for all those years ago. It was small. Simple. Traditional. At least for the Navajo, which was what his new wife, Kay, was. James wasn't exactly sure of all the things that made it "traditional." There was a lot of attention paid to which direction they were facing, and at one point James and Kay washed each other's hands. James's favorite part was that he got to ride in on a horse at sunset. The hero of the day. Ready to sweep Kay off her feet.

James knew what *wasn't* traditional about the wedding. The fact that his fifteen-year-old daughter, Molly, was there.

The fact that it was Kay's second marriage. The fact that neither one of them had parents alive to be involved. But Wayne and Barbara had gladly stepped in, along with Kay's friends from the school—the principal, an English teacher, an algebra teacher. James thought it turned out to be quite a nice day.

That wedding had been a few months ago. Now, he sat on the end of the couch, Kay leaning against him, feet on the cushion beside her, legs up and bent at the knees. Molly rested against her legs, her hair draped in Kay's lap as Kay braided it. The dog—the mutt, Private—lay on the rug beside them. They were listening to one of Molly's records, and Kay sang along softly.

"You know this song?" James asked her.

"Sure," Kay said. "Don't you know Rush? They're a good band."

"She's cooler than you, Dad," Molly said.

"I guess so," James said. Then, there was a knock at the door.

Molly squealed. "Oh! That's Paula!"

"Wait!" Kay demanded. "I'm almost done."

She did a couple more over-unders and tied the braid off with a hair band.

"Come in, Paula!" James shouted.

Paula swung the door open. "What's this? Family cuddle time?" She made a disgusted face, and Molly leaped off the couch and ran at her, wrapping her in a bear hug. Private stood and lazily wagged his tail, sniffing Paula's shoes.

"You know you want to join!" Molly cried.

Paula squeezed her back. "I will suffocate you, Molly Pinter."

Both girls giggled and then pulled back.

"What's the plan today, girls?" Kay asked, getting up from the couch.

"Grandma Beans is outside in the car. She's taking us to bingo." As a child, Paula hadn't been able to pronounce "Grandma Beatrice" and the nickname stuck.

Kay smiled and raised her eyebrows. "Bingo? Really?"

"Those old people are the best," Paula said. "They don't give two squirts anymore. They have the *best* gossip."

"I'm gonna grab my purse," Molly said, hurrying down the hallway.

"Plus," Paula went on. "Molly's . . ." She lowered her voice to a whisper, ". . . boyfriend . . ." She waggled her eyebrows, ". . . got a summer job at the senior center."

James straightened up. "Molly's *boyfriend*?" He didn't whisper.

"*Not* my boyfriend!" Molly yelled from her bedroom. Paula, though, grinned and nodded vigorously.

"The boy from the dance? I thought he was just your friend!" James yelled back.

When Molly returned, James thought her lips looked a little shinier and redder. She shoved Paula slightly.

"We *are* just friends."

Paula was still grinning. She winked at James. "See you later, Mr. P! Mrs. P!"

The girls hurried out the door, and James followed, calling after Molly, "Is that lipstick you're wearing?"

"Lip *gloss*, Mr. P," Paula replied, as she and Molly got into the car. James waved to Paula's grandmother in the driver's seat.

Molly stuck her head out the window. "It's just a little bit,

Dad. Love you!" She blew him a kiss, and the station wagon pulled away.

James sighed and went back inside. Kay was making tea in the kitchen. He sat down at the table. "Well. Seems like Molly's got a little fling going."

Kay turned to face him, one hand holding a mug of steaming tea, the other on her hip. She smirked.

"Ya think, Detective?"

"You knew?"

Kay shrugged. Picked the other mug up off the counter and brought it to him.

"There were clues. Little glances when he picked her up for the dance that gave her away."

James gripped the mug with both hands, hung his head between his arms, and chuckled. Then he raised his head again and looked at Kay.

"Guess sometimes dads just don't wanna know."

"She's almost sixteen," Kay said. "It was bound to happen."

James took a sip. "It's strange sometimes missing all those years. She was just a baby. A tiny thing. And now she's not. She's almost grown." He shook his head. "I missed all those in-between years, and I have only myself to blame. I was a damn idiot. Stubborn and stupid."

Kay put a hand on one of James's. "You have her now. You have us both. And maybe another little one soon. Who you *can* watch grow up." A smile crept onto her face. It was a little shy and sweet and it made James hungry for her.

"You're still sure about that?" he asked.

Kay laughed. "I'd say it's a little too late to ask me if I'm sure. I threw all those condoms away months ago."

"But you and Al didn't want a baby?"

"No," Kay said. She looked down at her tea. "But we tried anyway. At the very end. We thought it might save our marriage."

James was about to say that he was glad it didn't save their marriage, but Kay went on, "I did get pregnant. But I lost the baby before it was born." She still stared down into her mug.

James made his voice soft. "You never mentioned that."

"I know. I'm telling you now because it might happen again." She paused to look up at him. "That baby would have been five years old in July."

There were no tears in her eyes. Kay rarely cried and usually only when she was frustrated, James knew. But there was a deep sadness there. He scooted closer to her and held her face in his hands.

"I'm sorry," he said and kissed her lightly on the lips.

She smiled. "Maybe we can both get another chance."

He kissed her again. Longer this time. "I'd like that."

She kissed him next.

"Maybe right now?" he asked when he got a breath.

She smiled that smile and bit her lip again, and James was about to pick her up by the waist when the phone rang. He groaned.

"Hold that thought," he said. "Don't go anywhere."

"You got it, boss man."

He picked up the phone and cleared his throat. "This is James."

"James, it's Wayne."

"LT," James said. He looked at his watch. "Is it that time already?"

"Sure is," Wayne said. "She'll be at the station in thirty minutes."

"Copy that," James said.

He hung up the phone, went over to Kay, lifted her over his shoulder, and headed to the bedroom.

"Fifteen minutes, then," he muttered. "Before I gotta leave."

"Fifteen minutes?" Kay laughed.

"Girl," James said. "I don't need long."

[3]

WAYNE

THE CALL HAD COME in late the night before. The young woman had sounded shaken but resolute. She needed to report a suspicious death. Her friend Robin had died after Robin's husband, Russel, rushed her to the hospital three nights ago. The woman calling, Patricia, only learned of her friend's death when she showed up at Robin's house for their standing breakfast date on Saturday. She was in shock, but she was sure of one thing: She needed to report the events leading up to Robin's death.

Wayne asked Patricia to come to the station the next day so he could file an official report and hear why she was so convinced this was something the police needed to handle. But as soon as he got off the phone and mentioned the woman's full name to Barbara, he understood just how serious the situation must be. Patricia Dawes, Barbara told him, was the head of the Shiprock chapter of the group Women of All Red Nations, or WARN. WARN was not on the greatest terms with tribal law enforcement. The young women had a habit of stirring up frustrations on the reservation and had recently led a protest against the latest mining operation, resulting in fights and arrests.

Though Patricia had called late on Saturday night, Wayne knew it wasn't too late to call James and relay the few details he'd gathered regarding the potential new case.

Now, at the station, Wayne made coffee and set out some cookies, waiting for James. He'd expected James would arrive well before Patricia, but instead, the PI strode in with only minutes to spare and hung up his hat.

"Time got away from me, LT. Sorry about that."

The two men sat down. "So did this Patricia tell you what the hospital had to say about the woman's death?" James asked.

"Respiratory failure," Wayne said. "According to Patricia."

"What was she admitted for?" James asked.

"Patricia said Robin complained of intense stomach pain and a high fever to her husband, Russel. That's all she knew. We'll have to see if we can't get anything more out of the hospital."

Just then, the station's front door opened and the bell dinged. Wayne could hear the murmur of Officer Begaye's greeting and then two sets of footsteps coming down the hallway.

Wayne and James stood to greet the woman.

"Thanks for coming in," Wayne said, shaking her hand.

"Hi there, Patricia," James said next, extending his own hand. "My name's James Pinter. I'm a consultant here with tribal police. I understand you've got something to report."

Patricia nodded. She was young, no older than thirty, Wayne guessed, with a round, serious face. She wore jeans and a tucked-in T-shirt, her hair pulled into a low ponytail that fanned down her back. She sat in the chair Wayne pulled out for her.

"Do you mind if we record this?" Wayne asked, taking his own seat opposite her.

"That's fine." She waited until she was settled, her hands folded together in front of her, before speaking again. "My friend Robin Kinsel died on Wednesday evening at the Shiprock hospital. She was twenty-four years old and healthy. She had a baby boy." She took a long, shaky breath. "The woman at the hospital told me it could have been a handful of underlying things that killed her." Patricia shook her head. "Which I don't understand. Like I said, she was healthy."

She stared at her hands and her forehead wrinkled, and Wayne wondered if she was thinking deeply or just trying not to cry.

"Is that why you're reporting this?" James finally asked. "Because it seems unusual for a young, healthy woman to die so suddenly?"

Patricia shook her head. "I'm reporting it because she was threatened. Before she died. Someone messed up her car. They slashed her tires and spray-painted words on it."

"What words?" Wayne asked.

"On the hood it said, 'Watch your back' in English. On the driver's door it said, 'Yooch'iid' and on the passenger's door, 'Ana.'"

"Liar. Enemy or outsider," Wayne translated for James.

"At the time, I sort of suggested that she report it," Patricia went on. "But it was complicated. We'd been at the protest the night before, and Robin wasn't feeling very friendly toward law enforcement." She looked Wayne dead in the eye then. "None of us WARN members were, which is why *I* didn't report it at the time, either. We didn't expect to receive much help."

James jotted on his notepad as Patricia spoke. Wayne had not been one of the responding officers that night. It wasn't his district, and the Window Rock Chapter had been able to get the situation under control on their own.

"So, tell us what happened," James said. "When and where did she find the car?"

"She was with me. For our weekly Saturday breakfast date. Sometimes we go to Gallup or Farmington to a diner, but that week we just went to the deli up the street, grabbed some breakfast sandwiches, and went back to my house. I'd picked her up, so her car was at her house the whole time."

"Was anyone else home?" Wayne asked.

"I don't think so. I think Russel took the baby to his parents' house. Anyway, he wasn't there when we got back."

"And that's when she saw it?" James asked.

"Yes."

"Are you sure it hadn't been like that when you picked her up?" James asked.

"I'm sure. It was parked right out front. Obvious."

"And Russel is her husband, correct?" Wayne asked.

"Yes."

"Was he there when you picked her up?" James asked.

Patricia thought for a moment. "Yes. He might have been about to leave, too. I remember him being outside with the baby. Robin kissed the baby goodbye and then she got in my car."

"Okay, so you left the house, got breakfast sandwiches,

took them back to your house, and ate them. How long did this take you? How long was Robin gone from her house?" Wayne asked.

"Probably about three hours? Maybe a little more?" Patricia guessed. "I made coffee. We had a few cups. Talked about some things for WARN."

"And what happened when you got back to Robin's house?" James asked.

"We sat in my car for a while. Just kind of staring at the words. And then she laughed. But it wasn't exactly a funny laugh. More like the way you laugh when you're thinking to yourself, 'This is the last thing I need.'" Patricia paused. Looked over at some papers taped to the wall about keeping the station's kitchen area clean.

"They weren't swimming in cash, you know? And now she had to replace all of her tires and have the car repainted. I could see it all going through her head. All the logistical reasons why this was a pain in her ass. She looked kind of pissed off. But I was worried."

"Do you remember what exactly she said?" James asked.

"She didn't say anything until we had both gotten out of the car to take a closer look," Patricia said. "And then she stood there with her hands on her hips just breathing in deeply, looking at the sky. I thought she was gonna lose it. But eventually she smiled at me and said, 'Now I can paint the whole thing green!' And that's how Robin was. She could always turn a bad situation around." Patricia paused again and swallowed a few times. Trying not to cry, Wayne guessed.

"She sang, 'It's not easy bein' green.' And then we both laughed," Patricia went on. "Like, sat down on the ground and laughed until we had tears in our eyes. The words were green, but also, her son is crazy about Kermit the Frog. He bounces up and down whenever Kermit comes on the television. He dances to that stupid song. He can watch that frog for hours. He has a stuffed Kermit that he brings with him everywhere. Everything is about Kermit for that boy. And we both knew how much he would love a Kermit-colored car."

Wayne smiled. He and James let Patricia enjoy the memory for a moment.

"Robin got up, brushed the dirt off her butt, and that was pretty much the end of that," Patricia said. "We went into her house, and I said something like, 'Do you think the cops would do anything about it?' And Robin shrugged. Then, later in the week, I called to ask if she needed a ride to the WARN meeting, and she said no, Russel would take her. And then I called her again this past Friday. Before our breakfast date. She didn't pick up, though. And she didn't call me back, so I just showed up like I always do."

Patricia turned away, and now Wayne could see the tears brimming in her eyes.

"And then I found out what happened," Patricia finally finished. A tear fell down her cheek, and she wiped it away with the back of her hand.

"And then you went to the hospital?" Wayne asked.

"Yeah. Russel couldn't tell me much about what actually happened to Robin. He was upset and angry. Like, really angry. But the hospital didn't tell me very much, either. Just what I already told you on the phone."

"Russel was angry?" Wayne asked.

Patricia nodded. "Every time I asked anything about the hospital, he kept saying how much he hated that place and that they'd killed her. I was too shocked to really understand what he meant. But thinking about it now, I think he's probably grieving. It's a way of grieving, anger. Isn't it?"

Wayne nodded, and James's pen scratched the paper again. "What can you tell us about her relationship with Russel?" James asked.

Patricia sighed. "They were high school sweethearts. They fought a lot, but just about regular stuff. They both had big personalities. And opinions. Sometimes opposing ones. They both ran hot. But I think they really loved each other. I could still see it in their eyes. Even after everything."

James cleared his throat softly. "Back to Robin's car. Y'all never talked about who could've done it?"

"We didn't have to. I mean, there are plenty of people who don't like WARN. On and off the reservation. We know this. We're a national organization and Robin was a pretty public face. Like me." Patricia paused and Wayne saw her fear, then. A threat to Robin was a threat to Patricia. To any of them.

"If you had to make a list of WARN's enemies, who would they be?" James asked.

Wayne tried to hide his smile. He wondered if this woman had the guts to name them all.

"The mining company for one," Patricia said. "Any of the mining companies, actually. We've gone pretty hard on them this year."

"And those who are friends to the mining companies," James added.

"Sure," Patricia said.

"Anyone in Robin's life tied to them? Work for them?" James pressed.

"Russel. He's an equipment operator."

James's eyebrows went up. "What'd he think of the protest?"

"Who knows? Russel knew who Robin was when he married her. I don't think anything she did surprised him."

"Is that one of those things they fought about? His job?" James asked.

"Russel's only there for a paycheck. I think he's smart enough to know our protest wasn't going to bring the whole operation down. And Robin was smart enough to know that Russel couldn't exactly quit. Not if they wanted to keep feeding their family."

"What else can you tell us about Robin?" Wayne asked.

"She was active in the Native American Church. She was smart, even though she never graduated high school. She was a good person. A good friend." That last part came out quiet, and Wayne could see Patricia was just about at her limit. But James pressed anyway.

"Other than protesting the mining companies, what else has WARN been up to around the reservation?"

Patricia took a deep breath. "Just some community support, you know? We have job programs for girls in and just out of high school to help them find work. We focus on traditional Diné occupations, like sheep shearing or weaving or bead- and jewelry work. Training them, helping them sell their products. We also make sure women know about the health services they can access at the hospital. Yearly screenings, vaccines, birth control, that sort of thing." Patricia paused. "And we support political prisoners, too. WARN was born out of the American Indian Movement and most of those members are in prison now.

We write to them. And we write to the politicians and ask for pardons."

James wrote a few more things down. "That's certainly helpful for me to know," James said. "Thanks for that. Got any more questions, Lieutenant?"

"Do you know anything about what Robin had been doing or where she had been going this last week? Other than your breakfast date and the WARN meeting?"

"Not really," Patricia said. "She took care of her son most days. Sometimes she and Russel went out if her parents could take the baby. She would go to the rodeo to watch Russel if he had a competition. But I don't know specifically about these past couple of weeks. She didn't say anything to me about doing anything unusual or different."

Wayne nodded. "All right. Well, we appreciate you coming in today."

"What happens now?" Patricia asked.

"We're going to write up a report for you to sign," Wayne said.

"Do you think she was killed?" Patricia asked.

"That's hard to say without more information," Wayne said.

"Will you keep me updated? If I call or come by?"

Wayne glanced at James. "It depends. Sometimes the details of the case have to remain confidential until we're finished with our investigation."

"Okay." Patricia looked back down at her hands.

James put his pen down. "I'm sorry about your friend. We're gonna do everything we can to find out what happened."

Patricia nodded but still didn't look back up. She tucked a

loose strand of hair behind her ear, tugged a little at her T-shirt. Finally, she looked Wayne in the eye.

"Don't hold it against her, okay? Her being in WARN."

Wayne was quiet for a moment. "My job is to protect and serve the Diné people. That includes Robin. And you. And all the other members of WARN."

Patricia nodded again.

"I'll go get that report ready," James said. Wayne and Patricia waited for him in silence.

[4]
MOLLY

THAT MORNING MOLLY had put on a pair of denim cutoffs, a striped button-down shirt tied at her waist, and her Vans sneakers. She wanted to look good but casual—not like she was trying too hard.

Still, as soon as she stepped out of Grandma Beans's car, she felt self-conscious. She went to bite her nails, but stopped herself. She tried to listen to what Paula was talking about but only caught snippets here and there. She was looking for Joey but also not looking for Joey. She wanted to know he was there, but she didn't want him to see her looking for him. She wanted him to see her looking cool and unbothered.

It all took so much concentration that when Grandma Beans abruptly stopped walking, Molly almost ran into her.

"Well, well, well," Grandma Beans said to an older woman Molly didn't know. "Someone finally crawled out of her cave."

"Flew," the woman corrected her. "I'm becoming an old bat, and that's just fine with me."

The two old women laughed and hugged one another.

Grandma Beans stroked her own chin like she was thinking. "Four weeks since you've been to bingo?"

"Oh, Beatrice," the woman waved the accusation away. "Time is one big lie. You should know that in your old age. Besides, I got one of those headaches. You know how they go."

Grandma Beans frowned and patted her on the shoulder. "You poor thing. I'm glad you're back." Then she turned to introduce Molly and Paula. The woman's name was Charlie, she said, and then she told the girls Charlie's maternal clan— Molly was still learning all the different clan names in Navajo and she often confused one for the other. Still, Molly smiled and nodded politely and didn't interrupt.

"Molly's father works with tribal police," Grandma Beans said.

Charlie's eyebrows went up. "BIA?" she asked.

"Private detective," Molly said. "He has a P.I. business. Pinter P.I. I help out, too."

Charlie nodded with an exaggerated frown, like she was quite impressed.

"They helped find that missing boy last year," Grandma Beans added.

"Well, that was mostly Wayne. I mean Lieutenant Tully," Molly said. She knew not everyone on the reservation liked tribal police. She always tried to give Wayne credit when she could. "He and my dad are, like, best friends."

Just then, Joey walked by and Molly happened to look up and right into his hazel eyes. She felt herself blush. Joey was taller than she was. Taller than most kids their age. Most people, actually. He played basketball at school, and he was good. He wore his long hair in a low ponytail down his back and had a dimple on one cheek. Every time he smiled and his dimple appeared, it sent shivers down Molly's back.

It happened just then. The smile. The shivers. "Hey," he said to Molly.

"Hey," Molly answered.

"Get a room," Paula muttered, and then giggled.

Molly really could have smacked her, but Joey just laughed and said, "Good to see you, too, Paula."

Then, Joey looked at the old women and really grinned. He threw an arm around each of them and squeezed them one by one. "Grandma Beans! Auntie Charlie!"

Molly noticed that the Navajo often called people "grandma" or "ma" or "auntie" even if they weren't really related. She knew it was a sign of respect, but aside from Grandma Beans, she felt awkward doing it herself. Like maybe she wasn't allowed.

Charlie patted Joey's cheek. "Little Joey Baca. Always good to see you."

"Little!" Grandma Beans gasped. "Look at him! This boy has never been little one day in his life."

"Well, he's tall now, but don't you remember him as a little boy? So shy and cute." Charlie patted his cheek again.

"I remember him as a fat baby that gave his ma a hell of a time in labor!"

Joey ducked his head a little, still grinning. "You telling my secrets, Grandma Beans?" he asked.

"Nobody has secrets from me." Grandma Beans winked, and Molly knew it was probably true. She had been a midwife on the reservation for a long time and that was an honest job, as Grandma Beans always said.

"Better get back to work," Joey said. He looked right at

Molly again, into her eyes. Like he knew the power in those stares. "See you later," he said to her.

"See you," she managed to get out.

"If you couldn't tell, Molly's got a little crush," Paula said once Joey had walked off. Molly huffed, but she was used to Paula's inability to keep anything from Grandma Beans.

"Ah, good taste," Grandma Beans said, nodding. It made Molly smile. This was why Paula felt so comfortable with her grandmother.

"Was he really a fat baby?" Molly asked.

"The fattest! As soon as he came out. He was a strong baby, too. Crawling at only a month!"

"No, Grandma. Not a month," Paula said.

"Maybe not quite. But he came out like a cow's calf. Ready to take on the world already."

The four women walked into the event hall and found a table at the center of the room. Paula got them all cards and chips, and they sat drinking iced tea as they waited for the room to fill up and the game to start.

"When did you stop being a midwife, Grandma Beans?" Molly asked.

"Oh, it's been years and years. I guess I started to get old. My arthritis. My eyesight. And I couldn't get an apprentice, either. No one wanted to go out to people's homes anymore. It used to be a revered job until these hospitals got so big and these clinics started popping up in every reservation town." She shook her head.

"Paula's mom didn't want to do it?" Molly asked. Paula didn't always like to talk about her mom, who was back on the reservation now but always seemed to be coming or going. Paula was in deep conversation, though, with an older man at the end of the table and didn't hear Molly's question.

"No, she was not interested. Maybe even a little afraid. Some of those women that I would have made my apprentice went off to nursing school. But Paula's mom always hated school."

"Did you deliver Paula?" Molly asked.

Grandma Beans frowned. "I tried to get her to come home for the last month of her pregnancy and give birth here. But she wouldn't. She wanted a fancy Albuquerque hospital." Grandma Beans sighed. "At least she brought back Paula's umbilical cord like I asked."

"You can take that with you?"

Grandma Beans shrugged. "She did. Which is good. I buried it here on the reservation so Paula will always know where her home is."

"So she's connected to the land," Molly said. That was a nice idea. She liked it. It was a beautiful place.

Paula leaned into her grandmother. "Can you two stop talking about my umbilical cord? It's creeping me out."

Molly smirked. "Paula seems like she's up for midwifery. Maybe she can be your apprentice!"

Paula's mouth fell open. "Don't you volunteer me to be handling slippery babies. No thank you!"

Grandma Beans smiled but shook her head. "Luckily, things are starting to come full circle. Women want to know about traditional birthing again. I'm grateful that I lived to see the day. I'm teaching classes now at the community center about giving birth and taking care of the baby. And listen to this! I have also just agreed to help teach classes for a new midwife certification program. Right here on the reservation! My ancient wisdom won't die with me after all."

"That's rad, Grandma! Congratulations!" Paula exclaimed.

Grandma Beans patted Paula's arm. "Thank you, granddaughter. I assume 'rad' is a good thing."

"All right, enough talk down there," the old man that Paula had been chatting with earlier said. "Bingo's starting."

Paula rubbed her hands together. "You're goin' down, Larry! This is *my* week."

The old man smiled. "We'll see about that."

[5]

JAMES

JAMES AND WAYNE entered the Shiprock hospital through the surgical wing and told the woman at the front desk that they were there to see Dr. Ciccone. After a few minutes on the phone, the woman hung up and said to them, "Great timing. He's got about an hour until his next surgery. You can meet him in his office on the third floor. The ladies up there will show you the way."

"Much obliged," Wayne said.

Wayne stopped for a soda at the vending machine next to the stairs. James stood with his hands in his pockets looking at the corkboard on the wall filled with notices and fliers. One asked if patients felt safe at home and had numbers to rip off if they didn't. Another advertised a free first aid class at the community center in a few weeks. There was a pink piece of paper about a flea market selling newborn baby clothes. And lastly, an advertisement for addiction meetings held in the hospital's basement on Friday nights.

James pointed to the first flier. "I assume this number isn't for the police."

Wayne shook his head. "Some organization."

"Do you know it?" James asked.

"There are a few around we work with. The main one is through ONEO."

"Where Byron Cody works?" James asked.

"Same ONEO."

Wayne finished off his soda in three large gulps and threw it in the trash. Then they walked up the stairs, their boots squeaking on the shiny, newly mopped tiles.

On the third floor, a young woman with slightly bucked front teeth and a long blond braid took them to the doctor's office at the end of the hall.

The office was small but tidy and professional. Books lined a shelf on the far wall—some medical in nature, some not. The doctor peered over his glasses at James and Wayne. The hair around his temples was starting to gray, but the rest was still a stark black. He had thick, bushy eyebrows and a crooked nose that reminded James of a boxer's.

The doctor stood. James stuck out his hand and the doctor shook it. Wayne did the same.

"Good afternoon, gentlemen," the doctor said. "What can I help you with today?"

"We're here about a recent patient of yours," Wayne said. "A woman who died here this past Wednesday evening, June the second. Her name was Robin Kinsel. I believe she was brought to the hospital by her husband. She complained of stomach pain and fever."

"Ah, yes. I remember her. Please sit."

James and Wayne sat while the doctor opened a filing cabinet behind him. "Let me retrieve my notes."

The doctor flipped through his files quickly, and after a

minute or so, pulled out a folder. He sat back down and riffled through the contents of the folder.

"Here we go," he said. "Robin Kinsel, twenty-four years old, female. What is it that you gentlemen would like to know?"

"Can you tell us a little bit about her symptoms when she arrived at the hospital? Relevant medical history?" Wayne asked.

The doctor lifted an eyebrow but went on. "Sure. She presented complaining of stomach pain, dizziness, and shortness of breath. On assessment she was found to be pale, clammy, and lethargic with a fever of 104.1. Her blood pressure was very low and her heart rate quite high. Recently recovered from a simple cyst removal operation..."

James interrupted him. "Cyst removal operation? Can you elaborate?"

The doctor looked at James over the top of his glasses and rested the paper on his desk. "Yes. Mrs. Kinsel had a history of ovarian cysts. The last time she visited us in April, she had a large cyst that was causing her pain, and so we removed it. Simple operation, fairly easy and quick recovery time."

"Got it," James said. "Please continue."

"When Mrs. Kinsel was admitted this time, we suspected her pain was originating from another cyst, perhaps one that had ruptured. If this happens, infection is possible, so to be safe, we gave Mrs. Kinsel an IV with antibiotic and pain medication. We were prepping her for surgery when she became increasingly short of breath and her oxygen saturation dropped to dangerous levels. We decided to intubate Mrs. Kinsel and place her on a ventilator, but before we could do that, Mrs. Kinsel went into respiratory arrest, and our attempts to revive her were unsuccessful."

The doctor glanced back down at the paper in front of him. "There are a few other things about Mrs. Kinsel's visit that you should probably know. The first is that I asked her when she was admitted whether she had taken peyote. You see, the drug has been popular among women on the reservation as a way to self-medicate. The hospital allows the use of peyote during childbirth, and many women with babies or young children will still have some of it around the house afterward and continue to use the drug for pain relief. Mrs. Kinsel admitted to taking peyote before arriving at the hospital."

"The hospital allows the use of an illegal hallucinogen?" James asked.

"It's not illegal on the reservation," Wayne explained. "It's allowed for religious purposes." He turned to address the doctor now. "Still, law enforcement typically understands this to mean the peyote may be taken during Native American Church meetings. How long have the women been using it here at the hospital?"

The doctor sighed. "For quite some time. At first, we fought the practice, scolded the patients, asked the families to please take the peyote away. But it's hard enough to convince some people on the reservation to come all the way to a hospital to be treated. For so long, they simply consulted a medicine man. We're trying to change that. We want them to seek care here. It's why we've opened clinics in some of the more remote areas of the reservation. And why, eventually, I accepted the use of peyote during childbirth. I witnessed its effects. The women were calm. In less pain. But we expect them to disclose this to us, not hide it. Once we have in our files that a patient has brought peyote to the hospital for childbirth, we know it's in their home. We ask in any subsequent visits if they have taken any and have noticed that the women do continue to use it to treat any and all severe pain. If ibuprofen doesn't work, they reach for the peyote."

"How do you believe taking the peyote affected Mrs. Kinsel's situation?" James asked.

"I'm not sure that it did," the doctor said. "But I wanted you to be aware that she had mescaline in her system."

"Which is not something that causes overdoses. Typically," Wayne added.

"No," the doctor admitted. "It's quite difficult to overdose on mescaline, that is true."

"What else did you want to tell us about her visit?" James asked.

"Her husband." The doctor sighed, took off his glasses, closed his eyes, and rubbed his temples. He stopped after a moment and opened his eyes again. "The man was quite hostile."

"How so?" Wayne asked.

"He was nasty with the nurses. He yelled at them. He was aggressive. Security had to escort him to his car."

"Did you notice any signs of abuse on Robin?" James asked. "Bruises?"

The doctor shook his head and put his glasses back on. "I didn't notice anything, no. But it was an emergency. I wasn't examining her for that sort of thing. And it was difficult to say after her death. The process of trying to keep a person alive in an emergency situation is quite brutal and many of the patients' bodies show bruising after the fact."

"And there's no history of abuse-related injuries in her files?" James asked.

"No."

"So, in addition to the peyote in her system, she was on at least two medications at the time of her death," Wayne said. "One for pain and an antibiotic."

"That's correct."

"Could she have had an allergic reaction to either of those medications?" Wayne asked.

"I suppose it's possible. Unlikely for the pain medication since she was given the same medication before with no reaction."

"And the antibiotic?" Wayne asked.

"Possible. But there was no swelling of the airways noted and no skin rash or swelling anywhere else, either. I don't believe anaphylaxis caused the respiratory failure."

"We might be able to learn more from an autopsy," Wayne said.

"Not regarding anaphylaxis," the doctor said. "That's very difficult to detect after death. But as far as sepsis or other causes, an autopsy could be helpful. That is, if the family agrees. Which is rare in my experience."

"We'll try anyway," James said. "Any nurses or staff we can speak with who assisted with Robin or who may have witnessed Russel's behavior?"

"Yes. Two of our nurses, Alice Peterson and Carole Sherborn were present, though only Carole is here right now at the hospital. Alice typically works the night shift."

"How about poisoning?" James asked. "Would you say her symptoms are consistent with some sort of poisoning from an outside source?"

The doctor nodded slowly. "Sure. There are a variety of drugs and substances that could be used to poison a person, some of which would cause symptoms like those Mrs. Kinsel was experiencing."

James glanced at Wayne and knew they had to get moving.

"Thanks for your time today, Dr. Ciccone," Wayne said. "Can we give you a call if we have more questions?"

"Sure." The doctor scribbled on his notepad, ripped the paper from the pad, and handed it to Wayne.

"These are the name of the nurses. The ladies at the front desk should be able to get you Alice's contact information."

"Appreciate that," James said. "Could we also grab a copy of your notes there?"

The doctor chuckled and turned the paper around for James to see. "If you think you can decipher this chicken scratch. But I've already relayed just about everything here. I'll leave that up to you."

James squinted at the paper. The doctor was right. It was barely legible. "I'll still take a copy, if you don't mind."

"I'll have one of my assistants run it through the copy machine and send it downstairs after you gentlemen," the doctor said.

James and Wayne stood and shook the doctor's hand again. "Thank you," James said.

The doctor smiled. "You're welcome. Please come see me again if you need anything else."

"The warrant for Robin's car should be ready," Wayne said as they hurried downstairs. "I'll go to Russel's. Execute the search. See if I can't talk him into an autopsy. I doubt he'll go for it, but I'll ask. You've got the nurse?"

"Affirmative."

Wayne glanced at his watch. "Meet me at the station later?"

James nodded. "I'll be there. Good luck."

James waited at the desk for the woman to get off the phone while Wayne left out the front door. The woman gave James a tight-lipped smile and about a minute later, hung up the phone.

"Can I help you?"

"Dr. Ciccone gave me the names of a couple of nurses. He said one of them would be here right now. Carole Sherborn. I'd like to speak with her."

"Oh, sure. Carole. Let me find her." The woman picked up a radio and spoke into it. "Carole Sherborn, you're wanted at the front desk." She waited a moment for a response, staring off into space with her thumb poised to press the radio's button again. But before she could, a voice said, "Copy."

The woman gave James another tight-lipped smile.

"You can sit down in our waiting area if you'd like. She'll be here soon."

"Thank you," James said, though he didn't sit down. He posted up against the wall, looking at things he hadn't noticed at first. A newspaper stand by the front door, stacked with copies of the *Navajo Times*, *The Gallup Independent*, the *Farmington Daily Times*, the *Arizona Daily Sun*, and the *Albuquerque Journal*. Magazines frayed and slightly torn at the edges on tables in between chairs. Caution: Wet Floor cones in one corner where they had mopped recently.

The laminate floors were clean but full of scuff marks from shoes and wheelchairs and the rubber bottoms of crutches. Stuck to the white-painted cement block walls was a sticker that read *God Loves You*, with a smiley face. One patient waited, holding a towel to his forehead, leaning forward on his knees. Another had her head tipped back, eyes closed, mouth open, snoring.

Finally, a tall woman with shoulder-length blond curls wearing scrubs appeared at the front desk. James watched the two women whisper to one another, and when they looked his way, he lifted a hand in greeting.

Carole—a woman in her late thirties, James guessed as she got closer—wore clogs on her feet and a cross necklace. She stuck out a hand and James shook it.

"Thank you for waiting, sir. I understand you're with tribal police?"

"Yes. Name is James Pinter and I'm a private investigator. I contract with the tribal police on occasion."

Carole nodded. "What can I help you with today?"

"I was hoping to get some insight into how the hospital handles medication administration and pain management in emergencies. Dr. Ciccone referred me to you, so I imagine you must really know your stuff. Are you one of the nurse supervisors?"

"The head nurse supervisor," Carole said.

"If you don't mind, I'd like you to show me your medication system. How you keep track of what is used when and by whom. Myself, I've been trained to respond to emergencies. But only out in the field with limited resources. I haven't got a clue as to how y'all do it constantly with such precision and with so many options. I bet you've got to know exactly what each medication does and how it reacts with all the others. And some of them sound so similar too."

Carole chuckled. "That's true. Who knows who comes up with these names? Some of them are tongue twisters."

"I promise not to give you a pop quiz." James grinned.

Carole glanced around nervously. "I guess I could give you a little peek. What's all this about anyway?"

"It's related to an investigation," James said. "I'm trying to picture in my mind what it might look like here when a patient shows up with an emergency. What happens behind the scenes."

Carole's forehead was wrinkled with concern.

"Just something on my checklist," James assured her.

Carole nodded. "I see. Well, follow me, then."

James followed Carole down a long corridor, through three different doors, which she opened with the key hanging from her lanyard.

Finally, James found himself in a large, cold room lined with shelves of vials and bottles behind locked glass. At the end, against the far wall, were industrial-sized refrigerators.

Carole grabbed a clipboard that hung from the wall.

"Anyone who needs medication for a patient comes to me first."

"What if you're not here?" James asked.

"They'll go to whoever the charge nurse is for that shift. The charge nurse reports directly to me and turns her key over after each shift. For night shifts, it's usually Dawn Harvey. But if one of us isn't here, another charge nurse is assigned."

"All right. So the nurse or maybe doctor comes to you or another charge nurse if they need medication."

"Rarely doctors," Carole said. "Usually another nurse."

"And then what?"

"And then we come to this room together. The nurse fills out this sheet with the medication they need, the dosage, the patient's last name and room number, the attending doctor, and the procedure or condition. They sign here, and then I initial beside it. We go—together—to the area where the medication is kept. I use my key again to unlock the glass or the refrigerator door and the nurse takes what they need."

"They take the whole vial with them? What if they have medication left over?"

"If we are drawing the medication from a vial, what is left is disposed of," Carole said. "For pills, they're placed in a small paper cup. The exact amount needed."

"So there are two sets of eyes—yours and theirs—making sure the correct medication gets taken."

"That's right."

"And only one key."

"Two. Dr. Ciccone has the spare."

James looked at the clipboard.

"How about stocking when a new order comes in? You do that as well?"

"Yes."

"Were you working this past Wednesday evening?" James asked.

"Let me think. Well, I had to stay a little later than normal. I went home around midnight. Dawn and I were both here for a few hours. Sometimes our shifts overlap like that. But I gave her the keys when her shift started at 7 p.m."

"Dawn Harvey, you said her name was?"

"That's right."

James pointed at the clipboard. "Do you have Wednesday night's log there?"

Carole looked down at the clipboard. She turned a few pages back.

"Patient's last name is Kinsel," James said.

Carole scanned the paper, flipped to the page before it, and then went back to the first.

"I'm sorry, you've got me a little jittery," Carole said. "I didn't realize you were looking at a specific patient. You can imagine how important this part of our job is. If someone made a mistake, it could be very bad for them. For all of us. I could lose my job."

Her hands shook slightly.

"Please, Carole," James said. "Take your time. Don't worry about all that right now. I'm sure everyone acted professionally. Just as they should. I just have to cross my t's and dot my i's and I appreciate you helpin' me."

Carole nodded and took a deep breath. She looked at the clipboard again, this time moving her finger down each sheet of paper before moving onto the next.

"Right here," Carole said. "Kinsel. Alice got the medication. One vial of vancomycin—that's an antibiotic—and one vial of morphine, the pain medication."

James looked over her shoulder. It was all there—the time, the medicine, the procedure, the doctor, Alice's signature. Dawn's initials.

"How often do you inventory?" James asked.

"Once a month. It's a process, because we order more medications as we need them. I have to square that with this."

Carole held the clipboard up. "And then that." She pointed at the shelves.

"And it comes out even?" James asked.

"Usually. It's rare to have discrepancies, but occasionally we come up short on pills that are accidentally lost in emergency situations. We try to oversee all ingestions but sometimes it isn't possible. We do our best."

"Makes sense. Patient drops a pill by accident. One falls on the floor in the hallway or somethin'. How about in those emergency situations? How have you got time to write all this down?"

Carole's gaze darted to the door behind James.

"Some of the information can be filled in later."

"So what's the important stuff?"

"Patient name and room number, medication name, and signature."

"Does that patient's name ring any bells? Kinsel?"

"Yes," Carole said slowly. "I believe it does. She was the one with the husband, right? He made quite a scene. He called me a..." Carole paused. Her face reddened. "Something not so nice."

"More of a scene than you're used to?" James asked.

Carole nodded. "He was a little frightening."

"Well, I'm sorry about that. That's probably not your favorite part of the job, is it? Dealing with people like him."

"No. It's certainly not."

"I appreciate this," James said. "Thank you for sharing with me, Carole."

WAYNE

THE BABY'S CRIES—SHARP and high-pitched—pierced the air all around the trailer. Wayne could hear them before he opened his car door. Before he had even turned off the engine. It had started raining outside, a slow drip, and when he got out of the car, he lunged up the three steps to the front door. He had the station's camera in a bag slung over his shoulder and some evidence bags stuffed into his back pocket along with the search warrant for Robin's car. He knew what he wanted to leave Russel's house with that day. How he would do it, he wasn't entirely sure. He was still working it out in his head when he knocked on the front door. He knocked again, ducked under the overhang, and wondered if Russel could even hear him over the child's screams. Wayne looked backed at his cruiser. Robin's car was no longer in front of the house like Patricia had described. That was good for Wayne.

"Russel?" Wayne shouted on the third knock. "Are you in there? It's tribal police!"

The cries got closer and the door opened. A young man with no shirt on stood in front of Wayne, frowning. The eighteen-month-old was on his hip, red-faced and soaked in tears. He had stopped wailing to study Wayne, but as he gasped for air, his bottom lip quivered. The TV blared behind them.

"Yes?" the young man asked.

"I'm Lieutenant Tully with tribal police. Do you have a minute?"

Russel shook his head. "This isn't a good time."

"I understand. And I'm very sorry for your loss. I know this must be a difficult time for you. But I'm investigating a vehicle vandalism. Your wife's car? A friend of hers reported the crime this morning."

Russel stared at Wayne. "Her car? That's what you're concerned about?"

"We are looking at all possible leads."

Russel scoffed. "Fine," he muttered. He turned and left the door open behind him. *Not ideal*, Wayne thought, *but good enough*. He took the invitation and stepped inside.

Toys covered the floor. A diaper was balled up on the counter. An empty but dirty bottle lay next to an open microwave. Photos covered the refrigerator door: the smiling young couple on horseback near the Canyon de Chelly; Robin gazing at the baby on her chest right after he was born, wrapped in the hospital blanket; Russel—Wayne assumed, because he couldn't see the man's face—fighting to stay on top of a bull in the rodeo arena. And then, Wayne saw a jar next to the stove. Still sitting on the counter. The peyote right in clear sight.

"So, what? You have questions for me?" Russel asked.

The baby was crying again, but Wayne could tell the fight was leaving him.

"Again, I'm very sorry about your wife." Wayne had to speak loudly to be heard over the TV.

Russel didn't respond, but he put the boy down. Russel watched the boy hobble over to his toys, then wiped his face with his sleeve. He picked up the remote control and turned the volume down.

"Her car was fucked with weeks ago. You can take a look if you want. It's in the backyard."

"Appreciate that," Wayne said. "Can you tell me about that day? What you remember?"

Russel took a deep breath. Looked at the ceiling. "I don't know, man. She went to breakfast like she always does on Saturdays. I went to my parents' house with the baby. When I got home, I saw the car. I was mad. We don't have money for that kind of bullshit. But Robin was always pissin' somebody off. So I wasn't that surprised. Just annoyed. Really annoyed that whatever she was doin' now caused that. The protest or whatever. She was already inside when I got home. She shrugged it off, which I also thought was pretty annoying, but I didn't even pick a fight with her about it." He stopped talking for a moment. Shook his head. "I rounded up enough spare tires to drive it around back. I don't need the neighbors lookin' at that shit every day."

Wayne tried to glance out the back window, but he couldn't see much through the one broken blind that stuck out like an accusing finger pointed right at him.

"Did you keep the old tires?"

"Nah. They were destroyed. Really slashed up. We burned them."

"How about the house?" Wayne asked. "Any signs it was broken into that morning?"

Russel shook his head slowly. "But the lock on the back door is broken. Has been for a while now. I guess they could've just walked in. Not that we have anything worth taking in here."

"So the person who did this to her car. They could've come into the house."

"Yeah. I guess."

"They might not have been looking to steal anything," Wayne went on. "But that doesn't mean they couldn't have tampered with things while they were here."

Russel narrowed his eyes now. "What do you mean?"

"This person clearly wished ill toward Robin."

Wayne watched the understanding wash over Russel's face. "You think they were trying to hurt her?"

"It's possible. For example, the doctor said Robin took peyote before arriving at the hospital. If that peyote was here, and out in plain view like it is today, it would've been easy for someone to contaminate it. Have *you* taken any of the peyote?"

"No." Russel's voice was quiet now. His forehead wrinkled.

"I think we ought to have that peyote tested. But I think there are other things we ought to check, too."

Russel still looked confused, or maybe just deep in thought, but he said, "All right," and Wayne took that as his best chance to get moving. He walked past Russel and the baby on the floor, who sat open-mouthed watching the television. It seemed the Muppets had finally subdued him, just like Patricia had described.

Wayne went straight for the bathroom, where he put on some gloves and collected the over-the-counter pain medication, some cough medicine, an old antibiotic prescription written for Robin, and a bottle of oxycodone written for Russel, and placed them in evidence bags. He took photos beneath the sink, where there wasn't much—some first aid type things. Band-Aids, rubbing alcohol, Vaseline. There was also a box of tampons and some toilet paper rolls.

He went to their bedroom next, and now, Russel was right behind him.

"You can do all of this," Russel said, though he sounded much more irritated now, "but it was the hospital that killed Robin. I know it. And I know you don't care, and you'll find anyone else to blame but them, but it was them."

"What do you mean, I'll find anyone else to blame?" Wayne asked. "Why do you think that?"

Wayne didn't need to ask which side of the bed had been Robin's. That bedside table was tidy. An unlit candle. A paperback romance novel. A tube of ChapStick.

"Tribal police are not interested in helping us. We all know it. You'll side with the IHS or the BIA or any other three letter government group that gives you money." Russel was getting louder now. More sure of himself. He was no longer in a state of shock, and Wayne knew that meant he had to hurry up. He opened the drawer next to Russel's side of the bed.

"Why are you looking through *my* stuff? I thought they would be targeting *her*?" Russel stayed glued to Wayne's side. There wasn't much in there. A few loose papers that looked like bills. Dirty tissues. Condoms in wrappers.

"Oh, sorry. This is your stuff?" Wayne said.

"Listen, you need to hurry up and finish whatever it is you're doing," Russel said. "I don't even know why I let a tribal police officer in here."

"I'm almost done." Wayne opened her drawer next. A lighter, a paper with some crayon scribbles on it—possibly her son's first work of art—and a note with a phone number that said, *On-call nurse.*

"Your wife had surgery a couple months ago," Wayne said. "Is that what this note's about?"

Russel looked down at it. "Seems like it, super sleuth."

Wayne doubted he could get away with opening Russel's dresser drawers at this point, so instead, he tried to get a good look at the closet on his way out. Clothes, shoes, shoeboxes.

"I'm going to grab that peyote and then I'm going to take a look at the car," Wayne said as he walked back down the hall. He could've kicked himself for not asking about the autopsy before Russel was annoyed, but he hadn't and he couldn't leave without doing it.

"We want to find out what happened to her," Wayne went on. "We'd like to perform an autopsy, with your permission."

"No." Wayne barely heard the response since Russel was turned away, watching the boy on the floor.

"If you truly believe the hospital is to blame, you should consent to this," Wayne said. "It could give us a definite answer."

Russel turned to face Wayne. "And what would you do with that definite answer? Anything you could to protect the hospital, that's what. That's why you're going through *my* drawers. Anyone but them."

"I assure you, that is not my intent. Whether the hospital

is to blame here, or the person who threatened your wife, I want to find out what happened to her. To hold the person who is to blame accountable."

Russell shook his head. "I don't want or need your help." When he paused and took a breath, Wayne could see his bottom lip quivering too, just like his son's. Russel touched his own chest. "I know in here that the hospital fucked up. You should've seen the way they treated me." His face hardened. "They killed my wife and there's nothing I can do about it. And there's nothing you're *going* to do about it. Take the peyote and get out of my house."

Wayne glanced at the baby. He now had a pacifier in his mouth that he must have found somewhere, and he lay face down on the floor, butt in the air, blanket clutched in his balled-up fist. His eyes were open, blinking and vacant. He was about to fall asleep.

Wayne walked into the kitchen, picked up the peyote jar, and tucked it under his arm. He then opened the back door and turned the lock. He jiggled the handle. Definitely broken.

"Thank you for your time and cooperation," Wayne said before stepping outside. "Whether you want my help or not, it's my job to find out what happened to your wife, and I'm going to do just that."

Russel didn't answer or turn around, and Wayne let the door close quietly behind him.

The car was tireless and sat at the back of the yard, a few feet away from a chain-link fence. The spares must have been returned to wherever Russel had found them. Luckily the rain had stopped, and Wayne walked through the still-wet weeds and soggy patches of dirt toward the trunk of the

Chevy Chevelle Malibu station wagon. The white car wasn't as dirty as Wayne would have expected, and he wondered how often Robin had cleaned it. Sure, the rain could've washed some of the dirt away, but even the bumper looked shiny. It looked well taken care of. He rounded the right side of the car and saw the *Ana*. The word was indeed green, though not the bright green of Kermit the Frog. It was darker, more subdued. Wayne circled around to the front. *Watch your back* was surprisingly legible with large, well-spaced letters. He looked for shoe prints on the hood and found a few scuff marks, but nothing else. He checked the other side and saw the *Yooch'iid,* which took up both the driver's door and the back door behind it.

Wayne took photos. Farther away first to capture the full scene, and then up close, to capture the details and scale. Next, he scraped the paint using a scalpel and a bag below to catch the slivers. And then Wayne dusted for fingerprints, estimating where one might have put a hand to steady themselves. The car was mostly dry by now, though he knew the rain and heat and sun could have destroyed much of what he would have found two weeks ago. Still, he found a few prints, and though it was possible they were Robin's or Russel's or Patricia's or anyone else's who may have touched the car between then and now—a friend who lent Russel a tire or even a neighborhood kid's—Wayne would process them anyway.

Wayne took his time walking back out front to his cruiser. He looked for trash or strange mounds of dirt where things could be buried but saw nothing. The yard was clean and flat.

A few drops of water on top of the hood of Wayne's

cruiser still gleamed in the sun. He placed the camera, peyote jar, and evidence bags on the passenger's seat, climbed into the driver's seat, and started the engine. He could see Russel watching him not at all discreetly between the blinds. Wayne raised a hand to wave goodbye, but Russel did not wave back.

[7]

DAWN

In the middle of a dream, Dawn heard the faint sound of her phone ringing. She knew she ought to get up and answer it, but she was so comfortable and she still had a full two hours before she needed to get up. So she ignored it and let herself fall back asleep.

But the knocks that followed sometime later were too loud to ignore. They sounded urgent and she jolted awake immediately.

She almost fell out of bed on her way to answer the door, briefly checking to make sure she was fully clothed before raking her hands through her hair and pulling a scrunchie around a crooked ponytail.

"I'm coming!" she shouted, but her voice sounded scratchy and caked with sleep.

The sun was bright and assaulting as she opened the door. She squinted and held her hand up to shield the rays.

A white man stood on her porch. "Hi there. Are you Dawn Harvey?"

"Yes."

"I'm James Pinter, here on behalf of the tribal police. Do you have a minute?"

Dawn nodded. "Have you got an ID?" The man handed her a tribal police business card.

"A badge?" she asked, handing him the card back.

He shook his head. "I'm a private investigator. A consultant."

"Give me two minutes," she said. She went back inside, changed into her scrubs, and grabbed the pistol she normally kept in the drawer of her bedside table. She tucked it under the upholstered chair, into the fabric where she had sewed an extra pouch, and then let the man inside.

Dawn sat in the armchair. She didn't offer the man a drink. "What did you say your name was again?" she asked.

"James Pinter."

"What is it that you need from me, Mr. Pinter?"

He sat across from Dawn on the couch, even though she hadn't invited him to do so.

"I understand you work nights over at the Shiprock hospital. I'm sorry I interrupted what little sleep you're able to get. Nights can get to you. I've been there."

"That's right," Dawn said. She wasn't about to accept this stranger's apology. He *had* interrupted her precious sleep.

"There was a patient Wednesday night," the man went on. "She passed away shortly after arriving at the emergency room."

Dawn waited for more. It was a hospital. People, sometimes, passed away there. Finally, she said, "I'm sorry to hear that. But I've really got to get moving. I have a few things to do before my shift starts. Is there something you need from me?"

"We're investigating the death. I have a couple of questions for you."

"All right."

"I understand that you were the charge nurse that night. That you handled medication approval. The nurse attending the procedure was an Alice Peterson. She would have gotten one vial of vancomycin and one vial of morphine. Do you happen to remember?"

Dawn nodded. "I remember bringing Alice back to get the medications, yes."

"Do you remember anything unusual about the interaction?"

"Unusual?" Dawn asked. She knew vague, open-ended questions could be traps.

"Are you certain Alice took the correct medications in the correct amounts?"

Dawn raised an eyebrow. "Did you see my initials on the log?"

"Yes."

"I take my job seriously. Of course I'm sure of what she took."

The cop, or whatever he was, eyed her closely. "And she took exactly what was entered into the log?"

Dawn gritted her teeth and tried not to roll her eyes. "Correct."

"Did Alice seem nervous? Unsure? Was she acting different in any way?"

"No," Dawn said, firmly.

"She must have been in a hurry. From what I understand, the patient was in a good amount of pain and thought to be septic. Was it one of those situations where Alice was only able to fill out some information and the rest had to be done later?"

That must have been Carole, Dawn thought, giving him that little tidbit. The woman was a blabbermouth with a shit poker face. And she was naïve. She didn't realize what a man like this could do with her words.

"Actually, the patient was stable. The antibiotics were important, but Alice had plenty of time to fill out all of the information requested," Dawn said. "You won't find blame with her or with me."

Dawn wouldn't go further to claim that blame wouldn't be found with other nurses or with the hospital itself or even with the doctors. There was plenty of blame to go around that place. But Dawn wouldn't share any of her misgivings with this man, because she didn't trust *him*, either. Alice was solid. A good one. Dawn could at least vouch for her.

"Of course," the man said. "We're just making sure we're looking at every angle here. We owe it to the family. I'm sure you understand. Do you attend births regularly, Miss Harvey?"

"We're understaffed, so we all do what's needed," Dawn said. "We don't have nurses assigned to specific wings like fancy hospitals might."

"Are you aware that Dr. Ciccone allows laboring women to take peyote, to bring it into the hospital with them?"

"Did Carole tell you that?" Dawn was starting to get annoyed.

"The doctor did."

Again, Dawn fought to keep her breath steady, her expression neutral. "Yes, I know the women take peyote. It helps alleviate the pain and the stress."

"I imagine some patients probably feel much more comfortable with you than with other nurses and doctors," James said.

"Because I'm Diné?"

"Yes."

Dawn shrugged. He wasn't wrong. She could understand the patients, speak their language—literally and figuratively. She knew they confided in her. Told her things they trusted she would keep to herself. And she did. As long as their life wasn't in danger, Dawn never felt the need to tell anyone else what her patients told her.

"Has anyone complained or reported unusual symptoms after taking the peyote?" James asked.

Dawn felt pressure behind her eyes. Her forehead creased.

"No. The women appreciate the peyote. I've heard nothing negative."

He handed her his card again. "Keep it this time. Please. And call me if you happen to remember anything unusual about Alice or about the patient from Wednesday night, Mrs. Robin Kinsel."

Dawn took the card. They both stood and she led him to the door.

"Thank you for your time today," he said as he left.

"Hágoónee'," Dawn said. She shut the door behind him. Robin Kinsel. Where had she heard that name before?

[8]

WAYNE

It was late and dark and Wayne was starving, but he waited until James arrived at the station to start eating. Earlier, Wayne had stopped at home to tell Barb how busy he had been that day—how busy he and James would probably be all evening—and she'd stacked two to-go containers with that night's dinner on top of one another in the passenger's seat before giving Wayne a quick kiss and a slap on the butt.

The station was basically empty except for Gene Begaye, who was helping Wayne process the day's evidence, packaging up what needed to be sent off to Albuquerque for testing.

James made a pot of coffee while Wayne microwaved the food, and the two men ate straight from the old butter tub and Cool Whip container Barb had used.

They didn't speak for a solid five minutes as they shoveled food into their mouths. Finally, they both wiped their chins and praised Barb's cooking.

"So. The autopsy," James said.

"It's a no," Wayne answered.

"Damn. For the usual reason?"

Wayne shook his head. "I made the rookie mistake of waiting to ask until he was good and pissed off at me for poking around his house. Regardless, he doesn't like the police. Doesn't trust us. Thinks we're just trying to protect the hospital."

James frowned. "Couldn't we just order one done anyway?"

An autopsy would have obviously made all of this much easier. Wayne didn't answer, but he did sigh.

James rubbed his palms on his knees. "We'll figure it out the old-fashioned way, then. How'd it go with the car? I saw Gene gettin' some packages ready."

"We're sending off a paint sample, the peyote, and some medications of Robin's I pulled from the medicine cabinet. We'll see if we find any matches on the fingerprints tomorrow. I also grabbed a bottle of prescription narcotics written out to Russel."

James raised his eyebrows. "Huh. How about photos?"

Wayne stood and left the room for a moment. He had kept the photos in his office while they ate, away from the food. When he put them in front of James, he tapped the one he had taken of the word 'Ana.'

"Interesting that only some of the message is written in Diné."

James squinted at each photo, studied it, and then pushed it away with the eraser end of his pencil. "You said you were able to lift some fingerprints."

"A few. Russel admitted to burning the tires and also told me their back door's lock was broken. It's possible the perpetrator could've walked right in."

"Well, that's convenient. For us, at least," James said.

"I'm not sure we have enough, but I could always try to get a warrant and go back to the house to finish the search that I started before Russel got antsy, but I doubt it would be very fruitful."

"He's destroyed anything that might look suspicious by now," James said.

"Exactly. His story of the day the car was vandalized lines up with Patricia's. He says, and I quote, he 'didn't even pick a fight' with Robin about it. Like it was her fault."

"How chivalrous," James said. "You get any details about the day Robin died?"

Wayne shook his head. "Like I said, the man wanted me out of his house. I was focused on gathering whatever evidence I could as quickly as I could."

"Understood," James said. "He doesn't know me yet. I'll give him a try."

"How about the nurses?" Wayne asked. "What'd you find there?"

"Not much. At least nothing they're willing to share."

"Can you blame them?" Wayne asked. "No one wants a dosing error on their record."

"I haven't seen or heard anything to make me think any of them made a mistake."

"You talk to all of them?"

"I did. One nurse at the hospital. She's the one in charge of medications during the day. She showed me the record with Robin's medication signed out and explained their system. Another nurse over the phone. She's the one who administered the medication. Then I visited a Navajo nurse at her house up the street after she didn't answer my phone call. She's the one who oversees night medication. Got the feeling she didn't like me too much."

"But you're so charming." Wayne grinned.

"Apparently not to Nurse Harvey."

"You think she's hiding something?" Wayne asked.

"Always possible. I got the feeling she also does not like her supervisor, the nurse I first spoke with."

Just then, the front door to the station opened and the bell dinged. "Hello?" Molly called out.

"Back here!" James answered.

Molly stopped in the doorway of the conference room. Her mouth turned down into a pouty frown.

"You didn't save any of Barb's cooking for me?"

"Didn't know you'd be comin'," James said. "Why aren't you in bed?"

"It's only 10 p.m., Dad," Molly said as she collapsed into one of the chairs around the table. "Kay and I just finished watching a slasher." She smiled and her eyes grew big. "Ax to the forehead! Anyway, I wasn't tired, and Kay agreed to drive me here."

Wayne pushed the photos over to Molly. "I assume you know all about the new case by now?"

Molly nodded. "Dad gave me the rundown earlier."

"Take a look."

She chewed her thumbnail as she studied the photos. "Hey, you know who could help us?"

"Who?" James asked.

"This guy Ricky," Molly said. "He's in my art class at school. He's a tagger."

"A what?"

"Graffiti artist," Wayne said.

"I mean, he might not talk to *you guys*," Molly said. "But he would probably talk to me. You should see his paint collection. There's no way he won't know exactly what kind of paint this is."

"You know where he lives?" Wayne asked.

"No," Molly said. "But his name's Ricky White. He's got to live around here if he goes to Shiprock High, doesn't he?"

"We'll find his address," Wayne said.

"You want me to come with you?" James said. "I'll be cool."

Molly giggled. "There is no way you would be able to be cool. You would definitely end up saying something very cop-like."

"Hey, now. I can be tricky," James said. "I used to go undercover all the time, you know."

Molly rolled her eyes. "I'll be fine, Dad. I'll bring Paula if you want."

"Bring Paula," Wayne said. "Every investigator needs a partner."

[9]

MOLLY

RICKY'S HOUSE was close enough to Paula's that Molly and Paula walked there.

"Okay, I have one," Paula said as she kicked a pebble down the street. "If John Travolta showed up at your house and asked you for a date, would your dad, a) Fight him, or b) Let him take you out to dinner?"

"Those are the only options?"

"Yup."

"Fight him. He's too old for me."

"He's only, like, ten years older than you!" Paula cried. "Okay, but who would win?"

"Obviously my dad," Molly said.

Paula cackled. "I would pay big money to see your dad kick John Travolta's ass."

The house that Paula and Molly stopped at was way nicer-looking than Molly had expected. It was not a house built into the ground like Kay's, the house Molly and James now lived in. It was a trailer like the rest of the houses on Ricky's street, but it was huge. And meticulously clean. And surrounded by a curated desert garden of various cacti and bushes. It had a large deck, too, and a doormat with a large sun printed on it. There was a metal butterfly hanging on the door. It was homey. Molly knocked.

An older man, probably around Grandma Beans's age, opened the door. Molly let Paula do the talking in situations like these. She was Diné, unlike Molly. Plus, old people loved Paula.

"Good afternoon, sir," Paula said. "We're looking for Ricky. We're friends of his from school."

The man lifted an eyebrow. "Who should I tell him is here?"

"Molly from art class," Molly jumped in.

"And Paula, Molly's friend." Paula grinned.

The man turned around slowly and shouted into the abyss, "Ricky! Some pretty girls are here!" He turned back around and winked. "That should do it, don't you think?"

Paula grinned but neither girl had the chance to answer before Ricky appeared behind his grandfather, slightly red-faced and combing his fingers through his shiny hair.

"Hey," he said to Molly.

"Hey," Molly said. "Um. There's something kind of random I need to ask you. Do you have a minute?"

"Sure. Come in."

"That's right," the older man said opening the door nice and wide for them. "Come in. Sit down at the table. I'll get you girls some cookies."

Ricky got even redder. "This is my grandfather."

"Call me Bill," the man said. Paula and Molly sat at the table with Ricky and waited for Bill to bring them a plate of cookies.

"Would you like some milk, too?" Bill asked.

"Oh, milk sounds delicious," Paula said. She got up again. "I'll help ya, Bill."

Molly smiled at Ricky. "Have you met Paula?"

Ricky nodded. "I think she was in my calculus class last year."

Paula and Bill came back with three glasses of milk. "Did you hear that, Paula?" Molly asked. "You and Ricky had calculus together last year."

Paula gasped. "With that awful witch? She was the worst, wasn't she?"

Ricky smiled. "I kind of liked her."

Paula looked at Bill with raised eyebrows. Bill nodded. "He can be a bit strange."

Paula sat down again and Bill pretended like he had something to do in the kitchen, but Molly could tell he just wanted to give them space.

"So, my dad is a private investigator," Molly said. "And he's got a case right now where somebody painted threats on this woman's car." She paused and thought about how much Ricky needed to know. Not very much, she decided. "I doubt the guy, or girl, who did it is an artist or anything. But I'm hoping maybe you can tell us something about the paint."

She leaned down and opened up the satchel she had brought. She took out a bag with the paint sample and the photos of the car. Ricky held the bag up to the light. "Definitely Krylon," he said right away.

"Really?" Molly asked. Ricky nodded.

"Not thick enough to be Rust-O and you can't really find any other brands around here."

He picked up the photos next. "Huh."

"Do you happen to recognize anything about the way the words are painted?"

"You're right. Not an artist. At least, no one I know from the rez."

"Because you would know their tag." It was supposed to be a question but sounded more like a statement.

"I would recognize them, yeah." He looked at the bag of paint chips again. "Can I touch the paint?"

"Sure," Molly said. She was pretty sure this sample was fair game. The rest Wayne had already sent off.

Ricky slid his hand into the bag and rubbed the paint between his fingers. Then he looked at them in the light. "It's new," he said. "Bought sometime in the last year or two."

"How do you know that?" Molly asked.

"It doesn't have any lead in it. The government banned lead in paint two years ago. Kind of a pain in the ass at the time because it caused a paint shortage. The old stuff used to leave this powdery white residue on your hands. It doesn't anymore."

"Language!" Bill shouted from the kitchen.

"Sorry, Grandpa," Ricky replied.

Molly couldn't help smiling. Ricky carried himself like a badass at school but his attitude toward his grandpa was sweet.

"Okay, so Krylon. Bought in the last two years. Any idea what color green it is?"

"Avocado. Definitely."

"That's the official name?" Molly asked.

"Avocado. Number 2009."

Molly jotted that down. "And where would one buy a can of Krylon Avocado, number 2009 around here?"

Ricky smirked a little. "If you're a punk kid like me, you mail-order them. But if you're *not* a punk kid, there's a hardware store about halfway between Gallup and Albuquerque. They've got a nice selection."

"But you don't buy your paint there?" Molly asked.

"Nah. The owner won't sell me any. Says he knows what I'll do with it." Ricky shrugged. "He's right, so I can't be too mad."

"Ha," Molly chuckled. "I guess that's true. What's the name of the store?"

"Hammer Away. It's right on the highway."

"Thanks, Ricky. This is really helpful."

Paula grabbed a cookie and took a bite. "Bill!" she cried after she swallowed. "I would never have guessed you were a baker!"

The man stuck his head around the corner and grinned. "I've been in the kitchen all morning slaving away at those." He pointed his finger at Ricky. "Don't let him tell you any different."

"You ought to bring these to bingo night. You ever go to bingo night at the senior center?" Paula asked.

"Do I look old enough to be playing bingo at the senior center?"

Paula shrugged. "I go every week. It's a good time! You should come." She nudged Ricky with her shoulder. "You too."

Molly watched Ricky go bright red. Tomato red probably, if it were a paint color. Paula and Molly and Bill chatted for a little longer before packing up and saying their goodbyes.

"I better see you at bingo on Friday!" Paula called before they left.

"We'll be there!" Bill said as he pushed a few more cookies wrapped in napkins into Paula's hands.

"You didn't tell me Ricky was cute!" Paula said after the door shut behind them.

"You should've known what he looked like! You guys had calc together."

"You make a great point. What in the world was I doing in that class?"

"Umm . . . paying attention to the teacher?" Molly guessed.

"Very unlikely." Paula sighed. "I think I might just like a sensitive type like that. An artist."

Molly giggled. "He was very sweet to Bill. Do you think Bill really made those cookies?"

Paula snorted again. "Those are from Whitethorne's Deli, no question. I know my rez cookies."

[10]

KAY

THE AT-HOME PREGNANCY test wasn't exactly cheap. Kay felt like a chemist inside the bathroom with a vial of purified water, a test tube with who knew what inside of it—"ingredients," according to the package—a medicine dropper, and an angled mirror. She waited a whole two hours to find out that the dizziness and nausea she'd been experiencing for the last couple of days was probably just due to heat and dehydration. According to the instructions that came with the test, she ought to still make an appointment with her doctor if she was confident in her pregnancy. She was not confident in her pregnancy. Not at all. What she was, was hopeful. She hadn't missed a period yet. It was probably coming any day now.

She had heard Paula and Molly talking about Grandma Beans's classes at the community center, and even though she was most likely not pregnant, Kay decided to go. The girls wouldn't be hanging around the community center because they were at the graffiti artist's house. And Kay wanted to hear what Grandma Beans had to say about having a baby on the reservation.

Kay walked into the white-painted, cinderblock room about fifteen minutes before the class was to start. There were rows of black fold-up chairs placed in the center of the room and at the front, a whiteboard with lots of writing. Grandma Beans stood next to it, scrutinizing what she had written and murmuring to herself. Kay came up behind her and lightly placed a hand on her shoulder. Grandma Beans turned and broke into a big smile. She hugged Kay.

"Kay Pinter! So good to see you! Are you staying for my class?"

Kay nodded. "Don't tell Paula or Molly, but James and I are trying for a baby. If we're not too old." Kay gave Grandma Beans a lopsided smile.

Grandma Beans chuckled. "I've seen older moms. You're probably just fine."

"Thank you for doing this," Kay said.

"It's my life's work." Grandma Beans gestured to the table along the far wall. "Have something to eat and drink first!"

"Thank you," Kay said. "I will."

Kay stood in the corner, nibbling on a muffin and checking out the rest of the attendees as they arrived, hoping none of them were her students, since that was the lie she had prepared in case she saw anyone else she knew. That she was there on behalf of a student. It wasn't out of the question. She frequently had pregnant students. Luckily, Kay didn't recognize anyone. No students. No fellow teachers. She finally sat in the back row and watched the other women file in.

"Welcome," Grandma Beans said loudly about five minutes after class was scheduled to begin. "Yá'át'ééh."

A few women muttered greetings in return. Some shifted

in their seats, getting settled. Hung their purses from the backs of their chairs.

"I am so pleased to see so many of you here today. I am glad you have chosen to spend your Saturday afternoon with me. And I hope by the time you leave, you will feel it was worth your time."

Grandma Beans glanced for a moment at the whiteboard behind her that was filled with bullet points and dashes and asterisks.

"So. You are all growing life inside of you! Baa shiłhózó. How wonderful! The future of the Diné people lives in this room."

Grandma Beans smiled wide enough to show her teeth, then. True happiness radiated from her being.

"When are you due?" she asked the room. The women were quiet at first. They looked at one another.

"Go ahead," Grandma Beans said. "Shout it out!"

Finally, a woman in the front row said, "In two weeks!"

Grandma Beans's eyes grew big. "Two weeks! That doesn't give me much time! Maybe you and I will have to have some one-on-one sessions." She winked at the woman and soft laughter rippled through the crowd.

"October!" another woman yelled.

"September 19!"

"How very precise!" Grandma Beans answered. There was some laughter again.

"I imagine many of you have a doctor you are seeing already established, is that right?"

Kay could see some heads nod.

"How many of you have doctors on the reservation? A show of hands?"

Nearly every hand went up. Only four women kept their hands down.

"Well, I will talk about the reservation hospitals first, then."

Grandma Beans stepped a little to the side to reveal more of the board behind her. Some women reached for their purses or bags and pulled out notebooks.

"Remember, this is not school," Grandma Beans said. "There will be no homework or tests. I wrote this up here because I'm old and tend to forget things. But please. Do not feel like you must copy it all down. I will give you my phone number and address at the end of class and I encourage you to come to me whenever with your questions and concerns."

She offered a soft smile.

"So you're in labor," Grandma Beans jumped right in, "and you have your packed bag ready with a change of clothes for you and a few outfits for your baby in different sizes. I've seen newborns the size of four-month-olds!"

Kay felt a small stab of pain in her chest at the mention of a big baby. Hers had been so small. Impossibly small. Kay had asked to see the baby when she came out of anesthesia and the nurse had looked torn for only a moment before nodding and bringing the lifeless baby to Kay. She would never forget that nurse's kindness.

"Now. How about other people?" Grandma Beans went on. "When the hospitals first opened, they only allowed the baby's father to visit the mother. Now, they allow two additional people and even allow some to be present during the birth. Whether it's your mom or your auntie or two aunties or your grandmother or your cousin, it's up to you. So, make sure everyone else has their bags packed, too. It might be a few days. Though your family can come and go as they please during visiting hours."

A hand shot up near Kay.

"Yes?" Grandma Beans asked.

"What if your baby's father isn't around?" the woman asked. "Can I bring three family members?"

"Yes, dear. Four adults including yourself."

Just then, the door in the corner cracked open and a woman walked in. She was short and not particularly thin but looked strong. Her face was quite beautiful, Kay thought. Her features sharp in a way that looked regal. The audience had mostly turned to look at her.

"Please continue," she said. "Sorry for the interruption."

Grandma Beans offered a smile and a wave, which the new woman returned. She did not sit down, but rather stood at the back against the wall.

"The hospitals have also changed another rule," Grandma Beans went on. "They will continue to offer twilight sleep if you want it. This means when it's time to give birth you will be given medication that will make you forget the pain of labor. You will feel like you slept through it and will be fairly confused when you come out of it. You will not actually be asleep, though. You'll still be able to respond to the doctor's requests."

Forget the pain of labor. How about the tears? Kay thought to herself. *The rushing around? The panic? The blood?* Everything had to be done so quickly to save Kay. Nothing could have saved her child. Kay could not remember much about the emergency c-section, either. She must have also been given twilight sleep.

"Twilight sleep may sound appealing," Grandma Beans

continued. "But if you would like my advice, I would suggest that you not choose this option."

A handful of women muttered to one another, and two raised their hands. Grandma Beans put one hand up.

"I know many of you want some sort of pain relief. Giving birth is no walk in the park. I've done it myself. I know." Grandma Beans took a deep breath. Her nostrils flared; her jaw worked. "But the medicine the reservation hospitals offer is not good for you and it is not good for your baby."

The hands still did not go down.

"Let me finish my thought and then you can ask questions. Some reservation hospitals *might* offer nitrous gas. I would encourage you to ask. That is a much safer option."

Kay watched the hands slowly go down.

"However, I know Shiprock does not always have nitrous gas available." She held up one finger. "But luckily, us Indians have been birthing with only natural remedies for quite a long time. Forever, would you believe it? I understand not all of you practice traditional Diné healing and do not have a medicine man and do not feel entirely comfortable visiting one. That's okay. There are other options, too." Grandma Beans looked straight at the woman standing in the back.

Another hand shot up. A different one.

"Yes?" Grandma Beans asked.

"Do you mean peyote? My friend used peyote to help her in labor. She said it worked well."

"The hospitals do allow peyote now. That's correct."

"How can we get some?" another woman shouted without raising her hand.

"I . . . I'll have to find that out," Grandma Beans stumbled on her words for the first time. "Perhaps Dawn." She nodded toward the woman, and all twenty-something attendees turned to look at her. "Dawn—a certified nurse midwife right here on the reservation, who we should all thank for putting this class together—perhaps she can find some more information for you all about that."

Wasn't the nurse from James's new case named Dawn? Had Kay only imagined that? Kay studied this Dawn woman for a moment, and just then, Dawn looked right at her. She smiled and nodded. Kay looked away, weirdly ashamed all of a sudden to be there at all.

[11]

WAYNE

Wayne had been working with Raymond Nez for almost a year now, gathering evidence of corruption within the Navajo Nation's government. It was slow and fairly uneventful, and they certainly didn't have enough proof of anything to bring a case anytime soon. Raymond's position as the head of the health department meant he was only invited to certain government meetings and only needed at certain times. But he was trusted by the chairman, Teddy Jackson—a member of the same clan, too—and he was willing to keep his eyes and ears open and report back to Wayne.

It wasn't a secret that Chairman Jackson and his cronies —most notably Cecil Cody—had a special relationship with the mining companies. Jackson claimed it was all in the name of progress and job creation, but Wayne and Raymond knew that wasn't the full truth.

WARN had become a thorn in the side of tribal law enforcement because of their tendency to stir up violence with their intense rhetoric. But Wayne hadn't taken the organization all that seriously before. Didn't think them organized enough or powerful enough. Perhaps he was wrong. Perhaps WARN—and women like Robin—*had* become a real threat to certain people. He needed more information, though. Insider information.

Aside from their working relationship, Wayne and Raymond had become friends. On that day, Wayne grabbed a tin of Barbara's teacakes to bring to Raymond. He liked Barbara's cooking, her baking. Everyone did.

Raymond stood and greeted Wayne with a smile and a handshake. "You brought me a treat."

Wayne patted his stomach. "Have to get rid of some of it so I don't eat it all myself. Got to watch my weight now that I'm getting older."

Raymond and Wayne sat down. "But you look great, Lieutenant! I'd be as fat as a cow if my wife could bake and cook like Barb."

Wayne chuckled. "It's a race against time at this point, my friend."

"So, what brings you to Window Rock today?" Raymond asked.

"I've got a new case that I'm hoping you can help me out with," Wayne said.

"Let's hear it."

"A woman from Shiprock died last week at the hospital. The doctor suspected sepsis from a ruptured cyst in her uterus, though we don't know for sure since the husband is refusing an autopsy."

Raymond nodded, his forehead creased in concentration.

"The death was officially reported to us by a friend. The woman who died, Robin Kinsel, had been threatened about two weeks earlier. Someone slashed her tires and painted all over her car, calling her a liar and an enemy and telling her to watch her back."

"So you think the threats could be related to her death?" Raymond asked.

"Could be." Raymond probably suspected Wayne wanted some sort of medical opinion at that point. Raymond had been a medic in the Vietnam War before being appointed head of the Department of Health on the reservation.

"Here's the thing," Wayne went on. "Robin was a member of WARN. A very public face for WARN, in fact. And her friend Patricia, who reported the death, is the chapter's president."

Raymond's eyebrows went up. "WARN, huh?"

"I can guess who WARN's enemies are here on the reservation," Wayne said.

"But confirmation would be better." Raymond sat back in his chair. Crossed his arms. "Tell me more about the death. If you can."

"The doctor said the husband was irate. Had to be escorted out of the hospital. It seems to me that could be a typical grieving response. But maybe not. For the doctor to mention it, perhaps it was outside of normal behavior." Wayne rubbed the back of his neck. "Robin admitted to taking peyote before coming to the hospital. Apparently, it's common now for women to take peyote during childbirth— and then to continue to use it for pain relief after the baby is born."

"During childbirth?" Raymond asked. "They bring it into the hospital?"

"That's right. The doctor basically conceded once he realized he wasn't winning any friends by banning it and might, in fact, have been driving women away."

Raymond frowned. "Not sure I agree with him on that."

"You think he should've taken a hard line?" Wayne asked.

"I think it invites all sort of headaches that the hospital isn't equipped to deal with."

"Fair enough. Well, I was able to confiscate Robin's peyote and have sent it off for testing in case it's been tampered with."

"Poisoning? I thought the doctor suspected sepsis."

"He said her symptoms could also be consistent with a possible poisoning, depending on what was used."

"What were her symptoms?" Raymond asked.

"Stomach pain, nausea, high fever."

"Which could be a million different things," Raymond said.

"Exactly. Apparently, Robin went into respiratory failure first before cardiac arrest."

"That can happen with sepsis." Raymond uncrossed his arms and sat up straighter. Leaned forward on the desk.

"If it *was* a poisoning," Wayne went on. "Aside from her husband, we need to identify possible suspects."

Raymond nodded. "Say no more, Lieutenant."

"Appreciate it. Not that I expect any talk specifically about Robin, although if you do hear that, call me right away. But anything about WARN you happen to pick up on. Keep me in the loop."

Raymond stood and shook Wayne's hand. "Hey, thanks

for telling me about the peyote in the hospitals. I wasn't aware. That's something I should know."

"Of course." Wayne pointed at the teacakes. "Don't eat all those at once."

Raymond grinned. "Can't make any promises there! Give Barb my love."

[12]

JAMES

THE DIRT at Window Rock's outdoor rodeo arena had been meticulously raked, and the soft lines were visible from the top of the wooden bleachers. James and Molly sat on splintered seats, watching attendees get settled. A group of teenagers to their right—ones Molly didn't seem to know—stuffed their hands into bags of popcorn and laughed with open mouths or behind their hands. In front of them, a mom and a little boy played a clapping game.

The announcers and other workers stood behind the gate on the opposite side of the arena, leaning up against the rails and sipping from Styrofoam coffee cups. James was looking for Russel Kinsel. Knew he was riding tonight but hadn't spotted him yet. He assumed he was in the practice corral behind the box seats. The side from which the bulls would be released.

"Do we even know what this guy looks like?" Molly asked.

"We'll know exactly who he is when they announce him."

"How do we know he's even going to talk to us?" Molly asked. "Wayne said he hates the law."

"We don't know, but we're gonna try," James said. "Besides, we're not technically the law, now are we?"

Molly raised her eyebrows. "What's your plan, Sherlock?"

"Well, I'd like to scope out his friends and family. At the beginning of the rodeo, they'll announce all the riders. Keep your eyes peeled for who cheers for Russel Kinsel. We might have luck with some of them. Besides, I'm assuming some of his friends were Robin's friends, too. If they're here tonight, they'll be good resources."

"So, we're just going to ask people about a dead woman and make sure they understand we're *not* law enforcement? That sounds . . . creepy."

James smiled. "We won't mention our ties to tribal police."

Molly shrugged. "I'm in."

Spectators continued to trickle in, filling up the seats around Molly and James. They carried hot dogs and smelled like fried food. Finally, the speakers crackled and the announcer welcomed everyone to the arena. He announced the kids first and Molly and James oohed and aahed as the small children expertly guided ponies between cones. Next was the woolly and steer riding, and boys slightly older than the first crowd, though not quite teenagers, held on tight or immediately slid off the animals as they were let out of the gate. Molly clapped a few times, visibly relieved that the boys were all right.

There was a break after that, and Molly and James got up to use the bathroom and buy some lemonade. James stood outside the bathrooms, beneath the box seats, while Molly went in. He could see the bull riders now, gathered just where he'd suspected they would be. Nearly all were young men about the same age as Russel. They all had chaps on and some wore cowboy hats. A few had short hair, others long and braided or tied into a bun behind their neck. One man's hair hung loose on his shoulders, and James thought he looked the oldest—not much younger than James himself. He was close enough to see their faces but too far to hear what they were saying. They leaned against the fence and laughed and smoked and shook their heads.

Lemonades in hand, he and Molly took their time returning to their seats.

"Did you see Russel back there?" Molly asked him.

"I have my guess which one he is, but I could be wrong."

"You didn't want to go up and ask?"

James shook his head. "It's not the time to distract the man. Not right before he gets on top of a bull."

"I saw a group of girls checking them out," Molly said. "Women, I guess. I don't know how old they were."

"Checkin' out the riders?" James asked.

Molly nodded. "Whispering about them. I couldn't hear what they were saying, but they were huddled together outside the women's restroom."

"I imagine some of those men are quite the bachelors."

"I can see the appeal," Molly said.

James raised his eyebrows. "You can?"

She giggled. "Sure. It's very brave of them."

"Brave, huh?" James asked. He wanted to call those young men reckless, but he couldn't deny that he probably would've been the first to hop up as a young man, had the opportunity presented itself. But he hadn't been hanging around rodeos at that age. He'd been investigating crime scenes in Vietnam.

"Probably fun, too," Molly said.

"I better not find *you* takin' rodeo lessons," James said. Molly rolled her eyes.

"I think you get me into enough trouble, Dad," she said.

He grinned at her. When they got back to their seats, James realized the crowd had changed. The parents of the little ones were gone, replaced with more people in their early to mid-twenties. It was getting louder now. Rowdier. The sun was setting, and the arena lights flickered on one by one until the whole space was lit up.

When the announcer got back on the intercom, the arena hushed before breaking into wild cheers at every name. Russel Kinsel was about halfway down that list, and a group of young adults at James's three o'clock hollered and clapped. His high score was impressive. Seventy-two. James knew enough about bull riding to know it took hard work to get a score like that.

"This feels too soon," Molly whispered. "For Russel to be doing this again."

James nodded. "Grief is funny like that. Something like this could be the only thing getting him out of bed these days."

"What about his son?" Molly asked.

James thought for a moment. He always felt inadequate answering a question like that, given his history as an absent father. But it was clear Molly wasn't thinking of herself at all.

"A responsibility is different than a passion," James finally answered. "I'm sure Russel loves his son. I'm sure he understands the boy needs his father right now. But this?" James nodded toward the open arena. "Maybe it simply reminds him that *he* is still alive."

Molly shook her head. "I don't know. It seems suspicious."

James swished the last of his lemonade around and drank from the straw before setting it on the bleacher at his feet.

"Noted," James said. "We'll keep an eye on him."

The first rider waited atop the bull behind the shut gate, gripping the rail. It was impossible to see the rider's face, but his anticipation electrified the whole arena. Finally, a buzzer sounded and the man inside the arena pulled the rope attached to the gate and scrambled out of the way as the bull came kicking and bucking from behind it. Some people cheered and shouted, but James noticed most of the audience seemed to be holding their breath. There was a digital timer lit up next to the box seats. The first man lasted 4.3 seconds, which James thought was pretty darn good, though he knew only riders who lasted eight seconds would get a score at all. The next couple riders lasted just about as long, and the crowd's attention clearly started to wander. There was more chatting and laughing, less breath-holding. But when they called Russel Kinsel, the crowd quieted. *Interesting*, James thought. He was known among the rodeo-goers, then.

"Go, Russel!" someone shouted into the quiet.

James could see Russel's hand gripping the rail, a bright-red sleeve disappearing behind the holding pen.

Red. In an arena with a bull. James shook his head. He had read somewhere, at some point, that bulls were actually color-blind. Whether Russel knew that, James wasn't sure. Maybe the man was suicidal.

This time when the man pulled the rope, the crowd *did* hold their breath. The whole crowd, it seemed. A woman behind them murmured the second count, even though the large digital clocked flashed right behind Russel. He looked like a rag doll up there, James thought. His one hand gripping the rope, his other up in the air like he was waving to them all. But his body flipped and flopped with the bull's movement. Six seconds, seven seconds, eight seconds. Finally, Russel was thrown from the bull and he scrambled to his feet as the rodeo clowns scurried to his side to protect him. Russel yelled in victory and the crowd was on their feet cheering for him. James stood and clapped too.

"He's good!" Molly shouted above the din. James nodded.

Three riders later, there was another break in the program. "Let's go talk to Russel's friends."

"Now?" Molly asked.

"Yep."

They stood and Molly followed James to the spot in the bleachers where he had heard the loudest cheers at the start of the program. No one noticed them approaching at first—or at least, they acted like they didn't—but when they got right up to the group, the two men and three women looked up at them.

"Hey, there," James said. "Do you mind if I take a seat?"

"We actually have two other people with us," one of the women said. "They're in the bathroom."

"Oh, I won't be long," James said, sitting a few feet from the group. "I wanted to ask y'all a couple questions about Robin Kinsel."

Molly climbed down one seat and sat in front of James, her body turned toward the group.

One of the men narrowed his eyes. "She isn't around anymore," he said. "She passed away last week."

"I know. And I'm sorry for your loss," James said. He took a pack of cigarettes from his shirt pocket and offered them to the group, but no one accepted. James slid one out for himself, lit it, and took a puff. "I see her husband rode tonight."

The group nodded, but most averted their eyes except for the young man who had spoken.

"What about her?" the man asked.

"We're a private investigation firm," James said. "And we're lookin' into the hospital's treatment of Mrs. Kinsel."

The man's eyes softened a bit. "You should talk to Russel," he said. "He knows they fucked up. They did it. It was their fault."

James nodded. He took another drag. "We're lookin' into it. They have suggested that her death had something to do with peyote she took before arriving there. Y'all see any merit to that?"

One of the women, the smallest and youngest-looking, bit her lip.

"No," another woman answered firmly. She was a larger woman. Wide shoulders. Tall. "The peyote is fine. She'd taken it before and was fine. It wasn't the peyote."

"She talk to any of y'all about who vandalized her car before her death?" James asked.

Once again, no one answered. They barely acknowledged his question. He waited anyway. Finally, the large woman spoke again.

"Robin didn't know who did that to her car."

"Who do you think it was?" James asked.

The woman looked him dead in the eye. "If Robin didn't know, why would I?"

"Maybe you had suspicions."

"I didn't," she said.

"What can you tell me about the hospital?" James asked. "Why does Russel think they're the ones that messed up?"

"You'd have to ask him," the first man said.

"It's because they always fuck up," the young girl spoke up now. "He's seen it himself when he's gotten hurt and when his friends here have gotten hurt. They're useless. All the reservation hospitals are."

"What's the next closest hospital?" James asked. "Off the reservation?"

"Gallup," the first man said. "Not too far, but far enough when it's an emergency."

"That place kind of sucks, too," the young girl said.

"Oh, I don't know. They treated me for a gunshot wound last year. I healed up just fine," James said.

They all stared at him again. He cleared his throat.

"Any specific prior complaints Russel had about the Shiprock hospital?" James asked.

"He's got *plenty*," the young girl said. "Really, you should talk to him."

James noticed the third girl slip away as they spoke. She didn't say anything, just turned, stood, and walked down the bleachers toward the bathrooms. Or toward the corrals. James dropped his cigarette on the ground and put it out with his boot.

"I will talk to him," James assured them. "All right, then."

He grabbed a stack of business cards from his wallet and handed out a few. "If you think of anything else I ought to know, give me a call or a visit." He tipped his hat and stood and Molly followed.

"Let's go talk to Russel," Molly hissed at him. "Like, right now! He's done riding."

[13]

RUSSEL

RUSSEL DIDN'T CARE about his award. He'd known he would win tonight. He could collect his money tomorrow. That wasn't what this was about.

Robin's sister had come to warn him about the white man and the girl asking questions and he wasn't in the mood. He'd told a buddy of his he was leaving early and then walked off into the dark parking lot to find his truck.

He carried his chaps and his hat in his hand and threw them in the truck bed. They stunk, he knew. He stunk. He got in the driver's seat and took a deep breath. Ran his hand through his filthy hair. He should've felt something, then. Pride. Relief. Robin's death hadn't changed his ability to win. He hadn't thought of her at all when he was on the bull. During those eight seconds, he had thought of nothing but his own body and the bull's movements. He didn't care about his shitty job or his empty bed or his son's incessant cries. And in the moments after he was thrown, as he stood on his two feet, wiping his hands along the side of his shirt, he felt intense love for that bull. The simplicity of the beast's existence.

But now, sitting in his dark, quiet truck, he felt hollow again. The rush had passed. He didn't want to go home and see his mother-in-law sitting vigil by his son's crib. He didn't want to wake up to one more day of his life without Robin. This wasn't how any of this was supposed to go.

Russel had been raised a Christian but considered joining the Native American Church right when Robin got pregnant. He'd been afraid then, he knew now, but it had felt something like a miracle. A miracle that he couldn't possibly understand. Suddenly, he needed to be sure of everything. It felt like it was his responsibility to understand the world, to explain it all to his son someday, and maybe joining the Native American Church would help.

Robin was, of course, all for it, but then something happened that gave him pause. It was the head of Robin's Native American Church chapter. The roadman. He was overly friendly with Russel. Too confident. Too aggressive. Russel didn't like him. But maybe he was just looking for a reason to back out. Maybe he subconsciously regretted expressing his feelings to Robin. Maybe it had been so long since the two of them had been on the same page about something, about anything, really, but especially something as personal and raw as spirituality, that it felt too unfamiliar, too uncomfortable.

Russel never went to a meeting, and now that Robin was gone, he was almost desperate for some sort of spiritual awakening. But he knew he wouldn't go to that roadman. And he knew that some part of him was still angry at Robin, bitter even, for introducing Russel to him. For pushing Russel away. How had he managed to make that her fault? How was it, he considered, that he could make almost anything Robin's fault, even now? Even with her gone?

He felt something, then. Pain. A sharpness in his chest that had nothing to do with being thrown from a bull. He took another deep breath and started the car.

WAYNE

Wayne happened to know the roadman at the Native American Church chapter where Robin would've attended meetings. Sort of. Clarence Draper's family had owned the trading post at the corner of Route 14 and Highway 491 for as long as Wayne could remember. Back when it was unusual for a trading post to be owned by an Indian. Back when trading posts were thriving.

Whenever he was in the area and needed something, Wayne tried to stop in at Clarence's trading post. He'd rather support the Drapers than a big-box store in Window Rock or Gallup or Farmington. The trading post sold snacks and coffee, magazines and soda like a gas station, and folks could pick up their mail like a post office. But it also sold rugs and jewelry made by Diné. Clarence always had the weaver or beadmaker's name listed alongside their maternal clan. Visitors from all over New Mexico—and even the country—were known to frequent Clarence's.

Wayne pulled into the empty parking lot before the sun was up. Half of the trading post had been built with logs and the other half added on sometime later and built with wood siding. He knew its contours, even though he could barely see it with only the light from the streetlamps. Wayne leaned his seat back just a hair. Watched a few cars and trucks drive by, their headlights flashing in his eyes before speeding off down the highway. He fiddled with the radio station. Listened to early morning talk radio—the polls were predicting a Ronald Reagan landslide win in November. He didn't know how he felt about that. He did know that Carter had screwed things up monumentally in more ways than one. But he also doubted a Republican president would make his life any easier.

Wayne switched the radio to the AM stations. KNDN. Navajo radio. They were talking about basketball. About Kareem Abdul-Jabbar. About how the US team ought to be winning a gold medal that summer, but because of the Olympic boycott, they were at home instead, getting fat on junk food and beer. Wayne chuckled and then turned off the radio when a car pulled in next to his. Clarence glanced at Wayne as he got out of his car, held up his hand in greeting. Wayne got out too and shook Clarence's hand. Clarence was only a few years older than Wayne but plenty shorter. He had wide shoulders but was thin at the waist, and he wore a loose T-shirt and long turquoise necklaces. He had a shy face that seemed to hide under thick eyebrows.

"Morning, Lieutenant," Clarence said. "Come on inside."

Wayne stood just inside the door as Clarence switched on the lights. Back lights first—a wash of yellow spilling out of the back office for just a moment before the main lights flickered on. The inside of the wood siding half of the post was tiled and white and bright. The other half, the half made with logs, was warm and welcoming, the items made by Diné hung on the walls with nails. The front door opened to the sterile side with racks of snacks and a coffee maker. As he waited for Clarence to clean up and restock and get the register ready for the day, Wayne made the coffee.

He was quiet as he watched Clarence pull snack-size boxes of Pringles out of a cardboard box and stack them on a shelf. The coffee maker dripped behind him.

"How's it going, Clarence?" Wayne finally asked.

"Good," Clarence nodded. "Business is good. Summer. Lots of tourists passing through."

"Glad to hear that. How's your family?"

"Good, good. Daughter is off to college this year." Clarence smiled a sad sort of smile. "Can't hardly believe it. House will be quiet without her."

"She the youngest?"

"Sure is."

Wayne turned to look at the coffee. There was enough brewed for a cup. He grabbed a paper cup and filled it, then placed the pot back under the filter. He blew on the steaming cup and watched the coffee ripple.

"I understand a member of your church passed away recently. I'm very sorry for your loss."

Clarence stopped what he was doing and looked at Wayne with pursed lips and squinted eyes.

"I'm sorry, too," he said. "Robin was a wonderful young woman."

"Her friend Patricia Dawes reported her death to us. She was concerned because Robin had been threatened a few weeks prior. Did you know anything about that?" Wayne asked, taking his first sip. Clarence looked puzzled.

"Threatened? In what way?"

"Her car was vandalized. She was told to watch her back."

Clarence raised a thick eyebrow and then turned away. He put the last of the Pringles on the shelf, ripped the tape off the bottom of the cardboard box, and started to break it down. His hands shook slightly.

"I knew her car was out of commission, but I didn't know there was any threat."

"Patricia said Robin was very involved with the church. What can you tell me about that?"

"Oh yes," Clarence said, still looking down at the flattened box in his hands. "Robin came to every meeting. She was truly a light in our community. She cooked and brought food for the mornings. She checked up on our members who were struggling and distraught. She had a real heart and a selflessness unusual in a person so young."

Finally, Clarence looked up at Wayne. There were tears in the man's eyes.

"I'm sorry you lost her so soon," Wayne said. "She sounds like she would've been a treasured church member for a long time."

Clarence nodded. He sniffled. "Please excuse me a moment."

He disappeared into his office, and Wayne heard him blow his nose. He figured he would give the man some privacy in his grief, and so he turned and drifted to the other side of the post, over to the wall with the rugs and the jewelry. Something had caught his eye. It was a smaller rug. Bright-red and white with a few black diamonds at the corners. Wayne stood in front of it for a while, admiring it. He eventually heard Clarence's foot-steps behind him.

"This is beautiful," Wayne said.

"Ah yes." Clarence drew up beside him. "We have some new weavers. This one is quite talented. Quite young, too."

Wayne looked at the price and did a little whistle. Clarence laughed.

"Like I said, tourist season. And they'll pay, too!"

"Good for you," Wayne said. "And good for . . . ." He squinted and squatted down a little to get eye level with the tag. "Lucille."

"I'd say weaving is about the most lucrative thing these women can do on the reservation these days," Clarence said.

"Was Robin a weaver?" Wayne asked, straightening himself up again.

"No. But she did help me find these artists. Through WARN."

Wayne turned to Clarence. "You're in contact with WARN members?"

Clarence scowled. "They're good girls. All of the ones I've worked with are good girls."

Wayne took another long sip of coffee. Sucked air in through his teeth after. "There's one more thing I wanted to ask you. In regard to Robin."

"All right," Clarence answered.

"Robin told the doctor when she was admitted to the hospital that she had taken peyote for the pain. When I visited her home, she had a jar of it in her kitchen. I'm not a member of the Native American Church. I'm a Catholic. So I suppose I don't know the specifics. But I thought I under-stood that peyote was only taken during meetings, in the teepee." Wayne paused. He hadn't asked a question but hoped Clarence would have something to say anyway.

"That's true," Clarence said. "It is not distributed in large amounts, only enough to be taken in the teepee." He cleared his throat and then opened his mouth slightly. A moment later, he closed it again. Wayne gave him time to say more, but he didn't.

"Do you have any idea where Robin might have gotten her peyote, then?"

"I'm not sure," Clarence said.

"She also took it while she was in labor with her son, which was more than a year ago. In fact," Wayne went on, "the doctor told me that women frequently bring peyote with them to the hospital when they're in labor."

Clarence shook his head. "That has nothing to do with me. I've never given a woman, or anyone, peyote when they leave the teepee. We take it together and that's that."

"Do you go to Texas yourself to purchase the peyote?" Wayne asked.

"I haven't for a long time," Clarence said. "Years, maybe."

"Why not?" Wayne asked.

"I haven't needed to. Cecil Cody or one of his sons purchase it for me. As they do for most of the roadmen on this reservation."

"And they are the only ones who do this? Who go to Texas?"

"Others accompany them sometimes," Clarence said.

"Do you know of anyone who's gone recently?" Wayne asked.

Clarence shook his head. "You would have to ask the Codys. Like I said, it's been a long time since I went."

"Could Robin have gotten hers from the Codys?"

"It's possible."

"But she never said anything to you about that."

"No."

Wayne stuck his hand out and Clarence shook it. "I appreciate your time," he said. "And I'm sorry about Robin."

"Do you think there was . . . foul play involved in her death?" Clarence asked, dropping his hand to his side. He blinked rapidly. Wayne couldn't tell if it was from fear or if he was trying to hold back tears again.

"It's possible. I'm looking into it."

Clarence stuck his hands in his pockets and nodded. His gaze jumped around. Over Wayne's shoulder, to the floor. He didn't say anything more, though, even after Wayne waited a minute, so Wayne said, "See you around, Clarence," and then left.

[15]

JAMES

HAMMER AWAY STOOD on its own on the side of the highway. James saw it maybe a mile away because of the giant hammer on the roof. Couldn't miss it. He held the front door open for Molly, who carried a side satchel with a drawing pad and some paper. The store smelled like metal and wood. Sawdust covered the floor. Molly blinked a few times when they walked in and then rubbed her eyes. James reckoned the store could use a better ventilation system. Or a few open windows.

The older man behind the counter wore a baseball cap with strands of white hair sticking out the bottom, and overalls—both stained with paint and primer and who knew what else. A pair of reading glasses hung from his neck. His nametag read, *Bud.* He nodded once at Molly and James. "Afternoon. What can I do for you folks?"

"Afternoon, Bud. My name's James Pinter and this is my daughter, Molly Pinter. We are private investigators over on the Navajo reservation." James stuck out his hand and Bud shook it. Molly did the same. "We've got a question for you about a customer, if it's possible to mine your memory."

Bud tugged at the back of his baseball cap, revealing slightly more of his forehead. James could see his greenish-brown eyes better that way.

"You can try." Bud grinned. "It isn't what it used to be, but I'll do my best to help you out. What's this about?"

"A threat made via vandalism. Nasty words painted on someone's car."

Bud's eyebrows went up. "That so?"

"We're pretty sure we know the make and model, so to speak, of the spray paint used on the car. Krylon Avocado, number 2009. Y'all sell that here?"

"I believe so," Bud said. "Krylon's got a whole hell of a lot of colors out these days, but why don't you follow me and we'll see what's back there?"

"Sounds good. Thanks, Bud." Molly and James followed him a few aisles from the cash register to a shelf filled with spray paint. Bud put his glasses on, leaned down, and muttered the names of the paint to himself.

"Here ya go," he finally said, picking up a can of paint from the shelf. "Krylon Avocado." He took his glasses off again and handed the can to James.

"Now here's the harder question," James said. "You remember anyone buyin' this paint anytime in the last couple of months? Particularly, anyone from the Navajo reservation?"

Bud sucked air in through his teeth. "There is a young Indian man that comes in here every so often to buy lots of different colors of this stuff. Always assumed he was a car mechanic. Doesn't talk much. But here." Bud turned around and tried to hustle to the end of the aisle, but it ended up looking more like a waddle. "Jeb!" he called. "You back there?"

He looked back at James. "My son. He's here pretty much all the time and has a much sharper memory than I do." He winked.

A young, muscular man in his early twenties with short brown hair appeared just a minute or two later.

"There ya are," Bud said. He guided them over, and Jeb looked James right in the eye as he gave him a firm handshake.

"These folks are private investigators, and they're asking about who might've bought this paint recently. Particularly any Indians."

James held up the spray paint bottle and Jeb squinted at it. Then he crossed his arms and slowly nodded.

"Few weeks ago, a man about your age was here buying that paint. He bought a few cans." Jeb paused and thought some more. "Before that, there was a young woman. 'Bout my age. Maybe a little older." He stopped again. Then shook his head. "That's all I can remember."

"That's good, that's real good, Jeb," James said. "Thanks for that. Is there anywhere we might be able to sit down, or even just have a little counter space up front so Molly can get their descriptions and draw a little sketch?"

"I would bring you to the back but heaven knows that table hasn't seen the light of day in years." Bud laughed. "Stacked up with one thing or another all the time. The counter is going to have more space."

The four of them returned to the front, and Bud drifted

off to help another customer as Jeb stood behind the counter and Molly got out her sketching supplies.

"We'll start with the woman," Molly said. "She was Navajo, right?"

Jeb turned a little red. "Some kind of Indian. I think."

"So, black hair? Or dark brown?"

James stepped away while Molly and Jeb hunched over the counter, drawing and talking. He went back to the spray paint aisle and scanned the shelf. There were two other shades of green and maybe close to fifty other colors. They were all Krylon brand. James supposed a store like this would only carry one brand. Specialize in it. Have some sort of loyalty discount. He thought about what Molly's friend had said. That the Krylon was a thinner paint than its competitor, Rust-O. He noticed Bud apologizing to the customer he had been helping out.

"We must've just sold the last one. But come back next week and we'll have more," Bud was saying. The man and Bud shook hands, and James caught Bud's eye, gestured for his attention.

"Your daughter is an artist, huh?" Bud asked when he got back to James's side.

"She sure is. She's darn good at it, too. A real asset to the business."

"That's just great. You always hope you've built something for them that they'll find worthwhile. Jeb is a big help these days. A big help."

"Can I ask you a question, Bud, about these paints?" James asked.

"Go ahead and shoot!"

"Any reason why you chose to carry this brand? This Krylon?"

"Oh, no. Not really. We looked into their competitor, too. Rust-O. But they were a tad more expensive. Think it's because they use whale fat oil in their paint. Can you imagine that? Their founder just happened to figure out that whale fat prevents rusting!"

"Huh," James said. "That's pretty interesting. Now, does this Krylon rust easy?"

Bud shook his head. "They claim to be rust resistant as well, and we haven't had any complaints saying otherwise."

"You strike me as a guy who knows his customers pretty well. Not afraid to have a nice little chat in the afternoon," James said.

Bud laughed. "I've always been called a talker. Even in school."

"Why is it that your customers who buy the spray paint don't just buy regular cans of paint?" James asked. "What're they usin' this for?"

"Well, like I said earlier, we get mechanics sometimes, who use it to patch up a little spot here or there. It doesn't drip like regular paint and it's easier to target a specific area."

"How about a young woman buyin' a can, like Jeb was tellin' us?"

Bud's face lit up. "They use it for all kinds of things. You wouldn't even imagine how handy women are these days." He did a little whistle. "They'll buy some spray paint and paint all the cabinets in their kitchen! Or paint over a table or chairs or a bench. Make it look brand new. Sometimes they'll use it to paint a fence or a mailbox—the spray paint is particularly good for outdoor jobs because of the anti-rust agents."

Bud stopped to glance over at the door. A customer had just left. He refocused on James. "And sometimes they'll use it to make little signs, too. Like a welcome sign outside their front door. But really any small repair job inside or out."

"That's some good information," James said. "Thanks, Bud. We really do appreciate you and your son takin' some time to talk to us today."

"I hope we've been helpful. I don't like hearing that any of our customers are capable of committing any crimes." Bud frowned.

"No, I imagine you don't. But there's no way for you to tell what type of person walks through your door. You've gotta give people the benefit of the doubt and assume they've all got good, normal intentions."

Bud nodded vigorously. "You're right," he said. "It's hard to do but it's what Jesus calls us to do." Bud held up a finger. "Now, except those teenagers that come in here buying only spray paint. I know exactly what they're going to use it for and I won't allow that. Back in my day, we respected public property, you know what I mean? We weren't just going to paint all over it, writing our names. Thinking that our name was something important! That takes gall! And now we all have to see it and spend taxpayer dollars cleaning it up!"

James chuckled. "I hear ya, Bud. Hell, we all did things during our teenage years that just didn't make a lot of sense, now didn't we? At least these kids aren't gettin' sent off to war anymore. That we can be grateful for."

"Amen," Bud said. "Amen to that."

[16]

MOLLY

IF THEY WERE GOING to have a gathering this large, Kay reasoned, they might as well all muck the stalls first. Work up an appetite. Barbara had brought the food—because, as Kay reminded everyone, her own specialty was scrambled eggs. Adriel was there, too, working next to Molly and making silly faces whenever he caught her eye. They stopped for a water break and Molly tried to mess up Adriel's hair, but he got away, giggling and leaping over haystacks.

"All right, I've exploited you all for long enough," Kay announced to the group. "Let's go enjoy Barb's cooking."

Wayne groaned. "Thank goodness. Any longer and you all might've had to carry me inside. My back is just not what it used to be." Barbara rubbed his back as the six of them headed for the house.

Adriel disappeared inside and Molly was right on his heels when she heard a car pulling into the driveway. It was Grandma Beans. Paula jumped out, and Grandma Beans honked, waved, and drove away.

"Typical!" Molly shouted at Paula. "Shirking your duties, showing up for the food."

Paula rolled her eyes and shoved Molly's shoulder lightly. "I would have *much* rather been shoveling horse shit than having that fight with my mother."

"Lucky me, then. I got to shovel some *solid* horse shit. Some not-so-solid horse shit, too," Molly said. She draped her arm around Paula's shoulder and rested her head against hers.

Paula laughed. "Gross. We're about to eat, you beast."

"And then play our favorite game—stump Barbara at who's who on the reservation," Molly said.

"She wins every time."

Molly did not think while she ate. She was way too hungry and Barbara's food way too good. She was vaguely aware of the "mmmm" sounds she made but wasn't embarrassed by them at all.

After, as they all sat back and sipped their drinks in a satisfied quiet, Molly finally pulled the drawings from her bag.

"Okay," she said. "Here are the two customers the man from the hardware store remembered."

"He also said something about a young man," James jumped in. "Assumed to be a car mechanic but not confirmed. Quiet guy it seems, who consistently buys various colors of spray paint. He wasn't able to give us a description other than 'a thin Indian fella, about twenty to twenty-five years old.' But other than that, he wasn't confident in anything from height to eye color to haircut and length to whether or not the young man had any scars, tattoos, or identifying marks."

"Under the radar, huh?" Wayne said.

"Whether intentional or not, seems to be the case," James said.

Molly held the drawings up to the group and then passed them around. She started with the woman, who James had already recognized.

"That looks like Dawn Harvey," Barbara said as she held the sketch out in front of her.

"That's what I thought, too," James said.

"You know Dawn Harvey?" Barbara asked.

"She's the night nurse in charge of medications at the Shiprock hospital."

"The one that didn't like you," Wayne said.

"The very one."

"She's got an older brother in federal prison, you know," Barbara went on. "LeRoy. He was arrested with a bunch of the other American Indian Movement leaders. After that trip to Washington, DC, to the Bureau of Indian Affairs head-quarters."

"That's right, I remember hearing about that," James said. "Didn't they wreck the place?"

"Well, they weren't being polite about their stay," Barbara said. "I think they called it an occupation and refused to leave. They hung a flag outside that read, 'Native American Embassy.'"

James chuckled. "The US government can get uptight about that sort of thing."

"They went through all the BIA's files and found some pretty damning admissions while they were there. They also took back some stolen artifacts. And at the end of the day, there was some property damage as well."

James whistled. "And Dawn's brother LeRoy was part of that?"

"He was. A lot of the American Indian Movement leaders went. All of them were arrested afterward."

Barbara had passed the sketch along and now Paula was holding it. "I think I know this woman, too," she said. She started nodding to herself.

"Yeah, this is the woman who sets up the classes Grandma Beans teaches. She's the one that's about to start the certified midwife program on the reservation."

"She is a nurse," James said. "Makes sense."

"All right," Molly said. "So, you all seem pretty confident that's Dawn Harvey. How about this one?" She handed the sketch of the man to Kay first. No one said anything until it got to Wayne.

"Hmmm," Wayne grunted. "Could be Clarence Draper." He rubbed his chin like he was putting on a thinking performance. "Or maybe it's because I just saw the man, so he's on my mind. But the eyebrows. The eyebrows are Clarence's defining feature, which this man has."

"Who's Clarence Draper?" Molly asked.

"Robin's roadman."

Molly knew she should probably know what that was, but she didn't, so she asked.

"It's like a priest or a pastor but for the Native American Church," Wayne said. "He leads the meetings and distributes the tobacco and the peyote."

"And you just saw him?" Molly asked.

"I went to his trading post to ask about Robin, since Patricia said she was involved in her church. It seems to me the two were fairly close. Though he claims he did not give

Robin the peyote I confiscated. He seemed to insinuate that it was the Codys, but didn't outright say so. He seemed a little . . . off. Upset, certainly. But maybe a little nervous, too."

"But you're not sure if this is him?" James asked, pointing to the drawing.

Wayne shook his head. "It's not exact, no. But like I said, the eyebrows."

Adriel had seemingly grown bored with the conversation and scurried off. Molly heard the TV switch on.

"All right," James said, leaning forward now in his chair. "So, we're pretty confident Dawn Harvey bought this same color spray paint and possibly so did Robin's roadman, Clarence. Now for the young man. 'Thin' is a relative term and could probably mean any young man on the reservation who isn't fat. Which could be Russel. Or Ronnie Cody. Hell, it could be anyone. It could, in fact, be a mechanic."

"But what does it mean that they all bought this same can of paint?" Molly asked. "They could've bought it for any reason, right?"

James nodded. "The hardware store owner said spray paints are popular with women for home improvement projects and the like. And Molly's friend only narrowed the purchasing time to the last two years. Our guy or gal could've purchased the paint a year ago—long gone from the memory of our friends at the hardware store—and only used it now."

"But this is a good starting place," Wayne said. "Especially the color. Avocado green. It's not like they purchased white or cream. You were at Dawn's house," Wayne turned to James. "See anything painted green?"

James shook his head. "I was only in her living room,

though. Didn't see her kitchen or bathrooms or anything else."

"Are Dawn and Robin connected at all?" Molly asked. "Other than the fact that Robin went to the same hospital where Dawn works?"

"Maybe they knew each other through Dawn's program. The classes and all," Paula suggested. "Robin had a son, right?"

Molly nodded. "She could've gone to the classes. But just because Dawn coordinates them, doesn't mean she's *that* involved in each one. Right?"

"You girls are on the right track," James said. "We do need to find out if Dawn Harvey had a motive to target Robin. I wonder if there was some friction between Dawn's programs and WARN. Some internal feud. Paula, do you have any idea who Dawn works with to hold these programs? I assume she's got some sort of connection for the classroom space."

"No clue," Paula said. "I could ask Grandma Beans."

"It would be really useful if we had someone on the inside of WARN," Wayne said, his gaze locked on Paula. "Someone who could go to their meetings, maybe. See what they're talking about, what they're worried about."

"Me?" Paula asked.

"You are a woman of a red nation," Kay said.

"So are you!" Paula replied.

"Pffff, I'm too old for WARN," Kay said. "And they know it. I don't have the energy anymore to be out there fighting cops."

"Yes, in your ripe old age of, what, thirty-five?" Paula asked.

Kay threw a napkin at her. "Thirty-six, actually."

"But I'm still a kid!"

"I think Kay's right," Barbara said. "They've got lots of members your age. And not many over the age of thirty."

"So what, you guys want me to go undercover or something?" Paula asked.

"Uh, yeah!" Molly cried. "That would be so cool!"

"And tribal police would, of course, put me on their payroll," Paula said. Wayne got a good laugh out of that.

"All you have to do is go to a meeting or two and report back on what they're saying and doing," Wayne said once he caught his breath.

"Sometimes I'm a real bonehead," Paula said. "But I think I can handle that." She smirked at Molly. "All right, fine. Sign me up for WARN."

DAWN

DAWN HADN'T SLEPT for thirty hours, and at first she blamed this for Carole's strange behavior. Maybe Dawn was simply hallucinating. She already didn't like the woman. Perhaps Dawn's brain was making things up.

Dawn and Carole rarely worked the same shift. They were like ships passing in the night, one exhausted, the other refreshed; one spent with effort, the other looking for the first problem to solve. There was the handing over of the keys. The sharing of information kept short and to the point. Dawn suspected Carole didn't like her, either, and she could guess why. But Carole was far too polite for confrontation, and Dawn didn't mind. She had enough to worry about. Carole was not a priority.

She had tried to force herself to sleep the night before, but of course, it didn't work like that for night-shifters. Bodies were not light switches but rather sensitive ecosystems in their own right. They took training and time to adjust to an unnatural circadian rhythm. Night nurses became like bats. Functioning on a completely different set of laws.

It was fine. Dawn had had too much to do anyway. About an hour into trying to sleep, she gave up, got up, and got to work.

Now, she was at the hospital for her shift and pouring what she thought was her fourth cup of coffee for the day, though she couldn't really remember, when Alice came bursting through the breakroom door with both fury and excitement in her eyes. Alice was small with slight features that were easily animated. She reminded Dawn of a cartoon character.

"You will *not* believe what Carole just said to a patient."

Dawn stirred a sugar packet into her coffee. "Should I sit down for this?"

Alice bit her lip and glanced over her shoulder. "You need to know. But I'm considering sedating you, actually, immediately after I tell you, so you don't kill her."

Dawn smirked and leaned against the counter. She crossed one arm over the other.

"No sedation needed. I might fall asleep forever right now. You know where the straitjacket is, right?"

"We do not have a straitjacket, smartass."

"Well then, you better come out with it and tell me already."

Alice shut the door behind her and lowered her voice anyway.

"So, she's telling this woman about tubal ligations. A woman, a mom, who came in with false labor pains, okay? Which, first of all, that's not what she's here for. So. The nerve. But you know Carole just cannot mind her own damn business or let the opportunity to assist in *any* surgery pass her by. Plus, the bonuses." Alice paused and rolled her eyes.

"It's like she was trying to plant the seed so when the woman does come back to give birth, she'll sign the consent forms to get her tubes tied, too."

Alice's voice was getting louder. She reached just past Dawn's left ear to get herself a mug from the shelf. Dawn passed her the coffee pot.

"Anyway, the woman is hesitant. She's not really buying what Carole's selling. So, Carole makes the point of looking at each of this woman's kids—she's got three of them with her —and she says, 'I understand you're unemployed. I would just hate to see the next one end up in foster care.'" Alice's eyes practically bugged out of her head. "Can you believe she actually *said* that?"

Dawn tried to slow her breathing down. Tried counting. Alice was right. She *might* need a sedative.

"I would *like* to be surprised, but we both know what an underhanded bitch she is hiding behind all that 'concern.'"

Dawn put her coffee down and rubbed her temples. It was quiet except for faint noises beyond the breakroom's walls. Alice took her first sip of coffee. She breathed in sharply through pursed lips as if she had burned her tongue.

"What should I do?" Alice finally asked.

"I think you have to address this one," Dawn said.

"How? She's kind of our boss."

"File a formal complaint with admin," Dawn said. She had meant to sound firm and convinced but it came out like a question.

"What if she retaliates?" Alice asked. "What if I get fired?"

"They won't fire you. I've reported her on multiple occasions."

"But they can't afford to fire *you*," Alice protested. "You're the only Diné nurse at this hospital. You're basically the interpreter in the operating room for some of these folks."

"True," Dawn said. "Sometimes we have to recognize when we have an advantage and use it. Which is why I've reported her so many times. It won't be like you're the first. Did you at least call her out?"

Alice took her hand back and put it on her own chest. "Of course I did," she said.

"What did you say?"

"I said, 'Mrs. Begay, having a tubal ligation is entirely your decision. You will still receive your Indian Health Services benefits if you prefer not to have the procedure done. The two are entirely unrelated and the procedure is only one option. There are other, more temporary methods of birth control.' I also told her that she's more than welcome to keep popping out as many babies as she wants. She can turn herself into a gumball machine for all we care. It's *her* family and *her* decision. She got a chuckle out of that."

Dawn smiled. "Sorry. I should've known you wouldn't let that slide. I really, really need some sleep."

Alice reached over and grabbed a chocolate chip cookie from the open plastic container on the counter between them.

"I about bit my husband's head off last week when I worked a double."

"How?" Dawn asked, in amazement.

"How would I bite his head off? I'd start with the ears."

Dawn laughed. "No. How do you eat sweets constantly all day and still stay as thin as a toothpick?"

Alice shrugged. "Talk to me in ten years when I have diabetes."

Dawn did not tell Alice the rest of her plan, which was to confront Carole directly. She knew Alice would've tried to talk her out of it and she knew Alice would've been right. But Dawn needed to say *something*. Maybe Carole didn't understand just how fucked up her comment was. Though Dawn doubted that.

When Dawn was finished her rounds, she stalked the hallways in search of Carole. She finally spotted her walking briskly toward the stairway at the end of the hall. Dawn wasn't about to run her down or yell at her, so she followed her instead.

Carole took the stairs down to the first floor and headed for the copy room, where she closed the door behind her. Weird. No one ever closed that door. Dawn hovered outside for a moment, deciding what to do. Finally, she tried to open the copy room door, but it was locked. Even weirder.

Dawn knocked quietly at first and then louder. "Carole?" she called. No answer. What the hell was she doing in there? Now Dawn pounded on the door.

"Hey, I saw you go in there! Can you let me in, please? I need to talk to you."

Still silence. Dawn huffed. She could hear Carole in there, moving things around or something. The soft hum of the copy machine. Dawn looked at her watch. Her shift was almost over. She ought to be leaving soon. She'd already turned the keys over a few hours ago when Carole first arrived. She didn't *need* the woman for anything. She knocked one more time. "Hello?!?"

Dawn even thought about going to find the key to the copy room. Maybe someone at the front desk had it and she could bust in on Carole. But she was tired. Despite her anger, this conversation could wait another day. There was probably some explanation for Carole's strange behavior, Dawn reasoned with herself as she walked away. It could be nothing, But she didn't think it was nothing. She thought it was most definitely something. The whole thing almost made Dawn want to call up that white investigator. But what would she say? "Carole locked me out of the copy room?" Whatever. Dawn let it go.

[18]

JAMES

THE PARKING LOT where James waited, leaned up against his car's bumper, was just past the giant hole in the ground— the surface mining operation where Russel worked. There was no avoiding him this time. James was alone. They would talk one-on-one, man-to-man. That was the goal, at least. Russel could certainly avoid James and speed off. But he didn't think Russel would do that. Maybe he hadn't been ready the night of the rodeo. But James knew his message had been passed on: He was looking into the hospital.

In the distance, James could see the monstruous machines, cumbersome and slow, creating clouds of dust and smoke. He thought of all the things he didn't know about Robin. About her relationship with Russel. All of the secrets, the motivations Russel might have to poison her. It would be convenient enough for a guilty husband to blame the hospital. Russel's family and friends seemed to already know how much he hated the place.

James supposed Russel could've contaminated the peyote. If he'd known about her pain. If he was positive she would reach for it. But there would have been other opportunities, too. No one knew what had happened between the time Russel left work that day and when he and Robin arrived at the hospital. No one but Russel.

The sun was low in the sky when the workers started to trickle into the parking lot. Russel spotted James and stopped walking. James lifted a hand in greeting. He came in peace.

Russel gave him a single nod and resumed walking, slower now.

"You found me," he said, standing about eight feet from James, hands in his pockets.

"I knew where to look," James said.

"What do you want?"

"To have a drink. Your favorite bar in Gallup. My treat."

Russel sighed. Looked past James. "That right? My favorite one? Out of all three?"

"I know you've got one," James said.

"I need to tell my mother-in-law. She's watching my son."

James nodded. "I'll follow you. You can ride with me. I'll drive."

He watched Russel hesitate. Weigh his options. But James guessed it had been a long time since Russel had been able to have a beer. And a ride home.

"Fine," Russel said. They both got into their cars and drove south.

Turned out Russel's favorite bar was a bit past Gallup. James made small talk on the drive, mostly about the rodeo. Yes, Russel had done woolly riding and steer riding as a kid. His grandfather had gotten him into it, though he'd been gone for two years, now. Passed after a battle with lung cancer. Russel had a collection of winning belt buckles. Was considered a top twenty bull rider in the whole Navajo Nation.

James didn't dare veer off this comfortable topic until they were settled onto their barstools at the Tomahawk Bar. Russel seemed to know half the place. The owner and his daughter and her husband, who tended the bar, and a couple who sat at the window and a kid who washed the glasses.

"So tell me about the Shiprock hospital," James finally said after they had both taken a few sips of their first beers.

"They ought to be shut down," Russel said.

"Tell me why."

"I've seen them be incompetent too many times. Negligent . . ." Russel seemed to be racking his brain for more legal-sounding words. He eventually shook his head. "Unprofessional. The last thing you want from someone who has your life in their hands."

"You got examples?" James asked, making sure his voice was soft. "Other than your wife, of course."

Russel took a swig of his beer. "A buddy of mine two years ago. Got kicked across the arena. Took eight hours to get him into surgery."

James let out a low whistle and Russel went on.

"The ambulance took forever. Then they couldn't see him at Shiprock because they didn't have enough surgeons. Drove him all around the damn reservation with a spinal injury." Russel paused and shook his head. "I had to go get him four hours away. Now I drive him to Albuquerque once a week so that maybe he can walk again one day. Still. Two years later.

You think his family has the time or money to take care of a full-grown man all day? Indian Health Services—you know, they run all the reservation hospitals—couldn't even get him a damn wheelchair. Had to find the money ourselves."

"How'd you do that?" James asked.

"ONEO. Some government grant."

"Is your friend making progress?"

Russel nodded. "They've got good doctors down in Albuquerque."

"Expensive, I imagine."

"He's in debt. They let you pay a little at a time. They don't tell you that. But we learned. If you're putting one dollar toward that bill every month? That's allowed."

"I've gotta ask." James sat a little straighter. Leaned over the bar. "Why didn't you take Robin over here? To a hospital in Gallup?"

Russel stared into his beer. "She was just in so much pain, you know?" He swallowed. "It was scaring me. It just had to be the closest thing. Gallup's another half hour. I didn't know if we could afford that."

James waited. He could tell Russel was holding something back. But instead of saying more, Russel took a sip of his beer and looked away. James waited a few more seconds before asking his next question.

"Tell me about that day. And if you can remember, the days leading up to it. Was Robin in pain then?"

"Maybe," Russel said. "I'm not saying she wasn't. I'm not saying there wasn't something medically wrong with her, you know? I just think the hospital made it worse instead of better."

"Did she tell you she was in pain before that day?" James asked.

Russel pursed his lips. "She had been in pain for a while. We'd been thinking about trying for another kid. But she was always telling me she didn't want to . . . you know, because it hurt. Most days she seemed fine. But some days, yeah. She was probably in pain." He shook his head. "I can't remember if the day before was one of those days. I was busy working."

"Did she do anything unusual in the days leading up to this? Go anywhere she didn't normally go? See anyone she didn't normally see?"

"How would I know? Like I said, someone had to pay the bills."

"And she didn't mention anything to you?"

"No. As far as I know, she and our boy sat around and watched TV all day and maybe went to see my family or her family."

"All right. So that day, what happened?" James asked.

"She called me at work, said she needed to go to the hospital. Like, right then. Neither one of us trusted the ambulance to come in time. All part of this shitty rez hospital system. I was a little annoyed, but my shift was almost over. I told the boss my wife was having an emergency and I left."

"And you went straight home to get her?" James asked.

"She told me it was an emergency and I believed her. I wasn't about to stop somewhere."

"What time do you think you got home and what time did you leave for the hospital?"

"I probably got home around 6:30. We left as soon as I got the baby's stuff together. Maybe twenty minutes later?"

"And this was Wednesday, June the second, correct?" James asked.

"Yes."

"And how did she look when you saw her?"

"Fucking awful," Russel said. "Like I said, I don't doubt she was having some sort of medical emergency."

"Did she take anything or tell you she took anything for the pain?"

"She told me she took peyote. Some tribal cop took it for his investigation. He said maybe she was poisoned, but she wasn't."

"And after taking the peyote, was she in less pain?" James asked.

"Yes."

"Did she seem strange at all to you? Did you notice any difference in her behavior after she took it?"

"She just groaned a lot. I think the pain exhausted her. I also think she was trying not to scare our son." He paused and narrowed his eyes. "The nurses. The doctors. When we got there, they made me feel like they would fix her, easy. No problem. They didn't seem concerned." Russel looked up at James. "What did they do to her?"

"I don't know what happened, Russel. I'm sorry, I don't have the answer yet."

Russel's eyes searched James's face for a moment, but it seemed he barely registered James's response.

"Maybe I should get a lawyer," Russel said. "Talk to legal services."

James scratched the back of his neck. "I think you'd need some proof first."

"Well, isn't that what you're doing? Trying to find proof?" Russel asked.

"I'm trying to find out what happened, yes."

Now Russel was really studying him. "Who do you work for, anyway?"

"Myself. Do you remember which doctor you talked to when you got there? Was it Dr. Ciccone?"

Russel raised his hand a little, and the bartender brought him another beer. He glanced at James, too, but James shook his head.

"Maybe," Russel said.

"Crooked nose like a boxer?" James asked.

"That was him," Russel said. "Yeah, that's him."

"And the nurse?"

"There were two of them. Some white ladies."

James nodded. "And what did they say to you after? When they came out and told you?"

Russel stared into his beer again and bit his lip.

"It was a little off, now that I think about it."

"What do you mean?" James asked.

"We were outside the room and one of the nurses came to talk to me."

"Not the doctor?"

"No."

"Did you see the doctor again?" James asked.

Russel nodded. "Only for a few minutes. When he stood there while I was being kicked out." He sighed. "The first nurse, she was real sorry. Real sad. I asked her what happened and she said something like, 'It's hard to tell sometimes.' She said they thought it was probably some kind of infection. From her past problems with her ovaries. But the next thing I know, some other nurse is walking up to us real fast. Frowning at me. She looked mean. And she gets right in between us. She says, 'Mr. Kinsel?' And I said, 'Yes.' I hoped she was there to tell me it was all a mistake. That Robin was fine. I thought maybe that's why she was mad. Because the first nurse got it wrong."

"But that's not what happened," James said.

"No. She started accusing Robin. Saying, 'Your wife used peyote, didn't she?' *Used*. She said it like that. Like it was heroin or cocaine or some shit. I'm not a church member, you know? But it was disrespectful. I *might* have called her a dumb white bitch." Russel cracked a small smile.

"And that's when you got kicked out," James said.

"The hallway just started filling up so quickly after that. I think I must've been yelling pretty loud."

"And the doctor was there?"

"Yeah. I remember looking at him like maybe my stare could stop his heart."

"And you think the hospital was hiding something," James said. "That it wasn't actually the infection that killed her. That it was a mistake on their part."

Russel nodded. "Do you believe me? That it was the hospital that did this?"

"I'm not a man of belief, Russel," James said. "I'm a man of fact."

WAYNE

WAYNE WAS on his way out the station door when Officer Gene Begaye told him he had a call from the lab in Albuquerque. Wayne answered it right there at the front desk.

"This is Lieutenant Wayne Tully," he said.

"Hi there, Lieutenant," a woman's voice said. "I'm from the state police lab down in Albuquerque. We have the results of your tests. All of the medications tested positive only for the chemical elements typically found in those medications. Nothing abnormal. The peyote, however, has tested positive for narcotics. Quite a bit of it, too. It does seem to have been contaminated. As far as the fingerprints go, we did not have any matches."

Wayne hadn't had any matches for the fingerprints, either. "Great. And you'll mail us those results?"

"Of course."

"Thank you for your time," Wayne said.

"We're happy to help. Have a wonderful day."

Wayne sighed as he hung up the phone. Someone *had* tampered with the peyote. Damn it.

Raymond had insisted that Wayne didn't need to drive out to Window Rock this time. He would be in the area anyway, so they met for lunch at the McDonald's that looked like a UFO just outside of Shiprock.

Wayne was savoring another skinny, salty fry when Raymond said, "I heard some WARN talk in Window Rock."

"Oh yeah?" Wayne asked.

"Apparently WARN was trying to establish an office there. Even though they're not a government entity, they can still request a presence in the capital if the government believes there is a benefit to both parties to be in close proximity."

Wayne popped another fry into his mouth.

"Turns out they were denied," Raymond went on. "I was included in the vote because WARN does occasionally raise awareness about health-related services on the reservation."

"Patricia mentioned that," Wayne said. "Vaccines and whatnot."

"Exactly. You want to take a guess at who voted against WARN?"

"All the usual suspects," Wayne said.

"Cecil actually called WARN dangerous," Raymond said. "He used their national status as a reason to argue that they're not actually interested in Diné problems. He said other tribe's priorities are not our priorities and that they would cause unnecessary headaches and could set back some of our most important projects."

Wayne grunted. "Projects. Exactly." He could almost feel

himself growing fonder of WARN as they spoke. "He didn't specify what these 'projects' were, I'm assuming."

Raymond shrugged. "He doesn't have to. We all know what Cecil or Chairman Jackson mean when they say something like that."

"Mining projects," Wayne said. "Oil and gas projects." Wayne looked out the long, narrow window that wrapped around the restaurant. "It seems as though Robin *was* poisoned."

Raymond put his burger down. "You can confirm that?"

"The test for the peyote came back positive for narcotics. They're sending me the results with the exact amounts, so I suppose we'll see if it was enough to kill the woman. Though I imagine it depends on how much she ate."

"And what medical emergency she might have already been having," Raymond said. "Shit."

"I know."

Raymond's eyebrows furrowed. He crossed his arms. "Have you told the doctor?"

"No, I just found out before I came here."

"He probably ought to know. It's one thing to make sure a patient discloses the presence of mescaline in their system. But narcotics . . ."

"I understand what you're saying. But I'm sure plenty of patients show up with narcotics in their system and they don't disclose that to their doctor or nurse."

"Of course, but it's always better to know. If there's a pattern . . ." Raymond didn't finish.

"I doubt that," Wayne said. "Robin was threatened. Her back door's lock was broken. Whoever painted that message most likely contaminated her peyote, too."

"Hmmm," Raymond replied.

Wayne looked at his watch. "Thanks for lunch, my friend," he said as he gathered his food and trash onto his tray. "Wish I could chat longer but I've got another meeting to attend."

Raymond stood and shook Wayne's hand. "I'll keep my eyes and ears open."

[20]

MOLLY

MOLLY KNEW it wasn't a coincidence that every time she went to an "official meeting" at the station, Wayne's candy dish was filled with Starbursts. It was her favorite candy and she knew somewhere, in one of those drawers, he kept a stash so he could make sure he was stocked up when she arrived.

She popped a pink one in her mouth when she sat down for the meeting and Wayne winked at her.

"I received confirmation this morning," Wayne said, "that the peyote was contaminated with narcotics. And not a small amount, either."

Just then, Paula pushed open the cracked door and crept in. "Sorry, sorry, sorry. I'm sorry I'm late. What did I miss?"

"The peyote was definitely contaminated," Molly said. "With narcotics."

"Oh shit!" Paula gasped.

"Exactly," Wayne said. "Now there is one person we know for sure had access to narcotics."

"Russel," James answered. "We've still got his prescription in evidence, correct?"

"Correct."

"I spoke with him the other day," James said. "Took him for a beer. He has a real hatred toward these reservation hospitals. I find it strange he took his wife to one when the Gallup hospital is only another thirty minutes down the road. He tells me he's seen the Shiprock hospital's incompetence over and over. Then, his wife needs serious care, and he takes her there? The same one he blames for putting a friend of his in a wheelchair?"

"I see where you're coming from, but thirty minutes is thirty minutes," Wayne said.

"It is," James agreed. Then he pointed at Wayne. "But he also said he was going to contact legal services to see if he ought to sue the hospital. He's considering legal action."

Wayne propped a foot up onto his knee. "So, the man . . . what? Poisoned his wife so he could take her to a reservation hospital where he could only hope they'd be incompetent enough for a lawsuit?"

"He was bettin' on it," James said.

"Maybe he didn't expect her to die," Molly offered.

"Maybe not," Wayne conceded. "He seemed distraught enough, and if anything, he tried to hide his tears from me. So let's say it was him, since we know the statistics. What were the threats on her car then? A distraction? A coincidence? A setup?" Wayne asked.

"An opportunity, maybe," James said.

"Which might explain his behavior when I went to his house," Wayne said. "Paranoid, yes. But he didn't try to stop me from taking the peyote."

"Are we even concerned about Dawn anymore?" Paula asked. Molly could hear her disappointment.

"Of course we are," James said. "She's another person who we know for certain has access to narcotics."

"So I still get to go to the WARN meeting?" Paula asked.

"Absolutely," Wayne said. "That's the main purpose of this meeting. To get you ready for tomorrow night. How are you feeling?"

"I feel great! Like I'm about to give an Oscar-worthy performance."

"We don't need Oscar-worthy," James said. "In fact, we don't want Oscar-worthy. We want as normal as you can get."

Paula narrowed her eyes. "I think you just called me weird."

"If the shoe fits, but listen," James went on. "Pretend right now in your mind that you're actually joining WARN. What about it appeals to you?"

Paula closed her eyes. "Ummmm. The potential for violence. Definitely."

Molly giggled. She couldn't help it.

"What else?" James asked.

Paula kept her eyes closed. "I guess it's pretty rad that they focus on traditional occupations. Like, screw *the man*, you know? I'm not gonna work at a 7-Eleven. No thank you. And then they actually help other women learn how to weave or make jewelry, which has got to be pretty damn boring but at least they're doing that for them. It's *their* money. They can be proud at night when they go to bed."

"That's good," James said. "So weaving and jewelry-making are not for you, but their mission is."

Paula opened her eyes. "Totally!"

"Think about that mission before you go into the meeting," James said. "And then maybe ask some genuine questions. One or two if the opportunity presents itself. Not too many. This is not the Paula show. Let's write some things down for you to keep your ears open for."

Molly already had a pen and her notepad out. "I can do that," she said.

"The last protest," Wayne said. "Or any upcoming protests. Any Navajo Nation government grudges they're holding. Especially since they were denied a presence in Window Rock. Anything related to Clarence Draper. Apparently, he sells some of WARN's rugs."

Molly drew some little asterisks and wrote those down.

"Obviously anything related to Dawn Harvey," James said. "Or her programs."

"And of course," Paula said, "anything about Robin Kinsel. I don't think you need to write that down, though. That should be obvious enough."

Molly did write it down. Then she ripped the paper from the pad and handed it to Paula. "Homework," she said. "Study up!"

"You'll do great," Wayne said.

Paula looked at the list and nodded. "I'm ready."

[21]

KAY

Even though it was summer and school was out, Kay was still at the high school almost every day tutoring kids who were in danger of failing out and not graduating. She wasn't getting paid to do it. None of these kids had the money for that. Some of them even had to lie to be there. They had to have summer jobs. They would tell their parents they were at work during those hours and tell their jobs they *couldn't* work during those hours. Others had parents who very much cared. Who brought Kay food and handmade socks and knives they had carved themselves to thank her. And then there was the last group. The ones who weren't failing at all but needed somewhere else to be. Anywhere else.

Kay glanced at the calendar on the wall on her way out of the classroom that Friday afternoon and sighed. Five months. She and James had been trying to get pregnant for five months and still nothing.

She found herself not driving home but instead driving to Barbara's office.

"Come in," Barbara said when Kay knocked on her door. She smiled and stood, and the women embraced.

"Are you enjoying your summer off?" Barbara asked once they were seated.

Kay chuckled. "I've been at the school all morning. And every other morning, too."

Barbara nodded. "We didn't exactly choose jobs we could clock out of easily, did we?"

"Neither did our husbands," Kay said.

"It's probably part of the reason we picked them. How is life as a newlywed treating you?"

Kay sighed. "I'm worried."

"Are you arguing?"

"No. Nothing like that." Kay glanced behind her to make sure she had shut the door. "We're trying for a baby."

Barbara's face lit up. "That's wonderful!"

"And we've *been* trying. Since before we were even married. So it's been months. Which I know can be normal and maybe I wouldn't be so worried if it weren't for my past." It all began to spill out of her, then. "Me and Al. We never talked about wanting kids in the beginning of our marriage, but we weren't exactly responsible about making sure it didn't happen. Which it didn't, until the end when we decided to really try. I stupidly thought it might save our marriage."

"A baby?" Barbara asked.

"Yeah. A baby."

The realization hit Barbara. Kay could see it in her eyes. "You were pregnant."

"I was pregnant," Kay confirmed. "But I lost the baby.

And that was five years ago. I'm older now. Maybe my body isn't meant to carry a baby. Maybe it never was."

Barbara stood from behind her desk and walked around to where Kay sat. She scooched the other chair closer to Kay and grabbed both her hands, facing Kay completely. This was why Kay had come to Barbara. She knew for certain that Barbara understood this particular sort of pain.

"First of all, I am very sorry for your loss."

Kay looked down at their hands and blinked back tears. "It was the final straw for Al and me," she said. "I think couples who truly love each other struggle through that. But that was not us. The bitterness, the blame, it grew quickly. He said some ugly things. Things he probably didn't mean. But I believed him. I couldn't fulfill the role gifted to me as a maker of life. What was I good for?" She paused. "I don't mean to hurt you. Perhaps you aren't as hard on yourself as I am. And I know Wayne would never utter something so terrible."

Barbara shook her head. "Wayne, no. But you wouldn't believe the nasty thoughts I've had about myself. Worse than that, I promise you."

"I'm afraid it won't happen for me and James, either. I think it's me. There's something wrong with me. It's obviously not James. He has Molly."

"You say that, but he's getting older too." Barbara raised an eyebrow. "I wouldn't jump to any conclusions yet. It takes some people a while. I know you feel like you don't have the time to be patient. I felt like that too."

Barbara paused, patted Kay's hand, and stood again, a bit abruptly. She walked to the other side of her desk and started flipping through her Rolodex. She found a card and handed it to Kay.

"I have no idea why and how I'm still holding on to that. He was my fertility doctor down in Albuquerque. It's a little pricey, since he's outside of the Indian Health Services system. But he's worth it. He can and will do tests that they don't do here on the reservation."

Kay stared at it. Doctor Hale. She swallowed. She shifted in her seat so she could put the card into her back pocket before her hand started to shake.

"Thank you," Kay whispered.

"It's up to you," Barbara said. "Whatever you decide, I understand. I won't be offended. You don't even have to tell me."

Kay smiled. "I know."

"And you can always come to me. For anything. Please. I know how lonely it was. How lonely it sometimes still is."

Kay stood too now and circled Barbara's desk to hug her. Kay almost asked what else Barbara had tried. Barbara was a Catholic but maybe she had been desperate enough to resort to anything.

Instead, she said, "My father would have told me to see a medicine man."

"Maybe you should," Barbara said.

"Do you think it would help?"

"I think anything that gives you peace is worth your time."

Kay studied her face, trying to see if it revealed anything, but of course it didn't. Maybe some things were too personal to share. Kay would probably never know.

As she sat in her truck in the parking lot of Barbara's office, she looked at the doctor's business card. There was a phone number listed. An address, too. But she wasn't ready for that yet. It didn't make sense, even to Kay, but if she went to that doctor, she would know for sure and maybe she didn't want to know for now. Maybe she needed to hold on to hope for just a little longer.

[22]

PAULA

THE MEETING of the Shiprock chapter of WARN was held in the basement of the high school. It smelled like gym class down there, and Paula was a little horrified that they hadn't found somewhere to meet that didn't stink like feet.

She recognized a few of the younger girls from school and gave a little wave. They acted excited to see her—as if they were friends, which they were not. They circled her, and one of them said, "We had no idea you were interested in WARN!" Paula gave them a big smile but then remembered James's words. This wasn't the Paula show. Instead of launching into full-on praise of the organization, she simply shrugged.

"My mom is always lecturing me about what I'm going to do with my life. I thought maybe this would shut her up."

The girls gave each other awkward glances, but one of them giggled. "Your mom likes WARN? That's stellar!"

"My mom likes paying the bills," Paula said. "I thought I'd check out some of the weaving stuff. Sounded like a way to make money. And also kind of interesting."

She could tell she was making them more and more uncomfortable, so she changed tactics. "Plus, the protests are way badass."

Their eyes lit up again. "It's like we're finally doing something important," one of them said with a sigh that Paula imagined had been rehearsed.

Luckily, the meeting was called to attention, and they all sat down in folding chairs facing a woman she knew to be Patricia, even though they had never met.

"Thanks everyone for coming tonight," Patricia said. "My thoughts are still a little scattered, so I apologize in advance if this meeting is all over the place." She took a deep breath. "We're all still feeling Robin's absence. She did so much for us." Patricia bit her lip, and Paula could see how raw her emotions still were. She wanted to hug the woman.

"Anyway, I guess since I'm already talking about her, I'll remind you all of her memorial next month. It'll be on the seventh at eight p.m. outside of the Shiprock NAC teepee. Just bring a candle and some flowers if you want. Mr. Draper will be offering prayers and songs."

A hand shot up in the front row far corner.

"Go ahead, Lori," Patricia said.

"I'm sorry to go a little off topic here," Lori said. Paula leaned forward in her chair to hear better. "But you mentioned Mr. Draper. Umm, I just wanted to let you know that he is *not* interested in working with Mr. Keegan on the rug auction in Nevada. He said he didn't want to work with any outsiders. None at all. He said, and I quote, 'I didn't get this far with the trading post to hand over profits to a white man and a stranger.' He wants Diné business partners only. I don't know if he's threatening to cut off our own partnership if we participate without him. I didn't ask."

Patricia tried to smile. "Thanks, Lori. I appreciate the update."

Paula had brought a notebook and pen, and even though some of the ladies were jotting down notes, Paula felt it would look pretty suspicious if she did the same thing considering this was her first meeting. She shifted in her seat and didn't write anything. Next time, she would ask for a recording device. Although she doubted a recording device would've picked up on Lori's tiny voice. *Damn it*. Now she was stressed about the competence of her memory. She didn't think that information about Clarence was relevant, but maybe it was? She tried repeating in her head, *Clarence doesn't like outsiders. Clarence doesn't like outsiders.*

"All right, I have an update for you all. It's not good news, but it's not the end of the world. WARN was denied a designated space in Window Rock. I don't know why, but I can guess. Anyway, we'll keep trying. I plan on being *very* annoying."

A couple women laughed softly, but Paula could see just how tired Patricia was. She could even feel it, all the way back in the last row. Patricia was exhausted.

Paula looked around to see if anyone would ask *why* they'd been denied, but no one did. Apparently Patricia wasn't the only one who could guess. This must have been something they had talked about before. Something that Paula was too late for.

For the rest of the meeting, Paula listened attentively as they spoke about signing up to knock on doors and to drive women to clinics or hospitals for checkups and screenings.

They spoke about the next class they were holding on jewelry-making. They spoke about supporting the creation of basketball teams for elementary-aged girls. But nothing about protests. No mention of Dawn Harvey or her programs.

It felt a little like a bust, and finally, at the end of the meeting, Paula wrote one thing in her notebook: *Robin's memorial. August 7 at 8 p.m.* Then she closed it, said goodbye to her classmates, and left.

[23]

MOLLY

MOLLY WAS TRYING to let it go. To breathe, to focus, to collect her thoughts, to think of something rational and productive she could do that morning instead of just stewing. But she was angry and her bike ride to the station took nearly half the time it normally did because she'd taken out her frustration on that bike. Pushed those pedals as if the very strength of her legs could crack open the earth. She knew it was irrational, but she felt like she was being pushed out of this investigation.

Paula was going to WARN meetings and Molly was not. James was going to meet with Dawn later that day and Molly was not. But James had been happy to use Molly the day before for the boring stuff. The phone calls and the mindless flipping through documents and newspapers to dig up all the dirt on Dawn Harvey they could find. But James needed to go to Dawn's house alone, he'd said. Something about establishing trust. But why couldn't Molly be there, too? What did Molly's presence have to do with trust?

She thought about her conversation with Paula late last

night after the WARN meeting. How Paula promised she had told Molly everything that had happened, everything that was said. And yet, after they hung up, Molly was annoyed. Did she think Paula was lying? Keeping something from her? Why would she do that? Maybe it was because Molly thought that she would've done a better job at the meeting. That she would've been able to find out more information.

She offered Officer Begaye a tight smile as she blew through the station's front door. She hadn't slept well the night before and she'd gotten up early that morning. Early, early. But she didn't want to just sit around the house. So here she was at the station, hoping to find some way to be useful.

"Morning, Molly," he said.

"Morning, Officer Begaye."

"Wayne's not in yet."

"I know," Molly said. "I'll wait for him in the back." She headed to Wayne's office. She was planning on posting up in the conference room to study her notes and make a plan, but she wanted some Starbursts first.

The only things left in the candy bowl were some Hershey's Kisses and Life Savers mints. Molly stared at Wayne's desk. She didn't want to snoop, but she knew the Starbursts had to be in one of his desk drawers. She wouldn't look through anything else.

But before she could even open a drawer, she noticed Wayne's answering machine light blinking. She stared at it for a moment. Of course Wayne had a message. He probably always had messages. It could be about anything. It could be personal. But Molly couldn't help herself. She wanted to be useful. Maybe she could get ahead of this investigation. She pressed play.

"Hey, Wayne. It's Raymond. After we parted ways the other day, I started to do a little research of my own. I know Robin was threatened. I know it seems like she was targeted. Still, the fact that it was the peyote that was contaminated and the fact that women have just been blatantly bringing it into the hospital . . . it just didn't sit right with me. Anyway, I've been going through death certificates and I've found three other young women who died suddenly at the hospital. So I called up your doctor, Dr. Ciccone, and he was able to confirm that all three women had admitted to taking peyote when they were admitted. I think there's a chance that something's going on there. I wanted you to know about these women and also that I'm happy to help you look into it. Give me a call back. Thanks."

The tape stopped. Molly sucked in a breath of still, hot air. Something was wrong with the peyote? Maybe *all* of the peyote? This was huge. She rewound the tape, waited for the light to blink again, but it didn't. Shit. Wayne needed to know the message was there. Molly bit her thumb's fingernail. She scribbled Wayne a note.

Your answering machine was blinking when I came into your office but now it has stopped. Weird! I think you have a message. —Molly

She hated lying, but she didn't want Wayne to know she had snooped. Now, she couldn't sit still. That morning she had felt useless and frustrated and restless. But after hearing that message, she felt ten times worse. She needed to *do* something. Maybe that's what her dad wanted from her, anyway. Maybe she needed to show him that she was ready for more responsibility. That she had her own ideas and wasn't afraid to act on them.

Something had been forming inside Molly's head for a few days now. Without James or Wayne or Paula, Molly felt like she had no connections, no real standing on the reservation. She wasn't Diné. She wasn't a real investigator in the eyes of the law or the state—or anyone for that matter.

But there was someone she could trust. Someone who might let her in on some secrets.

Molly grabbed a Life Savers, unwrapped it, popped it in her mouth, and left Wayne's office.

"Leaving so soon?" Officer Begaye asked.

"I thought of something I have to do. Will you please tell the lieutenant that I'll see him later?"

"Sure."

As Molly closed the station's door behind her, she thought of what she would say, how she would approach this. She had no idea if Joey was a member of the Native American Church. They hadn't gotten to that level of close yet. But she did know that Joey had a lot of friends. The basketball team and their fans, the after-school debate team he was on, the elders who he cooked and cleaned for, announced bingo for, joked with. Joey knew a lot of people.

Molly grabbed her bike's handlebars and lifted the kickstand with her foot. Then she faced it in the direction of the senior center, got on, and started to pedal.

———————

Molly was not religious. The only religious person she had

known growing up was her grandmother Rita, and Molly's mom had done her best to keep Molly and Rita distant.

So when Molly told Joey she was shopping around for a church on the reservation, she wasn't being truthful. Even if Molly were interested in going to church, she already knew where she would go. She had been to George's church a few times, and even though she had not forgiven him for his actions last year and she might never, she did like his church. It was a welcoming place and she particularly liked Fred, the assistant pastor.

A small part of Molly felt a little guilty for being disingenuous with Joey. She really liked him. A lot. She wanted to actually get to know him and for him to know her. But she knew when you were an investigator, sometimes you just had to do things like this. It was part of the job. Besides, she already flirted with Joey, and flirting often felt to her like an act. Like she was supposed to bat her eyes and flip her hair and giggle when what she wanted to do was talk to him. Really talk to him. Learn who he was. What made him tick. Find out if he'd actually read the novel for English class, *One Flew Over the Cuckoo's Nest*, and if he did, what he thought of the Indian character. To ask him how many hours a week he practiced that layup to execute it so flawlessly at every game. To find out if his mom still folded his clothes or if he did it himself, since his T-shirts were never wrinkled and never had lines down the center. But Molly knew this was not what she was supposed to do. These things were vulnerable and intimate and she had to do her time flipping her hair until . . . when? She didn't know when that next step came. Maybe today, she guessed.

"My dad isn't big on church," Molly was saying now.

"But there are so many around here. Everyone seems to go somewhere. Well, except Kay. She's into the traditional stuff."

"So she probably has a medicine man, then," Joey said.

"Maybe. If she does, she's never said anything to me about it." Molly liked how Joey looked at her when he talked to her. Actually paid attention to her, didn't just pretend to.

"My dad's family is Pentecostal," Joey said. "But my mom and I don't really go. We go to meetings at the Native American Church."

Molly's heart beat a little faster. "Oh. So, you don't really like the Pentecostal Church?"

"It's not that. The church was fine. It just didn't feel right for me."

"And the Native American Church does?" Molly asked.

"Yeah," Joey said. "It does." He paused. His eyebrows furrowed. Molly stayed quiet and let him think.

"I feel more . . . connected. And it's not just about the peyote." He gave Molly a half smile. "It's the fire right in front of me and the earth right below me. My family, my people, right there with me. All the extra stuff is gone. It just feels . . . real."

Molly couldn't take her eyes off Joey. She felt her breath get shallow and she couldn't speak for a moment.

"That sounds . . . pretty rad," she finally said.

Joey grinned. "You could come if you want. I don't know if you'll feel the same, since you're not Native. But you could still come. They'll let you."

"Really? I thought you had to be a tribe member?"

"Nope. You don't. Anyone can come. And actually, we're meeting tonight. My mom hasn't been feeling great, so I'm going alone. But you could come with me?"

Holy shit, Molly thought. Could she? Would she? Looking at Joey, Molly did not want to say no. She could tell he wanted her to come. He really wanted her to.

"All right," she said. "Does everyone do the whole peyote thing?"

"Usually. It's a big part of it. I don't think I've ever seen someone refuse it."

Molly swallowed the lump in her throat. "How do you take it? Do you smoke it?"

No," Joey said. He looked a little like he was holding back a laugh. "You eat it. Just a little bit. It's not dangerous. You won't get sick or anything."

Molly felt a little sick now at the thought. And now she knew Joey was going and that he could be in danger. He would go with or without her. She had to go now. She didn't know what she could do to help him. Maybe just watch him. Make sure he was okay. Get him help right away if something happened. And she could probably fake eating it herself, couldn't she? Just pretend to but actually spit it back out into her hand? Maybe she wouldn't even have to put it in her mouth. She would think of something. She forced a smile.

"Sounds awesome. Where should I meet you?"

[24]

WAYNE

THE ANSWERING MACHINE WAS OLD. Wayne was surprised it still worked as well as it did, so when he read Molly's note, he wasn't surprised that it might be starting to die on him. After listening to Raymond's message, he sighed. It could be nothing. A pure coincidence. But now he had to consider that there could be something wrong with all of the peyote on the reservation. This investigation was turning into a real clusterfuck.

He let his hair out of his ponytail for a moment. Ran his fingers through it. James would be there soon, which was good. Wayne needed someone to talk through all of this with. He closed his eyes for what felt like just a second, but when he opened them again, James was sitting across from him, grinning.

"Late night, LT?"

Wayne chuckled. "No. I'm just getting old, I guess. And I was greeted this morning with a less-than-pleasant message. Are you ready for it?"

"I'm ready. Let's hear it."

Wayne rubbed his eyes, sat forward, and rewound the tape. He let James listen.

James grimaced. "How likely you think that is? That these women's peyote was contaminated, too?"

"I have a hard time buying it," Wayne said. "I'm inclined to believe it's a coincidence, but I guess we can't assume."

"No, we can't," James agreed. "All right, so what does this mean if it's more than just Robin's peyote that's a problem? We haven't heard anything outside of these cases, correct?"

"We have not, but why would we have heard anything? If these women, and maybe some men, are dying because the peyote is contaminated, no one is making that connection."

"We would have heard *something*, LT. People could be dropping as they leave their meetings. What about your friend Clarence? He didn't mention anything, did he?"

"No."

"So maybe right now we focus on the women."

"The women who are getting their peyote from somewhere. Where, we don't know yet," Wayne said.

"Could they be getting it themselves? From the source?" James asked.

"It's a hike to go all the way down to the border of Texas and Mexico," Wayne said. "Some serious gas money. Which is why it's usually a small group. Almost always the Codys. Sometimes by themselves, sometimes with a few others."

"Peyote isn't grown any farther north than that?" James asked.

"Nope. I've been to a few houses that have tried, but peyote grown outside of that area does not have the mescaline levels you would want. It's almost useless."

"So the women are getting it directly from the Codys," James said.

"Possibly. Clarence claims he doesn't distribute it outside of the teepee."

"And Robin had a decent amount of peyote. More than just a few slices she could've slipped into her back pocket," James said.

"It sounds like they all do. Remember what the doctor said? They use it in labor and then continue to take it."

"Would the Codys have any qualms about distributing the peyote outside of the teepee like Clarence does?" James asked.

"It would be bold of them," Wayne said. "Everyone knows Cecil is a traditionalist at heart. He's got a relationship with the roadmen and he's probably been to a meeting or two, but he's not an NAC member. Not really. It isn't his place to be in control of the peyote."

"But the roadmen trust him to purchase it for them. And I assume he continues to do so because that puts him in control over the spirituality of a large percentage of the reservation."

"Still," Wayne said. "They wouldn't continue to put their trust in Cecil if he was careless with the peyote. They have to believe he reveres it, too. That he understands its importance."

"I see what you're saying, but these are pregnant women, LT. What's the harm in him giving these ladies some peyote?"

Wayne sighed. "So, what? It's all word of mouth? These women tell one another to go see Cecil when they're pregnant?"

"Or Ronnie. Or Byron," James said.

"Say they are getting it from the Codys. Why would the Codys contaminate the peyote?" Wayne asked.

"Maybe it's targeted. Maybe Cecil had a bone to pick with each of the victims."

Wayne shook his head. "He wouldn't use the peyote to punish them. Or get rid of them. Like I said, Cecil understands how revered the plant is. He wouldn't jeopardize his own standing in the community."

"Would he have to? Up until now, no one's put two and two together. He might have relied on everyone's assumption that peyote overdoses just don't happen."

Wayne cracked his knuckles. "Maybe. But why would Cecil's enemies go to him for peyote? If Cecil was targeting these women, why would they trust him at all? I wouldn't eat something Cecil gave me. Not any day of the week."

"That's a good question, LT."

"Who else could be distributing it?" Wayne asked.

"Well, Clarence could be lying," James said.

Wayne nodded. "He could be."

"Say the peyote is going through a middleman," James said. "Say it's Clarence. Cecil would have to be pretty damn comfortable with the man to make sure specific jars of peyote go to specific women. That's suspicious behavior right there. Clarence would almost have to be in on it too. Or at least willing to look the other way and not ask questions. He would have to not care about these women at all."

"So who do we know Cecil trusts?" A smile crept onto Wayne's face.

"You tell me, LT."

"Victor Black."

"Who is Victor Black?" James asked.

"Cecil's medicine man. The best medicine man on the rez, many would say."

"And that's not the same as a roadman?" James asked.

Wayne sighed. "No, my friend, it is not. A roadman is the Native American Church's head pastor. A medicine man is specific to traditional Diné beliefs. They are different religions. The Native American Church was established in Oklahoma in the late 1800s by a Comanche man and spread from there. It incorporates parts of Christianity. The Native American Church is intertribal, and peyote is and always has been an essential part of that religion. But traditional Diné healing does not use peyote. There are other things a medicine man might prescribe, but peyote is not one of them."

"And yet you believe a medicine man is doing just that right now to these pregnant women?" James asked.

"If it were anyone else but Victor Black, I would say it's not possible. It wasn't that long ago that peyote was completely outlawed on the reservation and not because of US or New Mexican law, but because of *our* law. People felt it was not for Diné. It's not our ways."

"But because Victor and Cecil are so close, you think Cecil would trust Victor with this task?" James asked. "And you think Victor would take it on?"

"He might. Plus, the relationship between a person and their medicine man is incredibly personal. Intimate. Discreet. And plenty of women consult a medicine man when they're pregnant or when they're trying to get pregnant or right before they give birth."

"You think Victor is trusted in a way that Cecil isn't," James said. "This still assumes Victor knows exactly what's going on and is okay with it. This also assumes a scenario that seems unlikely. Robin, an enemy of Cecil's for whatever reason, and an NAC member—which I assume means she doesn't practice traditional Diné healing—went to Victor Black for peyote."

"Unlikely, maybe. But possible. If it was the only way for her to get ahold of peyote for her labor."

"Fair enough," James said. "Humor me for a minute, though. Dawn Harvey. She works at the hospital. She's a nurse midwife. She speaks the Diné language. Say the women are going to her for the peyote? And she's going to Cecil. Maybe she goes to Cecil for each patient. Gives their name or whatever Cecil might ask for. Then Cecil gives her the peyote to distribute. She wouldn't have to know that he's targeting the women."

Wayne leaned back in his chair and crossed his arms. "Doesn't it seem convenient that all these women are pregnant? Cecil has these women that he's targeting and he's just, what, waiting for them to get pregnant? That doesn't seem efficient."

"Do we know if these other women were WARN members, too?" James asked.

Wayne shook his head. "I don't know much of anything about them yet, but that does seem like the most likely scenario."

James held up a finger. "And we know Robin's peyote was just fine when she gave birth. Nothing was wrong with her peyote then. The women are coming back for more after they use up what they have."

"So they trust it," Wayne said. He leaned his elbows on his desk and put his hands on top of his head. "It seems elaborate. Maybe it is just a coincidence. Maybe Russel poisoned his wife's peyote and everyone else's peyote is just fine." He looked up again and folded his hands together.

"Maybe," James said. "But you know we can't write it off."

"I know," Wayne said.

"I was already plannin' on payin' a visit to Dawn Harvey later. How are we gonna find out more about what Victor Black is up to these days?" James asked.

Wayne stood up. He walked across the room, squatted down, reached into a low drawer, and pulled out a booklet. He set it down in front of James. It read: *Medicine Man Directory*. "This has caused quite a scandal recently. I think we can use it to our advantage."

"You've got an idea?" James asked.

Wayne nodded. "I've got a little bit of a plan forming."

[25]
JAMES

JAMES SAT in his car in front of Dawn Harvey's house. Her car was in the driveway, so she was home. She would be leaving for her shift at the hospital in a few hours. James grabbed the doughnuts and the steaming cups of coffee he had picked up on the way, got out of the car, and walked up the three steps to Dawn's front door. He held the bag of doughnuts and stacked coffees in one hand and knocked with the other. He waited a bit and then knocked again. Just as it had the first visit, it took Dawn a minute to answer.

She took in the sight of James and rubbed her eyes. "You're back."

"You never called," James said. Dawn took two steps back into the house and did not shut the door in his face. He took that as an invitation and walked in, setting the doughnuts on the coffee table.

"You have a way of knocking on my door like a damn SWAT team when I'm in my deepest sleep," Dawn said.

"You've gotta go to work in a bit. I got you black coffee. You struck me as a black coffee kind of person. But if you want cream or sugar, I got some of that too." James gestured to the doughnuts. "In the bag."

Dawn took one of the coffees from James's hand. "Black is good."

They both sat and sipped for a moment.

"You figure out what happened to Mrs. Kinsel yet?" Dawn asked.

"No."

"Is that why you're here? I don't know what else I can tell you."

"I'm here because I feel like we did not get properly introduced the first time. I want to tell you a little story about myself."

Dawn raised an eyebrow and did not smile. James went on.

"I'm a private investigator now, but I was trained in the Army. First as a military police officer and then as an agent in the criminal investigations division. I mostly investigated crimes committed by members of the military. My last case was My Lai. Maybe you've heard of it. I spent months looking at photographs, listening to accounts of some of the most horrific shit you can imagine—told to me by both the families of the victims and the soldiers who committed the acts. I tried to get justice for those people, but ultimately I failed. Much of what I did in the Army punished fellow soldiers for crimes. But there was a good number of cases, including My Lai, that involved cover-ups from the high rankers. The brass. Even all the way up to the big US of A war machine."

Dawn's expression hadn't changed much, but she crossed

her arms, so James knew this was a good time to pause. To leave some dead air.

"And you think," Dawn finally said after a moment, "that's going to make me like you? What, because my brother is in federal prison? Set up for some bullshit crime? My enemy's enemy is my friend sort of thing? But they weren't your enemy because they were paying you."

"Not anymore," James said.

Dawn scoffed. "A radical now, are you?"

"I didn't say that."

"But you did say you failed."

James nodded. "I had some wins. Before My Lai and more recently."

Dawn took a sip. "You have until I finish this coffee to get to the point."

"What I'm saying is, if you know something about what could have happened to Robin—or even if you know about something strange going on—and you're afraid to say it, don't be. I know how to handle this."

Dawn frowned. "Why are you on the reservation anyway? Working with the tribal police, I know. But why?"

"I like it here. It's my home now."

Dawn snorted. "It's your home now, huh? That's how it works, isn't it?"

"I was invited to make it so and I did."

"Tell me about those wins you've had. Would I find any of them interesting?"

"Maybe. Both murders. One tied up in the uranium spill last year. The other related to the cover-up of an ICWA violation."

"Huh," Dawn said. She almost sounded impressed, James thought.

"Why didn't you tell me you were a certified midwife?" James asked.

Dawn shrugged. "I like to keep things to myself when I can. It didn't seem relevant."

"Pretty relevant when I asked about delivering babies."

"I thought if you were a good enough investigator, you'd figure it out on your own," Dawn said.

"Well, I did. Found out you were an excellent student. Top of the class in your nurse midwife degree program at the University of Utah. You were a part of the Maternal-Child Nursing Project in Shiprock. First Diné CNM to work in a hospital on the reservation. And you're only twenty-seven. Impressive."

"Plenty of Diné have been midwives before me. We've had midwives since the beginning. I'm not special because I'm 'certified.'"

"Now, you know that's not true or else you wouldn't have gone through all the trouble. And you wouldn't be goin' through the trouble now to certify more midwives on the reservation through the program you've created."

James could see Dawn's jaw clench.

"Fine. But it's only important to Indian Health Services and outside the borders of this reservation," Dawn said.

"In other words, it's necessary in today's world."

Dawn took another long sip. She uncrossed her legs and leaned her forearms on them.

"I hope there isn't a threat under there."

"A threat?" James asked, but thought, *Damn. She's quick.*

"To strip my license."

"Why would I do that?"

"You're looking for someone to pin this death on. I don't know why. People die in the hospital all the time from all sorts of causes. But for whatever reason, this Robin, her death is important. And a nurse's error would be convenient. You've been going after us since day one. But I also know that Robin took peyote before coming to the hospital. You asked me about the peyote the first time you came here. You, the doctor, Carole, you all see it like it's a street drug. But it's not. It's medicine to us. It's sacred. I'm the only one at the hospital who understands that and who encourages our patients to use it like I would encourage them to use any medicine that they're comfortable taking that heals or alleviates pain. And that alone makes me suspicious. You think you can put this woman's death on me when I had nothing to do with it."

James sat back in his own seat and sighed. "I'm thinking someone who has worked as hard as you have would never put all that on the line over something that wasn't worth it. You wouldn't need someone like me to threaten you. You know the stakes."

"I care about my Diné patients, Mr. Pinter. And that is all I care about. I care about the fact that I am the only Diné nurse at the Shiprock hospital. The only one who can truly understand their needs. And you're right. I will not let you or anyone else jeopardize that. I will not abandon those women to the reservation hospital system."

"Women like Robin?" James asked.

For the first time during their conversation that morning, Dawn looked away.

"What do you want?" she asked, quietly.

"I want you to know that Mrs. Kinsel's peyote was contaminated. She was poisoned."

"Shit," Dawn hissed. "Really?"

"Yes," James said. "Now, Mrs. Kinsel was also threatened a couple of weeks before her death. We thought she was specifically targeted. But now we've found other cases. Other young, healthy women dying at the hospital after taking peyote."

Dawn looked back at James. "But you don't know whether *their* peyote was contaminated."

"We do not. Not yet. We can ask their families if they still happen to have the peyote, if we can test it. But I'm not sure how successful we'll be there."

"You should try anyway," Dawn said.

"We will."

Dawn looked a little shaken. "You all right?" James asked.

"What can I do?" she asked.

"I would not let one more patient take that peyote if I were you." James leaned forward in his seat. Put his hands on his knees. "Wherever it's coming from. Not until we know more."

Dawn was quiet. Didn't confirm she had even heard James, though he knew she had.

"And if you know of anything or if you see anything suspicious, you should call me." He stood and picked up his coffee. It was light. Just about all gone. He put his hat back on.

"By the way," James said, pausing at the door. "I read your brother's case. It was bullshit. All of it. I'm sorry they did that to him."

Dawn did not respond or even meet James's eye. When he left, he shut the door gently behind him.

[26]

DOUG

In the bathroom mirror, Doug adjusted his starched collar and unrolled his sleeves. He buttoned them at the wrist, brushed a piece of lint from his elbow, and headed back down the hallway to his office.

Officially, Doug Ahasteen kept the books for the new, fledgling Navajo Health Authority—which was his cousin Shawn's brainchild. Doug had experience in accounting—plus, it didn't hurt that he was also a practicing Diné healer.

The health authority had been a bear to handle so far. Grants had to be written to justify its existence. And Doug's own idea, the Medicine Man Association, had certainly helped with that. There had never been anything like it, and while Doug found himself taking on more and more work—as was often required in nonprofits—the MMA was important to him. It was a priority.

Back in his office, Doug took a deep breath and looked down at the list on his desk. He was calling each member who had agreed to be a part of the association and asking for dues. He was only asking for a small amount. Just enough to cover the booklet that had already been printed and paid for out of Doug's own pocket, and the radio ad he was hoping to air next month. But he didn't like making the calls. The other healers were smart. They knew what Doug was asking was fair, and they all hoped his efforts would bring in more patients. But the whole reason for the association in the first place was because of how badly the healers were struggling these days. They didn't want to give up a cent, and Doug didn't want to ask for one. Besides, Doug had never been very good with people. It was the hardest part of being a healer. His mind was methodical. It thrived on the properties of the herbs, the dosing of the medicine, the discipline of the ritual. But often when he sat with a patient in their home, listening to their stories, he had to bite his tongue to keep himself from finishing their sentences for them, hurrying them up.

If only Victor Black would join, Doug thought bitterly. He could probably fund the entire advertising campaign alone.

He shook his head and was about to pick up his phone when there was a knock on his office door. Nearly everyone Doug worked with came in without announcement or invitation, so he knew it was not a colleague.

Doug stood, smoothed down his shirt, and opened the door. His heart beat a little faster when he saw a tribal police uniform on the man before him.

"Hello, Officer," Doug said. "What can I do for you?"

The man stuck his hand out and Doug shook it.

"Lieutenant Wayne Tully," the man said. "Can I borrow a few minutes of your time?"

"Of course." Doug stepped back to let the lieutenant inside. Once they both sat, Lieutenant Tully spoke again.

"I appreciate what you all are doing here," he said. "With this Medicine Man Association. I don't practice traditional healing myself, but I know those in the community who do, or who might want to, will appreciate this. There are plenty Diné younger than myself who never had an elder teach them the old ways but are still curious. Something inside them wants to connect."

Doug felt his grip on his chair's armrest loosen just a bit.

"Thank you," he said. "We appreciate the support. What brings you here today, Lieutenant?"

"I've got a somewhat unusual question for you."

The lieutenant leaned back and laced his fingers together in his lap.

"Have you had any fellow healers speak about young women—specifically pregnant women—asking for peyote?"

"Peyote?" Doug felt the crease in his forehead wrinkle. "Perhaps you're not familiar, Lieutenant, but traditional Diné healing does not involve the use of peyote."

"Oh, I'm familiar," the lieutenant said. "But you see, we've got something happening on the reservation. Pregnant women are obtaining peyote to use during labor and are continuing to use it to self-medicate after they've given birth. Nothing wrong with that. The hospitals are aware. It seems to be quite effective. But we've had some deaths recently with no discernable cause. Their commonality is peyote. They all took peyote before going to the hospital. We're trying to find out where the women are obtaining it."

"And you think it could be from a healer?" Doug asked. He adjusted himself in his seat. This could be an embarrassing start to the MMA. It was certainly not the kind of attention they needed.

"Could be. Their roadman denies distributing it. Many of these pregnant women might trust a healer. And many of the healers have close and unique relationships with members of the community."

The lieutenant's stare bore into Doug.

"I haven't heard of anything like it," Doug said. "There's been no mention of peyote from anyone."

"Mr. Ahasteen, I would rather not speak with every single healer in your association. No one at all comes to mind when you hear of this?"

Doug felt nervous again. He cleared his throat and swallowed twice. He racked his brain trying to think of anyone who would've given him any indication they would do something like this. He didn't want to think poorly of any of them. It wasn't good for the fragile unity he had recently created.

"I uh . . ." Doug started to say. But then he realized what was happening. Doug knew exactly who the lieutenant was thinking of. He must not know, Doug thought. He must not have realized that Victor Black was not a member.

At one point Doug would never have done what he was about to do. He'd considered Victor a friend. No, a mentor. Victor had been a mentor to nearly all the healers at one point or another. But after the last few months, Doug no longer held the same respect for the man. He hadn't understood Victor's decision at all. And Victor had only made Doug's life more difficult. He no longer felt much loyalty.

"Victor Black," Doug said, "is not a member of the association."

The lieutenant's eyebrows went up. He moved his head back like a turtle retreating into its shell.

"Victor Black isn't a member?" the lieutenant asked.

Doug gritted his teeth. "He is not."

"That's strange," Lieutenant Tully said. "I would've thought he'd be one of the first to sign on."

"He feels it's too modern. And impersonal. He called it the healer's phone book. He said he's only ever reached people through relationships and he doesn't intend to become a pharmacy."

Doug realized after he said it just how much he'd been wanting to complain to someone. Not that this lieutenant was the person for it.

"That must be frustrating," Lieutenant Tully said.

Doug inhaled and let out a long breath. "It's not ideal."

"Did Victor's decision . . . upset other healers?"

"Some. More than I'd hoped but not as many as I'd feared. Most healers on the reservation want to do anything and everything they can to keep doing what they love. They don't have the luxury Victor Black does to be picky about their patients."

Doug hated how bitter he sounded. But it was true. Victor could afford to do whatever he wanted and the rest of them couldn't.

"It's too bad he isn't a member."

"I haven't quite given up on him," Doug lied.

The lieutenant wrote down his phone number on Doug's pad of paper.

"Well, if you happen to speak to Victor or to anyone and they mention anything about peyote, please do give me a call."

"Will you be questioning all of the healers, then?" Doug really hoped he wouldn't. He didn't want anything scaring them away from this new project. From the attention they were about to get.

"I'll be discreet in my investigation," the lieutenant said.

Doug nodded. "I appreciate that."

The lieutenant stood up. He shook Doug's hand.

"Keep up the good work. And don't forget to call me if you learn anything."

Doug swallowed the lump in his throat. He gave Lieutenant Tully a small wave as he left and tried to steady his shaking hands enough to call the next number on the list.

[27]

MOLLY

Molly's first thought as she sat on the ground inside the
teepee, her back against the canvas wall, was that she should
have told the truth to *someone* about where she was going.
She had told James she was at Paula's and she'd told Paula
nothing because she knew James wouldn't question it,
wouldn't call Paula's house or stop by. He wasn't that kind of
parent. She'd thought both of them would have been likely to
stop her—to try to talk her out of it or flat out forbid her to go.
She actually couldn't think of one person in her life who
would not have tried to stop her. That probably should have
told her something, but once she knew Joey would be taking
the peyote, she had to come.

The meeting had a purpose, which was something Molly
didn't realize about Native American Church meetings. Most
were called for a reason, though not all. A neighbor and
friend of Joey's had asked for this one. Her son struggled with
addiction, had been in and out of recovery, rehab, using. He
had relapsed again and the woman was feeling low and
helpless.

"We have tried to get him to come before," Joey had said to Molly as they drove to the meeting. "It can really help with recovery, you know. The meetings, the peyote. It's medicine. It works. But he always brushes us off."

"Taking the peyote isn't, like, bad for drug addicts?" Molly asked.

Joey shook his head. "Not the way we take it. We don't take that much. It's called a hallucinogen, but I've never hallucinated. I don't think anyone does. At least, I've never heard of it."

Molly nodded. She felt less afraid hearing that. Still. It might've been like that in the past, but no one knew if *this* peyote was different. Molly's nerves were on a roller coaster. One minute she felt calm and comforted by Joey's words and presence and the next she remembered the danger they could be in.

When they entered the teepee, Molly studied the roadman. This must be the Clarence guy Wayne had talked about. He looked pretty average. Not too tall. Not too big or skinny or old or young. Unremarkable except for his particularly bushy eyebrows.

On their walk from the car to the teepee, Molly had noticed how easily everyone was talking, laughing, smiling. But now, inside, seated, waiting for the man with the giant peyote cactus to begin, everyone was much more serious. They were quiet. Some seemed to be concentrating on something Molly couldn't see. Maybe something inside of themselves.

A fire burned in the center of the circle, and Molly shifted on the blanket Joey had brought for the two of them, trying to get comfortable.

Molly noticed something being passed from person to person on her left. It was coming her way. Her chest tightened. Joey leaned into her slightly. She could smell something on him. Soap? Cologne? She liked it, whatever it was.

"Tobacco," he whispered, and Molly's shoulders relaxed. Each person brought the corn husks to their mouth and inhaled. Molly could handle tobacco. It worried her, though, that she hadn't been paying enough attention to see it coming earlier. It was just so smoky in the teepee. Molly was already sweating. Her back, her temples, down the middle of her chest.

She shifted again to take pressure off one of her legs and noticed how motionless everyone else was. Maybe they were used to it, but Molly's foot was already falling asleep. She tried to sit still as she took the corn husk–wrapped tobacco from the man to her left. She'd thought she would stand out at the meeting, be a spectacle. But no one seemed to care. They barely acknowledged her. Not like at school, where every person's differences seemed to be on constant display, her whiteness the loudest and most obvious of all.

She was clumsy with the husks but managed to inhale a little bit of the tobacco smoke. She passed it to Joey and then studied the peyote cactus next to the roadman. It was large and she had no idea how they would eat it. Would he cut it open? Every time she thought of what she might do when the peyote was given to her, her head swam.

Once everyone had smoked some of the tobacco, the roadman began to speak, reminding everyone of why they had gathered. The woman spoke next about her addicted son and Molly listened. She spoke of the fights, the lies, the missing jewelry that had been in the family for generations, the day she'd found him face down in his own vomit, the resentment, the morning she'd assumed he was dead. The woman paused multiple times as she sobbed. Molly felt awful for her. She could see the woman's pain, could hear it in her strained voice. She thought about Adriel and his mom, who had struggled with addiction when he was a baby. Linda was Kay's sister, and apparently, they'd been very close. Their own mother had died when they were kids, but Molly wondered right then if Kay had gone through something similar to this woman. It broke Molly's heart to imagine it. Linda was gone now. Murdered. Hers was the case that had brought Molly and James to the reservation in the first place.

Molly didn't know what she ought to be doing once the songs and chants started. She barely knew any Diné, so she didn't know what they were saying. But she guessed that thinking about Linda was probably appropriate. Honoring her life, her legacy, what she had left Molly—which was the greatest cousin Molly could have ever asked for. Linda *had* struggled, but she'd also recovered and was a wonderful mother to Adriel before she was killed. Molly imagined Linda sitting there with them. She imagined thanking Linda for such a wonderful little boy. And even though Molly hadn't taken any peyote—no one had yet—she found it surprisingly easy to picture Linda beside her. Sometimes a wave of uneasiness came over Molly when she tried to picture Linda. She had only ever seen her dead body, after all. But Molly didn't feel any of that now. She only felt a deep gratitude.

But now the roadman was bent down, retrieving something from a bag, and Molly knew in the pit of her stomach that the peyote was coming. Her heart raced. She thought of

Robin Kinsel, a woman she had never met but who had died —possibly due to ingesting the same plant all these nice people were about to eat. Robin had also had a little boy, who was now without a mom, just like Adriel. Molly couldn't bear for one more woman to die. For one more little boy to lose his mom.

"Stop!" she shouted. Now she was most certainly the center of attention. Everyone stared. The fire crackled. The roadman turned slowly to face Molly.

"Excuse me?" he asked.

"Please. I'm sorry. I didn't mean to—" She grasped around her for words in the still tension, "—interrupt. But you can't eat that peyote. Please. Something could be wrong with it. A woman died. Women have died."

A wave of murmurs rippled through the teepee. Molly did not look at Joey, but she could feel his stare and her already hot face grew hotter.

"What?" the roadman asked. Molly thought she saw annoyance in his face, but no. Looking closer, she could see it was anger. The words tumbled out of her now, the desperation behind them rising.

"My dad is an investigator with the tribal police. Multiple women have died in the hospital after eating peyote. They don't know yet if the peyote is to blame, but at least one woman's peyote was contaminated. Please. I don't want anyone here to get hurt."

More whispers. Molly watched the roadman take a deep breath. Compose himself.

"We are very welcoming to outsiders here at the Native American Church. But I do not appreciate the outburst or the unsubstantiated claims."

Molly wanted to protest, but she bit her tongue. The roadman's glare did not leave her face.

"If anyone here is bothered or concerned about this sacred plant that I hold, let them leave with our guest." He held up a small paper bag now, and Molly wondered that if the peyote was in there, what was the giant cactus doing behind the fire?

She wanted to disappear. She wished the earth would open up and swallow her.

"But I can attest to its safety," the roadman continued. "I will ingest some myself now to assure you of my faith."

The roadman tore his eyes from Molly, reached into the bag, and popped a piece of dried peyote into his mouth. He chewed, swallowed, and smiled at the group.

"I'm sorry," Molly muttered before standing and stumbling out of the teepee. She hoped Joey would stay behind. She had no idea how she would get home, but she'd find a way. She'd rather walk all the way home in the dark desert alone than face him.

But Joey followed. Molly did not want to cry, but the tears crawled down her cheeks anyway. She did not turn to look at him but heard his footsteps behind her, and then, beside her. Finally, she stopped walking and faced him.

"I'm sorry. I'm very, very sorry. I can't believe I embarrassed you like that."

Joey tilted his head to the side.

"Is that why you wanted to come? To warn people? You could've just told me."

"I know. I should have. I don't know what I was thinking. I wanted to protect you, I guess. But I'm not really supposed to tell people about the case."

Molly looked back at the teepee, expecting it to still be full of people. But actually, a small group of women stood outside now, talking to one another. They must have left the meeting, too.

"Shit. I really caused a scene, didn't I? And my dad's gonna be mad, too."

Molly crossed her arms and looked down at her feet. Joey took a step closer. Close enough to touch.

"Hey," he said, his voice low. Like a purr or something. Molly looked up.

"You were trying to help. You have a good heart."

Molly let out a breath of relief, and Joey took another step forward before wrapping his arms around her. They stood like that for a moment, Molly's head against Joey's chest, listening to his heartbeat.

"They probably won't let me bring white girls to meetings anymore, though," he finally said. They both laughed.

"I'm not the first and only?" Molly asked.

Joey pulled away and grinned. "You didn't know? That's kind of my thing."

Molly laughed again. She turned, and they began to walk again, his arm around her shoulder, as she leaned into him. "Liar."

When they reached Joey's car, he spun her toward him and stared into her eyes. "Promise me you'll come to more places with me and cause absolute chaos. I think it's pretty cute."

Molly smiled. "Promise."

Then, Joey leaned down and kissed her. It was slow and gentle and sweet, and Molly wanted it to last forever.

When Molly closed the door behind her as quietly as she could, the only light she could see was the digital clock in the kitchen, which read 12:24 a.m. On the way home, she'd thought about waking up her dad and telling him what had happened. Getting it over with, getting it off her chest, facing the consequences right away. But now that seemed like a bad idea. He would think she was having an emergency, probably, and what could he do about the whole thing right then, anyway? Go back to the meeting himself? Molly doubted that would make anything better.

She thought briefly of not telling him at all. She had yet to do something like this. Something she knew would disappoint him. But she knew she had to fess up. She cared about the P.I. business and knew this would affect the investigation. James needed to know.

She sighed and went to the kitchen to get herself a glass of milk. She doubted she'd be able to sleep. Not with all these thoughts and feelings swirling around inside her.

She opened the fridge, took out the gallon of milk, and poured herself a glass. She was sipping it, leaning against the counter, when she heard a noise. A door closing, but not the front door. She could see that from where she stood.

Damn, someone was up. Molly held her breath, hoping maybe they would go to the bathroom and back to bed without even noticing her. But then Kay appeared in the kitchen doorframe. She was squinting with only one eye open and her hair was disheveled.

"What happened?" she asked, her voice thick with sleep. "I thought you were staying at Paula's."

Molly let her breath out in a long gust. "I don't want to keep you up."

Kay shook her head. "It's fine. Once I'm up, it takes me a while to fall back asleep."

"Sorry," Molly said.

Kay smiled. "Don't worry about it. Do you want to talk about your night?"

"James is gonna be so mad at me," Molly whispered.

Kay nodded toward the living room. "Go sit. I'm going to make some tea. Do you want some?"

"Sure," Molly said. She placed her empty milk glass in the sink and went and sat on the couch. She let herself relax into it but didn't feel sleepy.

When Kay came in, she handed Molly a mug and joined her on the couch, tucking her feet beneath her.

"So," Kay said, "where were you really?"

"How did you know?"

"Well, you said James is going to be mad at you. So, I assume you lied."

"I did. But I wish it was just that. I probably totally screwed up the investigation."

Kay's eyebrows went up. She blew on her tea and sipped. "Okay. Start from the beginning."

"I wanted to help more with this case. I've been feeling . . . I don't know. Left out, I guess. It sounds silly but Paula's been able to do so much more than me."

"Like go to the WARN meeting?" Kay asked.

"Exactly. So I thought maybe I could find out something from Joey. Maybe he knew something that could help me."

Kay sucked air through her teeth.

"I know, I know. I really shouldn't use people I care

about. And I wasn't trying to. He's just a connection to the community."

"So is Paula."

"Right. But Paula's already doing her part. And I already know everything Paula knows."

"So what did Joey tell you?" Kay asked.

"That he's a Native American Church member. And that there was a meeting tonight and did I want to come?"

Kay's eyes grew wide. "No," she whispered in disbelief. "You went?"

Molly nodded. "I had snooped earlier and heard a voice-mail message for Wayne. It was Raymond Nez. He found three other women who died after taking peyote. Three! I just wanted to protect Joey. I didn't have a plan, really. I thought maybe if I was there and something happened with the peyote, I could get him help faster. I would know what the problem was. Maybe."

Kay leaned closer. Narrowed her eyes. "Did you take some?"

Molly shook her head. "No. Of course not! Actually, I panicked and told everyone there not to take the peyote and then I told them why and the roadman was really angry and he took some himself right there in front of everyone and told me to leave."

Kay gasped and brought her hand to her mouth. "Oh, honey."

"The meeting was for a woman whose son struggled with addiction. It made me think of your sister and then of Adriel. And then I thought of Robin and her little boy. I just didn't want one more young mom to die. Not if I could help it."

Kay grabbed Molly's hands. "I understand. You probably thought of your own mom, too. I'm sure you miss her."

Molly did not want to cry. Maybe she *had* been thinking of her own mom. She knew how it felt to lose a mom. She nodded instead of speaking.

"Thank you for thinking of Linda, even though you never knew her. She would've really liked you. She had a big heart—just like you do."

Molly swallowed her tears and smiled. "Sometimes I feel like I did know her. Because of Adriel, you know?"

Kay nodded. "I see her all the time when I look at him. When he gives me little smirks."

"He's such a good kid," Molly said.

"He is," Kay agreed.

"Anyway, a few of the women *did* leave after I said something. I hope everyone else is okay."

"Was Joey upset with you?" Kay asked.

Molly was glad the light was dim. She could feel herself blush.

"No. He's, like, a really nice guy."

Kay let go of Molly and picked her tea up again. "He is. He's a good catch."

Molly giggled. "I don't know if I've caught him yet."

"He isn't your boyfriend?" Kay asked, a playful smile behind her eyes.

"I don't know. But he did kiss me tonight."

Kay almost spilled her tea leaning forward so fast. "What!"

"Shhh," Molly laughed. "You'll wake my dad up."

"How was it?" Kay asked.

"Perfect. Amazing."

Kay snorted. "I think it's safe to say you've caught him."

"How mad do you think James will be?" Molly asked.

"About the kiss?"

Molly giggled again. "No! I'm not telling him about that! About the rest of it."

Kay shrugged. "At first? Maybe pretty angry. But your dad loves you. He'll forgive you. And I doubt you've ruined the entire investigation."

Molly sighed.

"We all make mistakes," Kay said. "It could've been worse."

"It could have?" Molly asked.

Kay started to laugh. "Maybe?"

Molly couldn't help it. She laughed too.

[28]
JAMES

It had been some time since James and Molly last smoked cigarettes together. James didn't want to encourage the habit, but Kay had assured him that morning that both he and Molly were going to need one.

Now, he listened to Molly list her wrongdoings, recapping her evening of lies and missteps. James tried not to lose his cool. Most of them were stupid mistakes. Typical for an amateur. For a teenager. But listening to Wayne's voicemail message? That made James angry.

"You don't ever do anything to jeopardize your partner's trust, you understand?" He turned to face her. "Especially something as unnecessary as that. Wayne is our partner. We need him. Not only that, he's our closest friend."

Molly's face turned red. She stared at her shoes. "I know. I'm really sorry, Dad. I shouldn't have done that."

James tapped his cigarette. "Joey forgave you because Joey . . . he likes you. But there was no reason to disrespect Clarence Draper. We ought to be building relationships, not creating enemies." He paused and took a deep breath. "I understand your judgment was clouded because of Joey. But if you would've stopped for just a minute and spoken to me about it. Or hell, even just thought about it yourself, you might've realized that we would've heard about it before now if *all* of the peyote on the reservation was contaminated."

He stopped. Belittling her wouldn't help things.

"But," Molly began. Her voice was small. Almost a whisper. "How are we supposed to know *which* peyote is contaminated?"

"That's the right question," James said. He took a drag of his cigarette. "Wayne and I talked it through and came up with some theories. What do all the possible victims have in common?"

"They're all women," Molly said. "Are they all WARN members?"

"Maybe. Seems likely. We've tasked Raymond Nez with finding out more about them," James said. "See if they were involved with WARN. Find out if they were church members. He's also going to see if any of the families happen to have any of the peyote left and ask if they'll let us test it."

Molly was still looking down, scuffing the dirt with her heel.

"Another thing," James went on. "I heard through the grapevine that Grandma Beans directed women in her class who asked about peyote to speak with Dawn Harvey. Now, I'm not sure if that's because Grandma Beans knows that Dawn distributes it, or because Grandma Beans knows nothing and only wanted to deflect. But we ought to have Paula pick her brain a little."

Molly nodded. She finally looked up at James and sighed.

"I'm really sorry. I feel like an idiot and a jerk. I don't know what I was thinking."

James took one last drag of his cigarette and then crushed it under his boot. He put his arm around Molly and pulled her in. "Just don't lie to me or to Wayne again, all right? And especially when you're about to put yourself in a risky situation. I need you safe."

"All right." Molly rested her head on his shoulder.

"You're not an idiot," James said. "Or a jerk."

Molly scoffed.

"You said some women left the teepee?" James asked.

"Yeah, a group of them. A small group. Maybe three or four?"

"I wonder if there's been talk among the women before today. Rumors or warnings." He shook his head. "We could really use some more women in the police field to do a little chitchatting."

"If *I* could stop making dumb mistakes . . ." Molly trailed off.

"Hey," James said. "Look at me." Molly turned to him. "Quit beatin' yourself up. We all make dumb mistakes. The important thing is learnin' from 'em and fixin' 'em. Now, come on. We've got some work to do."

[29]

KAY

HER TRUCK WAS STILL IDLING in the dirt road as it had been for the last ten minutes. She thought he might've come out by now. Knew that he knew she was there.

She told herself she had every right to be there. As far as Kay knew, he was a good man. The best medicine man on the reservation. Her best chance, she thought now, of getting pregnant.

He was also not Cecil Cody, despite his connections to the man. She felt a little guilty that she hadn't told James about this visit. She would eventually. Or maybe not. She didn't know yet.

Kay took a deep breath, rubbed her sweaty palms on her jeans, and finally shut off the engine. She walked up to the squat brown clapboard house. A warm light emanated from the front room, but the rest of the house appeared dark. She tried to steady her breath, but her heart still raced and she could taste something metallic in the back of her throat. She closed her eyes and thought of her father. Then, she knocked.

Victor Black was much darker-skinned than most Diné

Kay knew. It was—she assumed—how his family had taken on that last name. An identifier and point of pride.

Despite his old age, Victor's hair was mostly still a stark black streaked with silver. That day, he wore it pulled back in a low ponytail. His good eye studied Kay. The other was milky and dead.

"You're a Benally," he said, his voice smooth and calm. He opened the door wider. "Come in."

The bareness of Victor's home surprised her. There were a few chairs and a sofa, but no decorations and barely anything on the tables. Back where she assumed the kitchen must be, there was another room with plants and jars and bottles. He sat on one of the chairs and invited Kay to do the same with a sweep of his arm.

"You knew my father," Kay said, her nervousness subsiding.

Victor nodded. Kay's father had never brought her here. Growing up, they had visited a different medicine man. Her mother's family's medicine man, who died when Kay was a teenager. But Kay's father had known Victor and spoke highly of him.

"Your father visited me plenty. Your sister too, once."

"My sister visited you?" Kay asked. She didn't think Linda had kept secrets from her. At least, not until the time right before Linda was killed. Then there had been plenty of secrets. But still. Kay had always thought them drug-related.

"She did," Victor said. Kay knew he wouldn't tell her why. Medicine men were like doctors. Your secrets were supposed to be safe with them.

Kay hesitated. She opened her mouth to speak and then

closed it again. She didn't know why she felt silly or embarrassed. She had no reason to. Her visit was valid.

"I'd like to get pregnant," she finally said. "I'm getting older and I haven't tried in a while." She flushed for a moment. "But when I did, the only time I got pregnant, I miscarried. I want to get pregnant again, and I want to carry the baby to term this time. I want a child. But my husband and I are older. We might be too old."

Victor smiled. It was warm and comforting, and that surprised Kay. She had always thought of him as a cold and distant man. Mysterious in some ways. She felt her shoulders drop a little. Her tension slowly released.

"You aren't too old," Victor said. "And men are never too old. Until they're dead."

Kay smiled, too. Took a breath. "Is there anything I can do? Or you can do? To help make sure it happens?"

Victor's eyebrows went up. "Me? I might not be dead, but I *am* done fathering children."

They both laughed at that.

"Is your husband . . . open to our ways?"

Kay bit her lip. She wondered if she should tell him that her husband was a white man. But then she thought of all the stories and all the gossip he must hear. Of course Victor already knew. Were Victor and Cecil friends, or was their relationship strictly professional? If they were friends, how much did Cecil divulge? Had *he* mentioned James?

"I don't think so. I guess I don't really know. I haven't said anything to him."

"Perhaps you should. There are always more options when the man participates, too."

"Say he doesn't want to. What then?"

"There are some things we can try without his cooperation. I can give you some herbs for your overall health. Some things to help with nervousness. One must be relaxed to host life. I can also give you something to help protect you from illwishers. If you would like, I can perform a Blessingway ceremony. After all those things, if you're still having trouble, we can always try an Enemyway rite."

Kay knew there was a "but" coming and thought of cutting it off, but she didn't. Victor went on.

"But if your husband is in bad health or overworked or is the target of witchcraft, I cannot help with that unless he is willing."

Kay briefly had visions of slipping herbs into James's tea, but it felt a little extreme even for her. At least for now. Maybe, eventually, she would get desperate enough.

She nodded. "I understand."

Victor's expression was serious and imploring. Still, Kay said nothing more, and after a moment he said, "Please stay here while I prepare the medicine." Kay nodded again.

After he left, she studied the patterns in the woodpaneled walls. The spot that looked like a face. And another that looked like a flower. Victor knew her father. Her family. They had been here before her. She took comfort in that.

When Victor returned, he handed Kay a jarful of herbs.

"This will probably last you a few weeks. Prepare in a tea and drink daily."

Kay took it and thanked him again.

"Come see me for more. Think about whether you would like me to perform a ceremony. And perhaps bring your husband."

Kay was so relieved and hopeful leaving her meeting with Victor that she didn't notice the truck parked around the side of his house. She was getting her keys from her purse when someone called to her.

"Kay Benally. What a coincidence seeing you here. You're just the woman I was looking for."

Kay's heart almost stopped. How inconvenient that Byron Cody would be the one to catch her here.

"Damn it," she muttered under her breath. Why in the hell was he being so friendly? He was walking closer to her, with a shit-eating grin plastered on his face. She almost corrected him; it was Pinter now. But she wasn't sure she wanted to get into that conversation with a Cody.

"Why on earth would you be looking for me?" Kay asked.

Byron leaned on the hood of her truck, still grinning.

"Don't act like we didn't used to be friends, Kay-to Potato."

Kay did not smile. Or show any recognition of her old high school nickname. Byron was younger than Kay but not by much. And of course, he had been her dealer during her party days. And then Linda's dealer after that.

"Did marrying the white dude really turn you into a tight-ass?" Byron rolled his eyes. "*Mrs. Pinter*. There, is that better?"

Kay hated that she felt like Byron had just read her mind. "What do you want, Byron?"

"No time for catchin' up, huh? All right. I'm looking for some help with something. From a teacher."

Kay held up a hand. "I don't want to help you. You'll have to find someone else."

"You don't even know what I want yet. I think you'll be interested."

"I'm not. I promise."

Byron squinted into the distance. Scrunched his nose like he smelled something foul.

"I find it strange that your hubby allows you to come to Victor. You know, with this current investigation and all. Unless you're a mole."

"It's none of your damn business why I'm here. And believe it or not, James doesn't *allow* me to do things. I just do them. He knows I'm a human being and not a dog."

"How radical." Byron sighed. "This could've been so much easier."

"Don't threaten me."

Byron smiled again, but this time it wasn't good-natured. It gave Kay chills. He smacked the hood of her truck with his palm.

"See you around, Kay-to Potato."

[30]
PAULA

GRANDMA BEANS WAS nifty with a rifle. Way out back behind her trailer she had set up a platform for target practice. Cans lined the top of the platform and casings scattered the ground at Paula and her grandmother's feet. In the distance, storm clouds were moving in, but the sun was still blinding in the sky and they both wore baseball caps.

"Grandma," Paula asked as the woman reloaded. "When's the last time Grandaddy went to a meeting?"

The old woman stopped what she was doing for a moment and squinted into the distance.

"Oh, it's been some time," she said. "Maybe a whole year."

"Really?"

Grandma Beans went back to reloading. "Says he's getting too old. I think the last couple of times really knocked him on his ass."

Paula let her grandmother raise the rifle to her shoulder, aim, and fire.

"What do you mean?" Paula asked.

Grandma Beans lowered the gun and shrugged. "It's a long night, you know? The whole experience. It takes a lot out of a person. Your grandfather seemed a little shaken up last time. He stopped going after that. Said he didn't trust his heart to handle it."

Grandma Beans handed Paula the rifle. "Why? Did you want to go with him?"

Maybe she would have before all of this. Now, as curious as she was, she didn't want to die. Paula shouldered the rifle.

"I just miss his stories. Riding a giant turtle through the clouds? Did he really think he was doing that? Or was he just screwing with me?"

Grandma Beans chuckled. "You know that old man. He's never been serious a day in his life. But he did tell me once that he's never hallucinated on the peyote. He closes his eyes and sees shapes and colors sometimes, but that's about it."

"Why didn't you go to the meetings?" Paula asked.

"I'm a traditional girl. The story of Changing Woman."

She stopped speaking for a moment, but Paula knew she wasn't done. Paula took the opportunity to shoot the rest of the cans lined up on her side.

"I went once," Grandma Beans continued when Paula was finished. "I appreciated the experience, but they talked about Jesus a lot. It felt unfair to Changing Woman. This land. These mountains. That's what speaks to me. When a healing needs to be performed, I want a chantway."

"I'd like to go to one of those with you," Paula said. Her grandmother smiled and wrapped her arm around her.

"I'd like that."

A raindrop hit her grandmother's hand. Then Paula's

arm. The sky had grown dark, so they packed it up and headed back to the trailer.

"I'll heat up some soup," Grandma Beans said as Paula toweled herself off.

While her grandmother was in the kitchen, Paula picked up a framed photograph of her grandparents. In the photo, her grandfather had just returned from fighting in the Pacific. He wore his uniform, and Grandma Beans held Paula's mother, who was young, but big to be held. Maybe five or six years old. None of them smiled. Paula set it back down and walked into the kitchen.

She opened the fridge and grabbed a Pepsi.

"So, Grandma. How are your classes going?"

Grandma Beans had her back to Paula. She was stirring the pot, and wet, stringy gray hairs clung to the back of her neck.

"They're great. I've been having great turnouts."

"When do you start with that midwife program?" Paula asked.

"Soon!" Grandma Beans spooned soup into bowls. "Dawn called me just yesterday and said that we have eight women signed up for the fall semester, which is wonderful. I don't think she was anticipating that many."

"That's great, Grandma!" Paula sat at the table. "How did you meet this Dawn anyway? How did all of this get started?"

Grandma Beans carried the bowls of soup to the table and sat down across from her. "She found me. I suppose it's been about a year now since we started the classes at the community center. Someone must have told her that I used to be a midwife and she showed up here, knocked on my door, and told me all about her plans."

"Her plans? You mean the certified midwife program, too?" Paula asked. "Was she planning it then?"

"Oh yes," Grandma Beans dipped a saltine cracker into her soup. "Dawn has all sorts of plans for the Shiprock hospital. For the whole reservation's hospital system. She is plain sick of being the only Diné nurse. I can tell that much."

"What else?" Paula asked.

"Hmmm." Grandma Beans sipped from her spoon. "She wants to get to you young kids before you even leave school. Set you up on a plan to apply to a nursing program. Get a midwife certification for those who are interested in that. She's on a mission to keep the old ways alive. I like that about her."

"She should talk to WARN," Paula said, sipping her soup too. "They do stuff like that."

Grandma Beans gave Paula a funny smile. "I don't know if Dawn's that sort of girl."

"What sort of girl?" Paula asked.

"Radical."

"I went to a WARN meeting, you know." Paula grinned. "They don't *seem* radical. It was kind of boring, actually."

Grandma Beans raised an eyebrow. "You be careful hanging around those women. They get into trouble."

"So what, this Dawn, she's like super straitlaced or something?" Paula asked.

Grandma Beans rested her spoon on the side of her bowl and squinted into the distance. "I don't know if I know her well enough to say that. But she's a hard worker. She strikes me as someone who doesn't have time for nonsense."

"Does she ever teach classes?" Paula asked. "Or does she just organize them?"

"She only organizes them. She doesn't seem to think she has enough knowledge to share, which is just silly. But I think she's embarrassed no one ever taught her Diné ways of giving birth."

Paula bit her lip. She needed to be honest with Grandma Beans. She was probably the most important person in Paula's whole life.

"Okay, so James somehow heard that you were sending people to Dawn if they asked about peyote. Is that true?"

Grandma Beans chuckled. "I know exactly how James heard that. And yes, I have sent women to Dawn about peyote. But I have also sent women to Dawn about countless other questions that I couldn't answer. You think this old toad knows where to get peyote?"

Paula laughed. "You aren't a toad. So Dawn never mentioned anything about peyote to you?"

Grandma Beans shook her head. "And she responded the way she always does. She respectfully told them she'll find out and get back to them. I have no idea if Dawn knows how or where to get peyote."

Paula crunched into a cracker. She chewed and swallowed and nodded. "Well, that's not helpful at all, Grandma."

Grandma Beans barked a loud laugh this time. "Sometimes an old woman is just an old woman. Not a detective or an undercover agent. I'm sorry I can't help here."

"I know," Paula said. "And I wouldn't want to make things weird for you with Dawn. I wouldn't ask you to snoop. It's not your job."

Grandma Beans patted Paula's arm. "No, but one day it

might be yours. And I have a feeling you'd be pretty stinkin' good at it."

WAYNE

WAYNE UNDERSTOOD why James needed to make a big deal out of what Molly had done. But Wayne wasn't particularly bothered by it. As an overly curious kid, he'd often stuck his nose in places where it hadn't belonged—and then lied about it. Didn't all cops behave that way as children? Wayne assumed so, but he knew how important integrity was to James, and so he'd accepted Molly's apology as seriously as he could. He also slipped her a few Starbursts on her way out of his office.

Now, at the Shiprock hospital, he asked after Dr. Ciccone.

"Is he expecting you?" the woman at the desk asked.

"No, but it's important. If he has even just a few minutes, I need to speak with him."

The doctor was paged, then, and Wayne walked with him down the hallway in between surgeries.

"I believe you've spoken with my buddy Raymond in the health department," Wayne said.

"That's right," Dr. Ciccone said. "He asked me to look into some patient records. He specifically wanted to know about peyote."

"Yes," Wayne said. "The reason for that is because Robin Kinsel's peyote was tested and confirmed to be contaminated with a narcotic. We're concerned she's not the only one."

The doctor stopped walking and looked at Wayne with wide eyes.

"You think there's a problem with the peyote?"

"There might be," Wayne said. "I'm going to ask you to call me next time someone brings peyote into the hospital. I would like to speak with them and have their peyote tested if they'll allow it."

The doctor frowned. "And if they've already taken it?"

"Monitor them. Be prepared to treat them for a narcotic overdose. If it's possible to take a blood sample, that would certainly be helpful."

The doctor nodded. "Apologies for not catching this sooner."

"I know how busy you all are," Wayne said. "There would have been no indications from friends or family that you'd need to worry about a narcotics overdose. I'm sure your staff, your nurses, the other doctors, they're all doing their best. Just keep an eye out and I'll let you know when we have more information."

The doctor shook Wayne's hand. "Thanks, Lieutenant. Appreciate your diligence."

"Oh, and one more thing," Wayne said before leaving. "I'm going to ask for those women's full medical records downstairs. That shouldn't be a problem, should it?"

The doctor slowly shook his head. "It'll take a few days. Maybe longer. As you said, everyone here is busy. They'll have to gather the documents and copy them, and I'll have to sign off. But, no. No problem."

"Great. Thanks, Doctor."

[32]

JAMES

The door to Clarence Draper's trading post had a fresh coat of paint on it. A sign nailed to the frame warned: Wet Paint.

"Avocado green," James said to Molly. She stepped closer.

"Looks like it could be," she said.

James raised his eyebrows and opened the door. They stepped inside. Clarence sat behind the counter, reading a newspaper. He looked up and smiled for only a brief moment, and then, recognizing Molly, straightened himself. His expression grew serious.

"Can I help you?"

James waited for Molly to speak. He had made sure she understood that her apology needed to come first. Before any explanations or questions. They took a few steps closer to Clarence.

"I want to apologize," Molly said. "For my behavior last night. It was unacceptable and disrespectful."

Clarence took a deep breath in but said nothing.

"I was childish and emotional. Our business—Pinter P.I.

—operates here on the reservation in partnership with tribal police. I would never want to mess up the trust we've worked so hard to build with the community. I'm very sorry."

Clarence eyed James for a moment and then stared at Molly. Finally, he nodded.

"I accept your apology, but I will ask that you do not come to any more meetings."

"I understand," Molly said. Clarence addressed James next.

"Is it true that Robin's peyote was contaminated?"

"Yes," James said. "And it's true that we've found three more cases of young women dying in the hospital after having taken peyote."

Clarence pursed his lips. "This is concerning."

"It is, and we want to get to the bottom of it as quickly as possible. I know you've talked to tribal police, but I'm hoping there's something else, some detail you might've forgotten about or overlooked or thought irrelevant before that might be useful to us now."

Clarence squeezed his hands together. He let out a long breath and looked James in the eye.

"I have an idea of where Robin might have gotten her peyote," he finally said. "Maybe she was the one giving it to the other women, I'm not sure. But she went to Texas herself with Cecil and Byron a few months ago. I don't know why I didn't tell Lieutenant Tully. I just . . . was caught off guard, I think."

Molly reached into her bag as Clarence spoke and pulled out her notepad. Clarence watched her but didn't try to stop her from taking notes. He looked up at the ceiling. He was clearly distressed, maybe trying to figure out where to begin.

"Would you like to talk in the back?" James asked. "Or somewhere more private?"

Clarence nodded. "Let me flip the sign and write a note that I'm on break. My office is behind me. You all can set up in there."

Molly and James sat in an immaculate office with only a lamp lit. It was cozy back there. The table was made of real, solid wood and the chairs had upholstered seats. When Clarence came in, he shut the door behind him.

"You have to understand, I knew Robin was going to Texas and I knew why. I encouraged her. We were in on it together."

"In on what?" James asked.

"The Codys." Clarence still spoke softly, even in the fortress he had locked them into. "They're not exactly happy with me." He forced a chuckle.

"Why not?"

"About a year ago, maybe more, I started to understand something about the peyote. You see, we have a drug problem on this reservation, as I'm sure you know already. Cocaine, heroin. I guess it's everywhere now. Not just here. So, I have a lot of church members who come to meetings seeking help with addiction. Alcohol addiction too."

Clarence sniffled. "They come with hopes for prayers and peace. But they smoke the tobacco and eat the peyote or drink the tea if I prepare it that way. And they keep coming back and their addiction recovery improves. At first, I thought it was spiritual. But I observed addicts who attended the other Christian churches, and I didn't see the same results."

He looked down at his hands. His breathing had slowed a little, which was good.

"I believe it's the peyote itself that helps with addiction. The way we take it, just a little at a time, it seems to do something for these people. Physically. I started to offer support groups to try to reach more people. The more people who joined, the more people who came to meetings, the more it seemed to confirm this theory."

"How did it confirm the theory?" James asked.

"I kept up with them. The ones who stopped coming to meetings frequently fell back into addiction. The ones who continued to come stayed away from drugs and alcohol."

James nodded. "I imagine the Codys didn't like that."

"No. They didn't. They sent subtle messages that they were not happy with me. At first I didn't understand, but then I put it together. My support groups, my informal program to attract addicts to my meetings . . . it was no good for business."

"What were the subtle messages they sent?" James asked.

"They stopped telling me when they were going to Texas. I was no longer invited. I could go on my own, of course, but it's hard to explain why that's rarely done. The Codys are synonymous with the reservation. If a person who normally travels with the Codys now travels on their own, the peyoteros are suspicious. And the Codys would have been even angrier. I had become an outcast and yet, even more reliant on them than I had ever been."

"And did they threaten you at that point? Once you were under their control?" James asked.

"Not outright." Clarence shook his head. "But they were difficult to work with. They no longer came around regularly. I had to pester them for more peyote. I tried a little experiment. I stopped holding my support groups so openly and instead only visited individuals at their homes. I did this for a month or so and the Codys were much more cooperative during that time. I got the message."

"And Robin? She, what, agreed to go to Texas for you because the Codys didn't have any grudges against her?" James guessed.

"Yes, that's right. They didn't know Robin and I were working together. She was more behind the scenes. She was very passionate about what I was doing. I imagine she must have had an addict in her life, though I never asked. But that's how she worked, you know? Like it was personal. She didn't like the idea of the support groups stopping. They needed to be public, she argued. We could reach more people that way. She wanted me to be free of the Codys."

Clarence laughed a soft, incredulous laugh. "Free of the Codys. Can you imagine?"

"You don't think she was free of the Codys at all, do you?" James asked.

"No," Clarence said. "I'm more afraid than I've ever been."

Molly glanced at James before speaking. "But you ate the peyote last night anyway."

"I did," Clarence said. He lifted his chin a bit higher. "This is my calling. What else am I supposed to do?"

"So Robin went to Texas with the Codys," James said. "And what happened in Texas?"

"She went to Mrs. Amada Cardenas's with the Codys and purchased peyote from her. But Robin also went to a different peyotero on the last day when the Codys were occupied with a social visit of some sort. She purchased peyote from *that* peyotero as well and struck up a business relationship. When she came home, she told me that in the future, we could go on our own and seek out this peyotero. His name was Diego Reyes, she said. She gave me all the peyote she had purchased from Mr. Reyes to try out."

"And what did you think of it?" James asked. "How was the quality?"

"Good," Clarence said. "I couldn't tell a difference, honestly. It seemed to be of the same quality."

"And she kept the peyote from the Codys' peyotero for herself? From this woman peyotero?"

"*Peyotera*." Clarence smiled a little. "Mrs. Cardenas. A lovely woman. It's a shame she's so close with the Codys. I have enormous respect for her."

"Robin kept Mrs. Cardenas's peyote, then," James clarified.

"That's right," Clarence said.

James sat back in his chair and propped his foot on his other knee. "Any idea why Robin might have given these other women peyote?"

"Are they members of WARN?" Clarence asked. "Maybe they asked her for some."

"We're in the process of figurin' that out," James said. "But that would be our guess, too."

James chewed on a thought for a moment. "Do you think it's possible that these women might have been addicts and Robin was givin' them some peyote to help with that?"

"Maybe, but I don't think so," Clarence said. "Robin really seemed to believe in the community aspect of the recovery process. She humored me, but I'm not sure she was entirely convinced that it was all about the peyote. I think she was still doing her own observations in that regard."

"But clearly she believed in the peyote's ability to provide pain relief," James said.

"Well, yes. She'd experienced that herself. And she believed in its spiritual importance. But I think she was trying to understand what exactly about the church meetings and the support groups was so effective. To her, maybe it was the peyote, but maybe it was a combination of things."

"Did the Codys find out what Robin had done in Texas?" James asked.

Clarence cleared his throat. Shifted in his seat. "That was my first thought when I heard of her death, to be truthful. That they had found out and punished her."

"How about Robin's husband, Russel?" James asked. "Do you know him at all?"

Clarence shook his head. "Robin introduced us once or twice. She was hoping he would start attending meetings but he never did."

"Do you know for sure that the peyote Robin took before her death was the same peyote she had acquired in Texas? It had been a few months since her visit, correct?" James asked.

"I don't know for sure," Clarence said. "Peyote, if stored properly, can be taken up to six months later and still have the same mescaline levels. But I don't know how much peyote from the trip Robin kept for herself. She gave me quite a bit. She wanted me to stop relying on the Codys for a while."

"But if she ran out," James said, "wouldn't she come to you for more?"

"I would think so," Clarence said. "I would hope so. But like I said, she wanted me to have enough for meetings, for those in recovery."

James nodded. "Thank you, Clarence. For sharing all this with us. I know this is frightening. The Codys do not mess around. But I can promise you that this conversation will not leave this room other than to share with Lieutenant Tully, who is the lead detective on this case. And I can assure you that Lieutenant Tully would like nothing more than to stop the Codys from harming one more person, if they are to blame in this."

Clarence nodded but his shoulders were still raised, his jaw still clenched.

"And I'm sorry again," Molly piped up. "After hearing all of this, I can imagine that what I did and what I said was very damaging to your program." She paused for a moment. "I will try to think of a way to fix it."

Clarence's face softened just a little. "Thank you."

[33]

DOUG

DOUG KNEW BREAKING and entering was probably not the smartest course of action, but he was desperate to get into Victor's house and search it. He needed this peyote drama to stay far away from his new and fledgling association, and he was annoyed that Victor would bring scandal to something he'd refused to be a part of in the first place.

That's why he was there that morning, in Shiprock, outside of the police station, smoking a hand-rolled cigarette. It was damn hot already. And the sun wasn't even at its highest point in the sky.

Doug had just put out his cigarette and was about to go inside when Lieutenant Tully stepped out the door into the parking lot. He looked surprised to see Doug.

"Lieutenant," Doug said. He walked over to him and they shook hands.

"Call me Wayne," the lieutenant said.

Doug shoved his hands into his pockets. "How have you been?" he asked.

Wayne dragged a hand down his face. "Tired," he said.

Doug glanced over Wayne's shoulder at the station, wondering if he could see inside. Maybe something was going on there today. "Is now not a good time?"

"Now is fine," Wayne said. "Now is good. Would you like to talk here at the station? Or would you rather grab some food?" He squinted at his watch.

Doug had skipped breakfast that morning and the thought of lunch made his stomach grumble. He wanted to keep this quick, but food did sound good. "We can grab something to eat."

"Hop in," Wayne said, digging his keys out of his pocket.

"I'll just meet you there," Doug said. "I have to go straight back to the office after."

"All right," Wayne said. "Whitethorne's Deli? On Route 13?"

"Perfect."

The wooden bench outside Whitethorne's was newly painted white, and when Doug dripped mustard on it, he quickly wiped it up with his napkin.

"So," Wayne said. "You must have heard something about the peyote?"

Doug finished chewing and swallowed his bite. He shook his head. "I was planning on paying a visit to Victor. I'm happy to poke around in there for you. See what I see."

Wayne's sandwich rested on some foil in his lap. He stared at it and nodded ever so slightly.

"Maybe we can set a date and a time," Doug went on. "Sometime while I'm there, you could come knock on the door. Keep Victor occupied outside for a bit. I have a good idea of a couple places to look."

"I'm not sure I can officially sanction a search without a warrant," Wayne said. "However, if you tell me the date and time, I can show up with a few questions for Mr. Black. You've got to tell me you'll keep your hands to yourself first, though."

Wayne stared at Doug overtop his sunglasses. It took half a second too long for Doug to catch his meaning, but when he did, he nodded.

"If there happened to be something sitting out," Doug said, "and I happened to tell you about it, then the mystery about which medicine man was supplying the peyote would be solved, wouldn't it?"

"Possibly," Wayne said.

"Is having peyote a crime?" Doug asked.

Wayne let out a long breath. "Twenty-five years ago, peyote was completely banned from the reservation. If tribal police found it, we were supposed to destroy it. And then the Navajo Bill of Rights passed and now it's a tricky thing. But in short, no. Possessing peyote is not a crime."

The pit in Doug's stomach grew heavier. "What about selling peyote? What if I got Victor to sell it to me?"

"That would be foolish," the lieutenant said. "The existence of the peyote is what I need to know about. A medicine man in possession of peyote is not illegal, but it is suspicious. It would be reason enough to narrow my investigation."

"Would you stop looking into the rest of the MMA

members?" Doug asked. He hadn't even thought about how to word that question. About how suspicious it might sound. But Wayne smiled.

"Yes, I would stop."

[34]

DAWN

THE FIRST WOMAN who showed up at the hospital and hurried over to Dawn, worry wrinkled across her forehead, was there before Dawn's shift even officially began.

"Please," she said, shoving a bag of peyote into Dawn's hands. "Take it. I don't want it anymore. I've heard it's killing people."

Dawn took a deep breath. She smiled. "I'll look into it. I promise." She rubbed the woman's back as she walked her back out through the doors to the woman's car.

Dr. Ciccone had been supportive of Dawn's efforts thus far, asking for nothing, but she knew now was the time to bring him the official credentials of her midwife certificate program. The American College of Nurse-Midwives Committee on Curriculum and Approval had sent her the paperwork to verify that her classes would be legitimate. Part of that paperwork stipulated that the program would recognize all religions practiced by the Diné and that nurses who were a part of this program would consult religious leaders about childbirth and child-rearing. This was a freedom of religion issue now.

The doctor's office door was cracked when Dawn knocked. "Come in."

Dawn entered. "Hi, Dr. Ciccone."

"Hello, Dawn. How are you doing?" He looked up from his work.

"Great. I actually have here with me the official approval from the American College of Nurse-Midwives for my program. And I have the curriculum, too."

She set her backpack down and unzipped it. She got the papers out and handed them to him. Watched him scan them.

"I appreciate this. Thank you."

"Those are copies, so you can keep them," Dawn said.

The doctor nodded. "I am afraid we're going to have to pause with the peyote until the investigation into Robin Kinsel's death—and now the deaths of three others—has been concluded."

Just as Dawn had suspected. "I agree. I don't want to put the women in any danger."

She almost told the doctor she was going to look into the peyote herself but realized in that moment how little he would probably care. He was waiting for the investigation. The cops. He needed it to be formalized.

Dr. Ciccone gave her a tight smile, and the corners of his eyes wrinkled. "I'll keep this filed away for the future. This is exciting stuff. Thanks, Dawn."

She left his office with one more mission before the day shift turned over to night shift.

Carole was at the second-floor nurse's station sipping from a can of orange soda. Dawn tried to make her smile look genuine but not suspicious, though if Carole had any brains at all she should know Dawn never came to her bearing goodwill.

Carole smiled back. "You're early today." And there was the judgment.

"Not really," Dawn said. "Can I ask you something?"

"Okay," Carole said.

"It's about receiving deliveries," Dawn said. "Well, lab deliveries specifically."

Dawn could read relief on Carole's face after that. Then a little bit of confusion.

"Do we still use LabMed 1st?" Dawn asked.

"Yes," Carole said.

"They deliver the kits, we use them, and then send them the sample, right?"

"Yes," Carole repeated.

"And they do everything? Cultures, bloodwork, tox screens?"

"That's correct. Why?" Carole was clearly losing patience, but Dawn didn't mind. She'd waste Carole's entire evening if she could.

"About how many do they send at once?"

"Of each kit? I'd have to look that up."

"How often do they get delivered? Weekly? Monthly?"

"Is there a point to these questions?" Carole's eyes narrowed.

Dawn shrugged. "Just curious. I'm happy to help with deliveries if you need it."

"No thanks." Carole's voice was less friendly now. No longer open to discussion.

Dawn shrugged again. "Have a nice night."

[35]
WAYNE

ADRIEL AND MOLLY had the same look of silly anticipation
on their faces. Like they might burst into giggles at any
moment. Kay was teaching Paula how to ride a horse, and
every other word out of Paula's mouth was inappropriate.

"I'm sorry, Mr. P, LT! But this shit is terrifying!" Paula
shouted.

"Just focus on stayin' on the horse!" James shouted back.

Wayne had not been able to spend one more minute at
the station, so rather than call James and Molly in, he'd come
to them. The smell of the horses and the sun beating down on
his hat was about one thousand times better than his stuffy
office.

Just then, a car pulled up. It was George. Wayne watched
Kay lead Paula and the horse away, toward the mesa in the
distance. Not surprising. Kay and George still weren't on
speaking terms. Wayne turned to greet him, and the two men
shook hands. Then James and Molly shook George's hand.
Private greeted him, too. The dog held no grudges.

"How ya doin', George?" James asked.

"Good, thanks. You ready to go, Adriel?"

The boy grinned and hopped down from the lowest fence rail, where he'd been perched. He waved to Molly and the men, but then looked abruptly in Kay's direction. He looked at his father for approval.

George nodded. "Go ahead."

Adriel ran toward Kay, kicking dust in the air behind him. George took a deep breath, put his hands in his pockets.

"How's it going, Molly?" George asked.

Molly grimaced. "All right," she said.

"You glad school is out?" he asked.

"I guess."

George nodded. He stared at the stable. They were silent for a moment.

"How's work going?" Wayne asked. "Did they give you back your old route?"

"Not yet."

Adriel was coming back now and George smiled at him. "Let's go, kiddo."

"Have fun," James said.

"Bye, Adriel!" Molly called. Adriel waved again, and then father and son got in their car and drove off.

Wayne, Molly, and James went back to leaning on the fence, looking out into the vast desert expanse.

"You wanna go first, LT?" James finally asked.

"I want to hear about Clarence. How did he take the apology?"

"Well, he told me I was not invited to any more church meetings," Molly said. Wayne couldn't help it. He laughed.

Molly laughed too. Even James chuckled a little, shaking his head.

"And at the end of the meeting I promised him I would try to fix it, which I have no idea how I'm going to do."

"Fix it?" Wayne asked.

"Yes. What I did was even worse than it seemed at first." Molly sighed. "Clarence has been dedicating his time to finding alcohol and drug addicts and bringing them to meetings. He believes that going to the meetings and taking the peyote regularly is helping them to quit."

"And then you told them all that they might be doing the opposite and ingesting narcotics," Wayne said.

"To be fair, I did not specify *what* the peyote was contaminated with," Molly said. "Still, I definitely did some considerable damage."

"Clarence tells us that because of this addiction program, the Codys have been unhappy with him," James explained. "Apparently Robin was also involved, though the Codys weren't aware until she went to Texas with them and purchased peyote from a different dealer."

"Why did she do that?" Wayne asked.

"So they wouldn't have to rely on the Codys anymore. Or any of the Codys' associates."

"Hm," Wayne said. "Smart."

"Or stupid if you think, like Clarence does, that it got her killed," James said.

"He thinks the Codys found out?" Wayne asked.

"So he says." James squinted into the distance. "It could also be a very convenient setup. We know now that Robin and Clarence weren't just church friends, they were business associates. Who knows what went on between them, but if somethin' went sour, this scenario with the Codys would be the perfect opportunity for Clarence to kill the woman and pin it on them. Besides, the door to his trading post has recently been painted avocado green."

"You think the man would be dumb enough to use the paint to frame the Codys and then use that same paint on a door that everyone can see?" Wayne asked.

"You know as well as I do, LT, that you can never overestimate your average human being's stupidity."

Wayne watched Kay lead Paula and the horse back to the stable. Their session must've been over. "I suppose you're right about that. What about the other women?"

"Could've been an accident. Maybe Robin distributed it to them after Clarence contaminated it. We find out if these women were WARN members yet?" James asked.

"Talked to Raymond this morning. We know for certain that two of them spoke to their families about WARN. Either said they were going to a meeting or talked about their services in some way. The third woman, the family has no recollection, but Patricia Dawes seemed to recognize the name, so it's possible."

"Any luck getting some peyote to test?" James asked.

"No. Their families either had no idea where the peyote went or had already tossed it."

"Damn," James said. "They church members?"

"Yes," Wayne said

"All of them?"

"All of them. But not all of them would necessarily go to Clarence. Two of them live closer to other chapters."

"They might go out of their way for his support group, though," Molly said.

"Yes, certainly," Wayne agreed. "Especially if he's the only roadman doing that sort of thing."

"What else you got for us, LT?" James asked.

"Doug Ahasteen paid me a visit," Wayne said. "He's real eager to find some peyote in Victor Black's house. He's asked me to come distract Victor for a bit while he looks around."

"You feel comfortable authorizing that?" James asked.

"I covered my bases. Told him to keep his hands to himself."

James chuckled. "That'll be interesting."

"I also asked Dr. Ciccone for full medical records for the other three women. One of the administrative ladies said she would have those ready later in the week."

James nodded. "And there was no autopsy done for any of those women?"

"Nope."

Paula and Kay were coming over, Paula shaking her legs out as she went. "So that's your idea of a good time?" she asked them.

"Watching you almost fall off?" Molly asked. "Yeah." She giggled again.

"She did great," Kay said. "And she'll do even better next time."

"Next time?" Paula asked. "I doubt my ass will ever recover from *this* time."

"Ummm, Paula. Didn't you say that someone mentioned Clarence at that WARN meeting?" Molly asked.

"Yup," Paula said. "Why?"

"What did they say again?" Molly asked. "Something about Clarence not wanting to work with someone?"

"Outsiders," Paula said. "Clarence does not want to work with outsiders for the rug thing. He will not participate in some auction or something. I don't know if those WARN ladies were gonna do it anyway without him. They were thinking about it, maybe."

"Is that what he said?" James asked. "Or were those your words? Or her words?"

"Oh, no. The girl quoted. Like this." Paula held up her fingers and made little air quotes. "Clarence does not want to work with outsiders."

"Interesting word choice," Wayne said, glancing at James. "Interesting indeed."

[36]
MOLLY

James sprang it on Molly the next day: They were going to Texas. There was no discussion, really, just a statement, and Molly assumed he must have talked to Wayne about it the night before. It was annoying being a kid still. Sometimes they asked for her opinion and sometimes she had no say at all.

Not that she didn't want to go to Texas. Meeting the peyoteros sounded like something out of a movie. She was excited. But she was also nervous and sad about leaving Joey and Paula for who knew how long. James insisted that Wayne needed Paula on the reservation for WARN-related problems, which Molly understood, though she wasn't happy about it.

And what if Joey forgot about her while she was gone? What if he found another girl he liked better? Molly made sure to say goodbye to him that same day. She found him at the senior center, but then took him out to his car for a little privacy and another amazing kiss that she hoped he wouldn't forget.

She packed her bag that night, and the next morning she said goodbye to Kay, who had woken up with them despite the fact that James insisted she sleep. Then Molly said goodbye to the dog, who she assured more than once that she would return, and that Kay would take good care of him, and that she was going to miss him a lot. Private's tail thumped the floor every time Molly's voice rose in pitch until she gave him one last kiss on the head.

James gave the dog a quick scratch and said, "Keep watch while I'm gone. You're the man of the house." Private stopped panting and closed his mouth. Looked at James, alert. He seemed to understand. It made Molly want to cry. She missed the dog already.

Then, James kissed Kay. "I'll call you when we get to Sue's," he said.

"All right," Kay said, gently pushing them both toward the door. "Get going so I can go back to sleep."

The drive felt like a tour of rusty brown hills. All kinds. Some sharp and jagged like the plateaus on the reservation. Others like pyramids, their tiers and levels jutting out here and there. And still others were almost unnaturally smooth. The way Molly might picture the surface of another planet. The hills rose up on each side of the road, sometimes along with towns and cities, sometimes on their own.

They drove through El Paso and Molly remembered visiting there with her mom years ago. Not long after Molly's tenth birthday, her mom had wanted to go on a road trip. Molly was hoping for the beach. She and her mom had gone to Galveston twice before, and even though her birthday was in the winter, they could still walk along the water and eat ice cream cones or funnel cakes and fries soaked in vinegar.

But Molly's mom wanted to go someplace they had never been before, and in that case, Molly didn't really care. She didn't have opinions about places she'd never been. Not when she was ten, at least.

Molly didn't know why her mom had ended up picking El Paso. Maybe she'd taken out a map and closed her eyes and pointed. She never explained her decision, but Molly remembered getting up early that day and driving for a long time. The longest drive the two of them had ever taken. They played every car game they could think of. The license plate game—which Molly doubted anyone ever won in Texas—I spy, twenty questions, punch buggy, the alphabet game, would you rather.

At the time, she'd loved that last game. Impossible choices about the weirdest, grossest, silliest things you could think of. But she remembered her mom getting quiet when she asked her a would you rather about being trapped in a room with her grandmother, Rita. Molly had thought that making fun of Rita was just a fun game, but Dorothy got so quiet that Molly wished she could shove the words right back into her mouth. It suddenly felt like there wasn't enough room in the car for her and her mother and their suitcases and that question. The air became so big and thick that Molly rolled the window down. Which was when her mom finally let out something between a sigh and a chuckle and said, "Whatever the other thing is, I choose it."

Molly didn't remember much about the actual city of El Paso except for the view from up high. That was all she could remember doing. Sitting for a long time at an overlook above the city, just staring at it. At the horizon and the mountains and the clouds and the small buildings lined in neat rows below them.

"There's another city," Dorothy had said. "On the other side of the highway, on the other side of a river. It's in Mexico. They call it a 'sister city' to this one. Maybe even bigger than this one."

"Can we go there?" Molly asked.

"I don't think so," Dorothy said in a real low voice, and Molly didn't press her because she was happy just being with her mom. Sitting in the quiet.

Molly and her dad drove on that very same highway now, and she could sometimes see the Mexico side as the roads lifted and dipped down, over and under each other, ramps exiting and entering the highway.

The last town they stopped at before their last major turn down Big Bend National Park's road was so quaint that Molly bought a postcard for Joey there. The buildings were all in the old Spanish style; Molly didn't know exactly what period of history, but they were painted mostly white with sky-blue or rose-red or blush-pink borders. Even the gas station was charming with a retro Coca-Cola machine inside.

Molly grabbed a snack there even though James assured her Sue would feed them dinner. Molly was hungry, and she didn't want to be distracted by her growling stomach.

The sun was setting as they pulled up to the park employee living quarters area. There were dozens of buildings that all looked the same. Short, squat, brown, single-level buildings with slanted roofs and only a few windows. They found the building number Sue had given James, parked, and knocked on the door.

A lady opened it, her hair fully white and pulled back in a low ponytail, her face worn and wrinkled by the sun, but the rest of her body fit and muscular. She wore work boots and muddy khaki pants and a plain green T-shirt. She smiled wide and immediately pulled James in for a long, tight hug.

"Jimmy Pinter. A proper man now," she said as she pulled away. "Oh, it's good to see you."

"Sue. You look the same as the last time I saw you. Like a movie star."

She threw her head back and laughed. "Still the charmer. Thank you, but I know that's not the truth." Then Sue smiled at Molly. "And you must be Molly. I'm sure you hear this all the time, but you look just like your mom."

Molly suddenly felt sad. Like in some other universe, her mom and James had worked things out and Dorothy had never gotten cancer and the three of them were visiting this woman from their younger years. Molly rarely indulged in these kinds of fantasies, because she liked her life now. But something about this woman who had known her dad when he was a boy made Molly wistful for something she'd never had.

She gave Sue her best smile anyway. "Thank you. It's a compliment. My mom was beautiful."

"She sure was. I was very sorry to hear about her passing."

"Did you know her well, too?" Molly asked.

"Of course! When they came home from college for Thanksgiving they would all be at my house! My boy Gary and all his old football buddies. And all their girlfriends, too.

It just made sense. But Dorothy was my favorite. I adored her."

Molly felt better, then. A warmth spread all over her body. It had been so long since she'd talked to anyone other than James who had known and loved her mother. And James was different, because his relationship with Dorothy had ended on such bad terms he probably couldn't even remember loving her.

"She was wonderful, wasn't she?" Molly asked.

"I loved Dorothy so much that after that first Thanksgiving I gave her our phone number and told her to call anytime for any reason, and she did! For many years. We slowly lost touch as people do, so I never got to meet you in person. Until today."

Molly felt her smile grow even bigger.

"Well, anyway. We can talk about all of this some more over dinner. You two must be starving." She took the bag from Molly's hand and ushered them both inside. It smelled amazing. Sue set Molly's bag down in the hallway and called over her shoulder, "Chili! I know it's not really the season for it, but I remember how much you loved my chili, Jimmy. And I've got some baked potatoes in the oven, too." She pointed down the hall. "Bathroom is the second door on the left. Everything should be ready in about ten minutes, but you can wash up before if you'd like."

"Thank you," Molly said.

Sue's bathroom had a blue ocean theme that Molly found a little funny given that they were in the middle of the desert. But maybe that was why. Maybe Sue loved the beach despite living in Texas her whole life.

There was a fuzzy blue rug, a fuzzy blue toilet seat cover,

blue soap shaped like seashells, and brown fishing netting hanging from the wall with clothespins and photographs. Sue with her park coworkers, Sue with a family—probably her son Gary and his wife and kids. Those same kids again and again: hiking with Sue, cooking with Sue, grinning at the camera wearing Christmas pajamas. Molly washed and dried her hands and face and made her way back out to the kitchen.

She saw her dad sitting at the table and knew he was probably waiting for Molly before talking about the case, but Molly wanted to hear more about her mom or even about her dad in his younger years.

"Sue, have you always been a park ranger?" Molly asked. "Even when Dad was a kid?"

James smiled. "My turn to wash up," he said and got up.

Sue stirred the pot on the stove. "Oh, no. I stayed at home until the boys were grown. Mostly I spent my time in my garden. It was no easy feat growing the things I grew in Texas. But then the boys left the house, and not long after, my husband passed away. Stomach cancer. I handed over the house's deed to Gary and the garden to his wife and I took this job."

"I'm sorry about your husband," Molly said. Sue turned to look at Molly and smiled.

"Thanks, darlin'. I'm sorry too. He was a good man."

"What do you do as a park ranger?" Molly asked.

"Well, we preserve and protect! Meaning I deal with any hooligans that show up and cause trouble. Give speeding tickets sometimes. But I also take care of the park. Educate visitors about the land and its history."

Sue turned back around to get the bowls.

"Are there a lot of women who do this?" Molly asked.

Sue chuckled. "Only one other here at Big Bend. And she's a young thing."

James was back. He sat down next to Molly. "So. Peyote. Ranger Demick. Let's talk about the case," he said.

Sue brought the bowls, steaming hot with chili, to the table. Then she went back to the oven to grab the potatoes. She brought those over on plates with what she called "the fixin's" on the side: butter, cheese, sour cream, bacon bits, chives. Then a pitcher of iced tea and glasses with ice cubes.

"Dig in," she said. After a few bites, she wiped her face with her napkin. "Believe it or not, I saw a peyote button just yesterday. I'll take you to see it in the morning if you'd like. There are some theories about the peyote plants up here and how they're different from the peyote plants down where you're going. Same species. *Lophophora williamsii*. But the population up here in the Chihuahuan Desert seems to grow larger, heartier, and has higher levels of mescaline."

James made a sort of grunting noise since his mouth was full, and Molly and Sue waited for him to swallow.

"So why are all the peyoteros farther southeast?" he asked.

"More plentiful," Sue said. "The smaller *L. williamsii* grows in clusters. Could take hours just to find one up here."

"Huh," James said. "Still, I bet you've got people coming to try to find some up here."

Sue shook her head. "It's generally not worth their time. There just isn't a big enough difference between the size and mescaline levels, I imagine. I assume you could just . . ." She shrugged. "Eat more of it. And they've got more of it."

"How about the peyoteros?" James asked. "Know anything about them?"

"I do not," Sue said. "But Ranger Demick will be able to tell you plenty. He's got a list for you of all the peyoteros in the state. The ones that operate legally, at least. They're required to report it for the license."

"Tell me about this Demick," James said.

"Ralph's a good friend. He's in Weslaco, which isn't too far from where you're going. You'll have to drive about two hours past Mirando City. Almost to the coast."

James nodded.

"Sharp man," Sue said. "Originally from California."

"What brought him to Texas?" James asked.

"GI Bill, I believe. He went to school here. Some fancy degree."

James sat back in his seat. "That was some darn good chili, Sue," he said. "And Demick is expecting us the day after tomorrow?"

Sue smiled. "Or the next day. Take your time, if you want. He said he'll be in the office all week."

"We'll get there tomorrow night. Stay at a hotel. Visit him in the morning." James paused and looked at Molly.

"Now, how about you tell Molly some more about her mom? Maybe I'd like to hear those stories, too."

[37]

KAY

THE DOG HAD EATEN a bowl of his own food, two pieces of Kay's bacon from breakfast, and a slice of cheese, but he still begged for something more as Kay put her shoes on to leave for a tutoring session at the school.

"It's loneliness," Kay said to Private. "That's what you're feeling. You can't eat it away." She patted the dog's head. "They will come back. I promise. And I'll only be gone for a few hours. Stay vigilant."

Private lay down and rested his head between his paws. He sighed.

Kay locked the door behind her and turned the radio up in her truck. She drove to school with the windows down, despite the heat, because she liked the wind in her hair. She was in a good mood when she pulled up to the school, if a little sad because she missed James and Molly, just like the dog. But she had decided to schedule a Blessingway ceremony with Victor, and she was pleased with that decision. She wanted to feel like she had done everything possible—everything in her power—to get pregnant.

So the sight of Byron Cody's truck in the school parking lot caught her off guard and irritated her. She marched over to it, ready to investigate, when Byron's big, smiling face greeted her in the window. He rolled it down.

"Kay-to Potato. You've got to stop following me around. I could report you for harassment."

Kay pursed her lips. "What are you doing here?"

"That is, in fact, none of your damn business."

Kay gritted her teeth. "What if I were interested now. What if I wanted to help?"

"You're not. You don't. I can tell."

"You said you needed help from a teacher. Is that why you're here?"

Byron said nothing at first. Made no gestures, only kept smiling at her. A stupid grin. Finally, he said, "Like I said, mind your fucking business, Mrs. Pinter." He started up the truck, turned to look behind him, and backed away.

Kay glared after his receding truck. He'd clearly been meeting with someone. There were a few other cars in the parking lot. Some were probably janitorial staff. But a few might be teachers. No cars she recognized, but she was early, so she could do a little poking around. She readjusted the bag that hung on her shoulder and walked inside.

The halls were fairly quiet, as they usually were in the summer. She could hear the bumps and scuffs of the janitor's cart, the squeaky wheels in motion. Kay peeked into rooms, sticking her head through doorframes. Finally, she found a teacher. Not exactly a friend, but friendly enough.

"Hey, Earl," Kay said. "You have a minute?"

The man smiled, the wrinkles around his eyes stretching

nearly to where his hairline ought to be. He was almost completely bald, with a fuzz of hair on the crown of his head. "Sure. What can I do for you, Kay?"

"I was supposed to meet Byron Cody here today. But I didn't see his truck when I pulled in. Did you happen to see him?"

"Oh, yes. Byron was just here. We were talking about the nursing program he's starting. Is that what you all were meeting about?"

"I guess so," Kay said. "He just told me he had a good opportunity for some teachers here. What's it about?"

"He's trying to help high school students get into nursing if they're interested. Byron's ONEO program—I forget what it's called—is going to help students with their college applications: getting references, helping them write an essay, finding financial aid, that sort of thing. Hook them up with that maternal nursing program at the hospital if they want."

"Huh," Kay said. "That sounds like a great opportunity. Did you agree to help? I'm just wondering if he'll still need me. It's something I would definitely be interested in."

"I did agree to help, but he might still need other teachers. I'll pass along your interest and let you know."

"Thanks, Earl. You doing some tutoring today, too?"

"Just one student today."

"I've got three. All right, well. Sorry I missed Byron. Let me know if he wants my help."

"Will do."

Earl put his glasses back on, and Kay left the room.

Well, that reeks of Dawn Harvey, she thought. Either Byron was working with her or against her, but there was no way this new program didn't involve her somehow. She walked down the hall to her own classroom, noting all the broken lockers along the way. She would have to tell Wayne about this.

[38]

BYRON

They were behind. Byron didn't know whose fault it was that James Pinter and his daughter had managed to sneak away from the reservation and down to Texas undetected. It was his job—or maybe Cecil's, but definitely not Ronnie's—to know what that bilagáana was up to. And now they had to play catch-up, which was a real pain in everyone's ass.

Byron's brother Ronnie was not allowed to be in charge of much anymore, because he had fucked up so many times. More times than Cecil even knew. In ways Cecil could never imagine. It made Byron's head pound to think of everything his father didn't know. Byron was tired of it. Keeping secrets from both of them just to keep the fucking family intact. To keep their position on the reservation secure.

Cecil assumed he was the one holding it all together, and that one day it would pass on to Byron. But that day had already come and gone. Byron had never even stopped to consider if he was ready for the responsibility; it was forced on him and he did what he had to do, but he also didn't know how much longer he could do it. How much longer he could love and obey and deceive his family all at once.

Byron thought for a quick second of the things Cecil would do to him if he ever found out. But he didn't have time to be distracted right now. He had a team to assemble. Travelers who would make the trip to Texas with him to somehow get ahead of that private detective motherfucker who was—like Cecil's own son—a bigger danger to the Cody family than Cecil knew. Byron knew, though. And he knew he should have been keeping a better eye on him. He'd been too distracted lately. He needed to get his head out of his ass and focus.

Byron thought now of the people who had to be invited, no question. Pillars of the church on the reservation. Personal friends of Amada's. The same people who made the trek down every February for the big President's Day weekend pilgrimage. Byron would show real disrespect if he didn't invite them, and that was not the kind of mistake Byron made.

But there was someone else Byron wanted to invite. He chuckled at the thought. It cheered him up. It made his shitty situation slightly more enjoyable.

[39]

JAMES

IT WAS ALMOST NOON the next day when James and Molly turned down Texas Boulevard. They were only one mile now from Ralph Demick's office. Shops and restaurants and some real tall palm trees that reminded James a little of Vietnam lined the street.

It was hot down there. A special kind of hot. By the sounds the car's fan was making, it was struggling to stay cool. Molly scooped her hair into a ponytail and fanned herself with her hand.

James turned off Texas Boulevard and into a parking lot next to a four-story block of a government building with lots of windows.

"I could use a lemonade," Molly said, opening her car door.

"We'll get one after." They both got out and stared at the building for a moment.

"Texas Rangers," Molly said, squinting in the sunlight. "They're, like, a really big deal, right?"

James chuckled. "Yeah. Pretty big deal."

"You wanted to be one, didn't you?" Molly asked as they crossed the parking lot.

"Of course I did. What little boy growin' up in Texas doesn't?" He held the front door open for her. "I could've walked right into the next class after I came home from the war."

They passed through a shiny, tiled lobby and headed toward the elevators.

"Why didn't you?"

They waited for the elevator to come and then stepped inside. James rubbed the back of his neck. "I wasn't right, exactly," he finally said. "In the head, you know? I had seen some terrible shit."

Molly stared at him. She was waiting for more. What else could he say? If it were anyone else asking, he would've stopped right there. But for Molly, he could try.

"I had bad dreams. I thought I was still there sometimes. It made me sick and angry. Being a Texas Ranger wouldn't have helped with any of that. I needed to be far away from a justice system that I felt was broken. I couldn't handle it. Not then."

"So you bought your rig," Molly said.

The elevator doors opened and they stepped out into the hallway. James read the office numbers and arrows on the plaque in front of him and turned right.

"I bought my rig. I did a lot of driving. I needed to be alone. I needed to do a job that didn't require me to speak to many people. Driving even gave me an excuse to not sleep if I didn't want to. Did that for years. Until I felt like I was a different person from the one who'd come home from the war."

"And then I came into your life," Molly said.

"Best thing that ever happened to me." James smiled at her. "You helped me remember what I loved. Filled me back up again."

"Awww, Dad." Molly blushed. "All I did was find a dead woman."

James laughed. Gave her a quick side hug. "And became the best assistant a lawman could ask for."

They were at the office now. The Weslaco location of the Texas Rangers. James opened the door to a scene that looked a lot like other special investigation offices. A front desk with a hallway behind it, lined with doors to individual offices, and James guessed there was an open pit somewhere at the end. A young man sat at the front desk wearing a uniform and a nametag that read, *Bordewich*.

"Can I help you?" His voice had just a hint of a drawl.

"Name's James Pinter. I'm here to see Ranger Demick. He's expecting us."

Bordewich glanced at his watch and the notepad in front of him before picking up the phone.

"There's a Mr. Pinter here to see you, sir," he said. Then a moment later, "Yes, sir."

He set the phone down and stood up. "Follow me."

Bordewich knocked on the third door on the right. "Come in," a voice inside said. Bordewich gave James a nod and walked away.

James opened the office door. Ralph Demick sat behind a large oak desk, scribbling something as he tapped his foot and bobbed his head to the music that was coming from the record player in the corner—Fleetwood Mac, "Gold Dust Woman." Molly's eyes lit up. James knew she liked that song.

"One moment," Ralph muttered. He had thick blond hair and large glasses. Finally, he put down his pen, stood, and reached over the desk to shake James's hand. He was trim but muscular and about James's age, give or take a few years.

"Ralph Demick," he said. "Please, take a seat."

James and Molly sat and Ralph grinned at them. "James and Molly. Heard all about you two from Sue."

"Thanks for seein' us," James said. "We appreciate it."

Ralph held up a finger and stood again. "One second." He went over and lifted the needle from the record.

"Sorry about that. Music helps me think. Gosh, I love that band. Saw them in concert last year." Ralph whistled. "What a show."

Molly looked like she was about to explode with envy, so James said, "Molly here is a big fan, too."

"Is that right? You've got good taste, kid." He winked at her and then sat back down. "You've got business with the peyoteros, I hear."

"We do. We've got some suspicious peyote up at the reservation. Wanted to see what's going on down here in Texas."

Ralph's expression grew serious. He nodded. "Which reservation?"

"Navajo."

"Huh. Well, I can tell you the peyote is not on our radar. This is the first time I'm hearing of anything suspicious. Tell me more about it."

"We had a woman die shortly after taking peyote and being rushed to the hospital," James said. "Now, what we do know is that her peyote was contaminated with narcotics. We had it tested. Quite a high amount. What we do *not* know is whether she died from an overdose or somethin' else. However, in the course of our investigation, we found a few more cases of other young, otherwise healthy women dying after taking peyote and being admitted to the hospital."

"Huh. Contaminated with narcotics."

"That's right," James said. "Many of the women on the reservation have been doin' some self-medicating with the peyote. It's safe to assume they were all already in pain before taking the peyote."

"But the contaminated peyote may have been the cause of death for the women."

"Correct," James said. "No autopsies were done. It's against their beliefs, so we don't know for sure. What can you tell me about the drug trade down here?"

"It's funny. Drugs aren't supposed to be a large part of what the Rangers do. Our responsibilities are as follows: financial crimes, death investigations, missing persons cases, protecting public figures or going after them for corruption. Those are our priorities. But down here by the border, there isn't much anymore that isn't tied to the drug trade. Plus, Border Patrol just transferred one hundred officers from Texas to Florida to deal with the Cuban immigrant crisis."

"So you've got your hands full," James said.

"That's one way to put it. And I'll say this. The peyoteros are never a priority. They just don't cause problems."

"What do you see the most of coming through the border illegally?" James asked.

Ralph didn't hesitate. "Definitely cocaine. Although we've been seeing more and more heroin, too."

"You've got known gangs and gang members in the area," James said.

"Of course."

"Operating in the same towns as the peyoteros."

"Sometimes," Ralph conceded.

"What can you tell me about Amada Cardenas?" James asked.

"Mrs. Cardenas is beloved by everyone. Cooperative with law enforcement. Seems like she files all her papers on time whenever she's due to update them. A pillar of the community, from what I know." Ralph ducked down to open a side cabinet and pulled something out. He slid the paper over to James. "There are twenty-seven peyoteros registered as such within the state of Texas."

James looked at the list. Sure enough, there were twenty-seven names, phone numbers, and addresses listed.

"That's the most we've ever had," Ralph said. "Mrs. Cardenas used to be the only one. Now, I would say her biggest competitor is Mr. Diego Reyes."

"What can you tell me about him?" James asked.

"He's Mrs. Cardenas's antithesis. She's personal. Spiritual. Respectful. Traditional. Mr. Reyes is a businessman. He wants to find out the most efficient way to pick, to operate, to sell. He's got a whole mailing setup, even. He'll ship to anywhere in the country."

"How does that work, legally?"

"All he needs is a faxed photocopy of their tribal enrollment card with the same address he's mailing the peyote to."

"Enterprising," James said. "All these peyoteros Mexican?"

"Peyote does not care if it grows on this or that side of the border. These peyoteros come from families who have gone back and forth to pick and sell for generations."

"The peyote doesn't care, but surely the law does," James said.

"They're US citizens."

"Can you speak Spanish?" Molly asked.

"I can," Ralph said. "Sort of a requirement for this job."

"Have you always known how?" Molly asked. "Sue said you're from California."

"I am from California. Languages have always been my thing. I picked up Spanish just living around it, but in the Army I was a linguist. I can also speak Vietnamese, Mandarin, and Japanese."

Now that impressed James. "I bet you don't use those too often anymore."

Ralph grinned. "You'd be surprised. There is actually a somewhat sizable Vietnamese refugee population here in Texas."

"No kidding," James said. "Well, we'll get out of your hair." He picked up the list. "Thanks again for this. It's a huge help."

"Sue said you were CID. Now *that* must have been a tough job."

"It was," James admitted. "I still miss it some days. Not many, though."

The two men laughed and everyone stood.

"I mean this," Ralph said. "While you're down here, if you need anything, call me. Things could get hairy and you've got no backup. I'll be there."

James could tell Ralph wasn't just being nice. He shook the man's hand. "I appreciate that, Ranger. I really do."

DOUG

DOUG HAD THOUGHT he would be more nervous than he was that morning. He felt great, actually, on his way to Victor's. Well-rested. He had eaten breakfast. Whenever he started to feel guilty or strange over what he was about to do, he would remember Victor calling the MMA a pharmacy and then he would feel much better.

He even waved to the beautiful woman in the truck that passed him just before he turned into Victor's driveway. She didn't wave back, but Doug told himself it was because she was distracted. She certainly looked it.

He knew Wayne wouldn't be there yet. That wasn't part of the plan. Still, when Doug shut off his car, he looked in the rearview anyway, half-expecting to see the cruiser with its lights on. Nothing.

Doug took a deep breath. Maybe he wouldn't find anything. Maybe this would all be a waste of everyone's time. Doug had the startling realization that if this were the case, he would be disappointed. The idea of taking down Victor had infected him.

Pharmacy, he reminded himself as he stepped out of the car. He approached the chipped, orange-painted door and thought how, if he had Victor's money, he wouldn't repaint, he would knock the whole damn thing down and rebuild. He knocked.

"Did you forget . . ." Victor began to say as he opened the door. But then he stopped. "Doug Ahasteen. What a surprise."

"Good morning, Victor. Were you expecting someone?"

"No. No. A client of mine just left. I thought she had come back." He shook his head a little like he was shaking away a pesky bug. "Please, come in."

Victor took a few steps back into his house and Doug followed. He looked around the living room. It was neat and tidy and looked much like it had the last time Doug visited, which would probably have been about three or four months now.

"Sit," Victor said before disappearing into his kitchen.

Doug sat on the couch and waited. He looked at his watch. About five minutes to go. Doug was not looking forward to those next five minutes.

Victor returned with two mugs of tea.

"Thank you," Doug said.

"How is the MMA faring?" Victor asked.

Doug sighed. He could do desperate. That felt real enough.

"I wish it were doing better. We have plenty of interest, but we need more money."

"Have you come to ask for some?"

Doug would've liked to think the man was mocking him, but Victor's face was serious and somehow that was worse.

Doug chuckled. "Victor, I would not ask you to fund something you are not a part of."

Victor leaned back firmly against the couch. "You know my decision about that. It hasn't changed."

Doug nodded and sipped his tea. "I thought perhaps you might be interested in the conference I'm planning. In teaching some sessions."

"A conference you will hold with no money?"

"I'm asking for sponsors. In-kind donations. Catering donated. That sort of thing. I believe we can pull it off."

"And I would need to be a member to teach at this conference? And then you would like me to donate my time, too?"

Doug hated this. He knew how good Victor could be at making others feel foolish. He reminded himself that this was all a ruse anyway. A way to kill time. Doug knew these arguments wouldn't work.

"Come on, Victor," Doug pleaded. "If you don't want to be a member because you don't need the clients, then fine. Your directory listing can say something like, 'Inquire directly for services.' Or you can be left out of the directory altogether."

"What would be the point, then?" Victor asked.

"To support the rest of us! We are not in competition with one another. You know this and we know this. You are in your own league. We respect that. But don't you want to leave this life with the promise that all you've worked so hard for will continue on?"

"It will." Victor was steady. He had not raised his voice. He took a sip of his tea and Doug clenched his jaw, waiting for him to continue. "I've trained all of you. Left you all with my knowledge. Did you forget?"

Doug felt his face redden and bit the inside of his cheek. He needed to stay calm. He couldn't let Victor get under his skin. But Doug could not deny just how much of an asshole Victor was being.

"And so many of those men are struggling now. They don't have the money. The knowledge you gave them is going to waste."

"I think I've earned the right to keep my own clients . . ." Victor started to say. But then there was a knock at the door, and as Victor stood to answer it, Doug checked his watch. Wayne was one minute early. He heard the door creak open.

"Good afternoon, Victor," he heard Wayne say.

"Lieutenant. Another surprise. I have a guest at the moment, but you're welcome to join us."

"Actually, I'd like to speak with you outside," Wayne said. "It'll only take a minute."

"All right," Victor said.

Doug slid to the edge of his seat just as Victor appeared around the corner. "Just a few minutes, please," he said to Doug.

"Take your time," Doug said. He waited until he heard the door shut again. Until Victor and Wayne's voices began to fade.

Then he got up quickly and strode down the hall to Victor's office. The door was cracked and Doug pushed it open all the way. Surprisingly, the office was not as neat as the rest of his home. There were papers in piles on every surface—multiple stacks on his desk, more atop the filing cabinets, another on a chair by the window. Would he keep the peyote in here? Or in his bedroom? Or with the rest of his medicine? Doug left the office and hoped Wayne would give him time to get back if he needed to.

Victor's medicinal room was lit up by a sequence of large windows, all the blinds and curtains open. In the corner opposite, a storage unit stood in the dark. Doug knew the purpose of this room was to offer whatever environment a plant or object needed to thrive and retain its healing powers. He knew it required monitoring, that Victor came here multiple times a day to adjust the blinds or check the temperatures. Doug had a room just like it. What he didn't know was anything about peyote. How it was grown, stored, packaged, nothing. *Shit.* He scanned the room quickly. Once, twice. He saw nothing he didn't recognize, and his panic started to pull at him. He didn't have time to search the whole damn house.

He hurried back to Victor's office and started opening the desk drawers and shoving things aside. It was so messy. Papers everywhere, mints, staples, typewriter ink, but no peyote. As he turned to leave, he knocked a stack of papers to the floor. He scrambled to pick them all up and noticed one that looked like a contract of some sort. A word jumped out at him. *Peyote.*

Until an agreement can be made with a Native American Church (NAC) roadman regarding religious consultation, peyote will be obtained directly from cosigner, Mr. Cecil Cody. Consultations for Christian patients will be made directly through patient's church. All traditional healing consultations will be made through cosigner, Mr. Victor Black. Mr. Victor Black requires all clients to attend one in-person consultation as well as in-person follow-up check-ins. Treatments and medicinal remedies will occur between patient and medicine man only. There will be no third-party, middle-man transactions.

Doug stopped reading. Wayne and Victor's voices were growing louder. He scanned quickly down the page trying to figure out what it was all about. Victor's signature was at the bottom along with Cecil Cody's and then a third signature: Dawn Harvey. Was that one of the dead women? Doug couldn't remember.

He wanted to take the sheet, to read it in depth later, but there was no time now to figure out how to do that. He couldn't just crumple it up in his pocket. *Shit.*

He acted next with almost no thought, but as soon as he noticed the window and realized it opened to the side of the house where he had parked, he decided to lift it up and slip the paper through a crack, to retrieve when he was back outside. A man of Doug's intelligence should have at least considered the wind.

He managed to shut the office door just as Victor closed the front door behind him and called Doug's name.

[41]

WAYNE

WHEN WAYNE WANTED TO THINK, he liked to walk. Sometimes he fantasized about being a cop in a big city. Walking a beat. Saying hello to folks. Taking in the sights and sounds.

That day, Wayne walked a trail that went across the highway, looped behind the fire station, past a picnic bench, along the San Juan River, and toward the actual rock of Shiprock, though he wouldn't make it anywhere near that far. Wayne had forged this trail simply by walking this same route over and over throughout the years.

Wayne didn't know what to think of what Doug had told him the day before. He claimed that Dawn Harvey had signed some sort of contract about peyote coming directly from Cecil and rules about other religious consultations. Was the contract for her midwife program? It seemed likely. Was Dawn supposed to send patients to Cecil or was Cecil giving the peyote to Dawn to give to the patients? It was too bad the contract was missing now. Wayne almost laughed at how much of a failure Doug's visit had been. There'd been no evidence of peyote and Wayne suspected that Doug had been too nervous to do a proper search. He understood. Doug was not trained for that.

Wayne stopped and sat on a rock on the banks of the river, which, at this time of year, was almost dried up. Kay's visit yesterday evening confirmed that Dawn also had some connection to Byron. He was either working with her or in direct competition to recruit high school students to become nurses. But if his father had a signed contract, the former seemed more likely.

Wayne looked up and watched the tint of the sky change from a blue gray to a pinkish orange. He would need another cup of coffee once he figured out what he was actually going to do that day.

If Dawn was the distributor, regardless of which Cody the peyote came from, she must not have known that Cecil had targeted these women. But she knew now. What would she do? Was she in danger of becoming Cecil's next victim? No, Cecil wasn't that careless. He knew about the investigation.

Wayne leaned forward onto his forearms and clasped his hands together. He looked at the dirt on his boots. The small spider that perched on the shrub in front of him.

There was another scenario that Wayne considered. One in which Dawn's intentions weren't so pure. If *Dawn* had contaminated the peyote, maybe it wasn't because she had anything against the women, but because she had something against the Codys. The women could be random. The goal, in this case, would be to set up the Codys. Which would be bold, reckless. Someone would have to be either profoundly stupid or blind with hatred to target the Codys. Wayne thought of Dawn's brother, LeRoy. He hadn't looked much into the case. Not that there would've been much information available to him. It was a federal case. Maybe the Codys had somehow been involved. Maybe Dawn blamed them for her brother's imprisonment. Still, Dawn Harvey didn't behave like a person who had nothing to lose.

Now that the sun was rising and the faint morning light spreading, Wayne could see a few empty beer cans crushed and scattered on the other side of the riverbank. Some cigarette butts too.

What frustrated Wayne most about this case was how little they knew about the other women's circumstances. The hospital had yet to call to say their records were ready. Wayne would have to make them ready, then. If this was all a coincidence—if the other women's peyote was never contaminated and their deaths were from natural causes—then Russel was still the most logical perpetrator. But their records might not reveal anything. Wayne may never know what happened to those other women.

He sighed, put his hands on his knees, and stood. "Never give up on the husband," he muttered to himself.

JAMES

A LARGE IRON sign loomed over an open gate and a dirt driveway. Had James been in any doubt he was at the right house, this would've cleared it right up. The sign was a half-circle bordered by the words "Native American Church." In the center was an iron teepee, and from the teepee, other words branched out: "Spiritual," "Residence," "Hope," "Love," "Faith," "Charity." This was Amada Sanchez Cardenas's house. The church-appointed Texas delegate for the Native American Church and most prolific and longest-practicing peyotera or peyotero in the country.

James and Molly arrived midmorning, but the sky was dark and gray like a storm might be coming. James pulled through the gate slowly, his car jostling back and forth on the rocky dirt road. The small white clapboard house sat to their right, and to their left was a covered picnic area and some large sheds. Directly in front of their car sat a teepee, and next to it were two tents.

James parked and shut off the car but didn't get out yet.

"Do you think she'll talk to us?" Molly asked.

He took a deep breath. "We've got to try. And we've got to tread carefully. We'll appeal to her expertise in the field. She's been doin' this longer than anyone. We can learn from her."

Molly nodded but didn't say anything, and they both got out of the car. Before they could reach the house, though, the front door opened and four men emerged.

The first gave James a big shit-eating grin. Byron Cody. *Damn it.* The Codys had beat him there.

James barely registered the other men. It was Molly who gasped, "Joey? What are you doing here?"

Somehow, Byron's grin got even bigger. His gold tooth was dull and dark in the overcast light.

"My favorite bilagáana. Mr. Kay Benally now, I hear."

Byron rubbed his hands together, and Joey stepped closer to Molly.

"Byron invited me," Joey said. He looked eager. And young. So young in that moment. "We're getting more peyote. Since everyone on the reservation is sort of afraid of theirs now. You said you were going to Texas, but I didn't realize we were coming to the same place!"

James couldn't see most of Molly's face, but he could see the tips of her ears turning red.

"I got you a postcard. But I sent it already to your house. I guess you'll get it when you get back." She stumbled a little over her words.

Byron hadn't wiped that stupid grin off his face yet. Joey's gaze flickered to James now.

"Hello, Mr. Pinter. It's good to see you."

"Hello, Joey." James tried to sound even, unbothered, but

this was a giant fucking pain in his ass and he knew Byron knew it.

"I bet you're here to talk to Amada," Byron said. "But you see, I already told her that you're trying to undermine her operation here. She doesn't want to talk to you about her business."

"Now, that's just not true, Byron," James said. "I'm sure you and Mrs. Cardenas would agree that ensuring the peyote's safety and purity is a priority."

Byron snorted. "I don't agree with you on anything, bilagáana." Finally, Byron's grin faded. "And you're on sacred ground here. You're not a member of the church, and you're not welcome." Byron gestured with his head toward the gate. "Go on," he said. "I'm sure these two lovebirds can meet up some other time and place." Byron winked at Molly. "We'll be here for the week."

James tilted his head from side to side, stretching his neck. "We'll visit Mrs. Cardenas another day."

Byron's loud, train-like laugh rang out. "Good luck with that."

James tipped his hat. "Gentlemen."

"I'll see you later, then," Joey said to Molly and a look passed between the two of them that James recognized so well it was like a rock had been hurled at his chest. He couldn't get angry. It was what Byron wanted. He did not want to deal with this right now. He turned and headed for the car.

James did not idle this time but threw the car into reverse and drove off of Mrs. Cardenas's property. The car was quiet for a minute.

When James finally trusted himself to speak again, he said, "You all right?"

"Yes." It was so quiet it was almost a whisper.

"You think you can stay focused?"

"Of course." This time she was much louder. "I'm a professional."

"I'm glad to hear that," James said. He took a few more measured breaths. "And you know about condoms, right?"

"Dad!" Molly screeched. She covered her face with her hands. "That is *so* embarrassing. I can't believe you said that! It is *not* like that."

"It's not? Looked like it to me."

"We've kissed. Two times. That's all."

James sighed. "All right. All right. Just had to put it out there. I am not ready to be a grandfather. Hell . . ." He stopped before he could say more. It was clearly not the time to mention the baby he and Kay were trying for.

"I know," Molly answered. "And I'm not ready to be a mom. I know." She looked out the window, and though the silence between them only lasted for a moment, it was sharp.

"Listen," James said. "This was a calculation by the Codys. They heard about the meeting, your outburst. They brought Joey to distract you and to distract me. They might even be trying to get information or to feed us information through Joey. I know it's hard, but you can't tell Joey the details of this case, all right? And you can't trust what he tells you, either. Byron's lying to him."

Molly nodded, her face still turned away. "It's messed up," she finally said. "Can't I tell him how Byron's using him?"

"I don't think he'll be open to it. He might get angry with

you. I would keep it to yourself for now. Joey will learn for himself soon enough." James rested a little now in his seat and relaxed his arms. He didn't realize he had been so tense. "We know the Codys don't play nice," he went on. "I'm sure Byron has been all over this town already warning everyone and anyone not to talk to us. We've got our work cut out for us, but that's all right."

Molly finally looked at him. "How is it all right?"

"We just have to strategize. It might seem like everyone is a friend to the Codys, but it's never that simple. We'll keep pokin' around. Someone in this town is bound to have a bone to pick with them."

Molly was quiet. James could tell she was feeling deflated.

"In fact," James went on, "open up that map. See that red star? That's our next destination. Can you give me directions?"

"Sure. Where is it?" Molly asked, staring at the map on her lap.

"Diego Reyes's address. You remember who he is?"

Molly looked back up at James. "He's Mrs. Cardenas's biggest competitor. And the man Robin bought peyote from."

James smiled. "That's right."

There wasn't much about Diego Reyes's house that announced him as a peyotero other than the fact that it was larger and nicer than the others on the street.

Reyes's house was two stories, painted light blue, and sat close to the road. James parked on the shoulder, and he and

Molly walked through the small but meticulously maintained flower and shrub garden to the front door. James knocked. The man who opened the door was younger than James had expected. He wore bell bottoms and a short-sleeve, button-down silk shirt with three buttons open at the top and two gold chains hanging on his chest.

"The investigator," he said. "Come in."

"Are you Diego?" James asked as the man closed the door behind him.

"I am Diego. And you are Mr. Pinter and this is your daughter."

"Byron Cody has been to see you already."

Diego waved at the air like he was swatting a fly. "I don't like thugs and I rarely work with the Codys. But I am intrigued by what he told me about you." He raised an eyebrow and smiled. "Please go have a seat. I'll bring some drinks."

The floors inside Diego's house were all white tile and his sofas a plasticky yellow leather. James and Molly sat, and Diego quickly returned with Coca-Colas in glass bottles. He popped the caps off before handing them to James and Molly. Molly was perched on the edge of the couch like she might need to run away at any moment. James appreciated her diligence but reclined and let the fake leather squeak under his weight. He had both of his weapons on his person, and Diego didn't seem to care or notice or even ask.

Diego sat across from them and crossed one ankle over the opposite knee.

"Something is wrong with the peyote, eh?" Diego asked.

"We don't know for sure, but we aim to find out." James said. "A young woman died recently up on the Navajo reservation after being rushed to the hospital in pain. The peyote she had taken only hours before was tested and found to have been contaminated with narcotics."

"Only hers?"

"That we're sure about. However, we're looking into the deaths of a few other women who also died in the hospital after taking peyote. We don't know whether their peyote was contaminated. We weren't able to get our hands on any to test it."

"Peyote contaminated with narcotics. I've never heard of such a thing." Diego's knee bobbed up and down as he eyed James.

"Well, it's happened, and it could've been contaminated an hour before she took it or days or weeks beforehand. Or right after it was pulled from the ground. That's what we're trying to find out."

Diego whistled. "Not here. My operation is as tight as a mouse's butthole. In fact, I would love to show it to you. To, uh, ease your mind."

"All right," James said.

"Bring your drinks."

Molly and James followed Diego out the back door, across a small backyard, and toward a covered patio. Rectangular, raised, chest-high trays filled up the patio, and as the three of them got closer, James could see the trays were full of peyote buttons. Men and women stood behind the trays, chopping bright-green, freshly picked buttons into chips. On the far end, the trays were unmanned and the peyote chips were brown and drying.

"My cousin Luis and my aunt Maria," Diego said, gesturing toward the two people on the end.

"Hello," James and Molly said. The two offered smiles but said nothing.

"You can see, here is where the buttons are cut into slices and dried before they are sold." He pointed to a row of plastic buckets full of intact peyote buttons. "The pickers bring me full buckets. I pay by the bucket."

"How much for a full bucket?" James asked.

"One dollar."

"And how long does it take to fill up a bucket?"

Diego frowned. His forehead wrinkled a bit. "Three or four hours."

"One person can fill a bucket in only three or four hours?" James asked.

"I could when I was a picker," Diego said.

"How do you know the pickers don't take any for themselves?" James asked. The cousin glanced up just then at Diego, waiting for a response.

Diego shrugged. "I don't. If they take any, it's for themselves. They can't turn around and sell it. The Indians won't buy illegally, and getting the peyotero license is a pain in the ass." Diego laughed. "Most of us with a license, our families have been doing this forever. Picking, at least."

The sun was getting lower in the sky, and Molly put her hand up to shield her eyes.

"Come," Diego said, leading them to a tan truck about twenty yards from the peyote trays. "Get in. I'll take you to where it grows."

James felt his pistol at his waist and climbed into the truck. Molly sat in the back.

"You said Indians won't buy illegally," James said. "But the Codys might."

Diego sucked his teeth. "I don't think so. Some picker won't be able to undercut Cardenas's prices."

"But you can?" James asked.

Diego laughed again. "My prices are competitive."

"Tell me about Cardenas."

"What's there to tell? It used to just be her dealing. A long time ago, when she lived and sold out of Los Ojuelos. She's like the rest of us. She started picking because her husband and her father did it."

"If she was the only one," Molly said, "who did she pick for?"

Diego grinned into the rearview. "There were other peyoteros when she was a picker. And other peyoteros when she started dealing. I'll tell you what happened to the other peyote dealers at the time. Some white dude who hated alcohol and was in charge of something important on the reservations, he came down and bought every single button he could. The entire stock of every single peyotero. One hundred and seventy thousand buttons. That's how the story goes, anyway. And then he burned them! He burned all of it."

"Holy shit," James said.

Diego laughed. "He must've been high as hell burning all that peyote."

James laughed at that, too. And then Molly joined in.

"Anyway, some peyoteros kept going after that but some didn't. Eventually, Amada was the only one left standing. We've all worked for her at some point. As pickers."

"You picked for her? What's her operation like?" James asked.

"Similar to mine." Diego stopped the truck and shut it off.

"The Indians like her because they've known her for so long. She listens to their stories. She takes their sacred traditions seriously. She welcomes them into her home. Lets them have meetings on her land."

"And you?" James asked, as they got out of the truck.

"I can't do what Amada does better than her, you know? That's her thing. I understand the peyote is medicine and I treat it that way." The three stood outside the truck, Diego's arms crossed. "When I started out, I thought to myself, 'What about the Indians that can't make this trip or don't want to? Or what about the Indians who can't quite afford her prices but would never ask to pay less because it would be disrespectful?' I can help those Indians. There is plenty of peyote here to go around. I will show you now."

The three started walking through a path surrounded by trees and shrubs as tall as James.

"How do you think Mrs. Cardenas feels about all her old pickers starting their own businesses?" Molly asked.

"I think she's fine with it," Diego said. "She's getting older. She believes in the peyote so much she wants to still have peyoteros around for the Indians to buy from after she's gone."

They walked through the dry shrubland, the sun almost below the horizon now. James picked his feet up high to avoid some of the tangles, and Molly gingerly held thorny branches out of her way.

Diego pointed to a short, fat, prickly cactus to their right. "Don't step on that. Even with shoes on, it hurts almost as much as getting bit by a rattler."

James and Molly avoided it.

"You see up ahead? The hill?" Diego asked.

James would hardly have called it a hill. More like a slight incline. He nodded.

"And you see how there are many more rocks up there?"

"Sure do."

"That's where the peyote likes to grow."

"No pickers out here, though," James remarked.

"There might be a few to the east of us still. But many pickers are done for the day. Like I said, they make a day's worth of wages in half a day."

Diego picked up his pace a little, his strides becoming longer. He had spotted something. When he finally stopped, he turned to them and spread his arms out low as if he were a painting of Jesus or the Virgin Mary.

"Here," he said. At his feet were small, round button cacti. Peyote. Some had pink or white flowers growing from the top. Others didn't. Diego pointed to their left.

"Do you see how the ground there is slightly greener than the dusty path we walked on?"

"Sure. What's that mean?" James asked.

"Peyote was there. It's been picked recently."

James walked over and squatted down. It was hard to tell anything had been there at all.

"When you say picked . . . how do you do it?"

"With a machete," Diego said. "You cut. As parallel to the earth as you can. Better chance of growing back that way. It takes . . . hmmm . . . six to eight years for a peyote plant to grow all the way. You don't want to pick ones younger than that. They aren't ready. The mescaline won't be at the level you want."

"How can you tell how old it is?" Molly asked.

"Size," Diego said. "Nothing smaller than a quarter."

James stood. "This is helpful. Very helpful. I appreciate you taking the time to bring us out here."

Diego nodded. "I'm an open book. You can ask me anything. I want you to know that what I do here is not dirty."

"All right, then," James said. "Robin Kinsel. That's the name of the woman who died. Did you know her?"

Diego's eyebrows went up. "Mrs. Kinsel? She's the one who died?"

James was certain Diego had already known that. There was no way Byron hadn't told him. Still, the man was a decent actor.

"She is. How did you two know one another?"

Diego breathed out a long, slow breath. "Robin came to me a few months ago to buy peyote. She told me she wanted to be business associates. That she would be back every few months to buy more. Or set up a system through the mail." He shook his head. "It's sad she's gone. She was a nice woman."

"A few months ago, when she bought the peyote, was that the first time you two met?"

"Sure," Diego said. "She was a little nervous. She told me she wanted our relationship to be discreet. I assumed it was because of the Codys, but I didn't ask. I just knew she'd come with them."

"And how did you leave things?" James asked.

"With a handshake." Diego shrugged. "I gave her my phone number. Told her to call or come by anytime. Said I was looking forward to working with her."

James eyed the man. Diego shifted his weight from one

leg to the other. Hung his thumb through a belt loop. But he didn't take his eyes off James.

"Well, thank you again for showin' us around. If we need anything else, can we come by? I expect we'll be around for at least a few more days."

"Please. Mi casa es tu casa." Diego slapped James on the back. "You can stay for dinner if you'd like. My wife's cooking is out of this world."

The three headed back to the truck, and James saw in the distance—to the east in fact, just where Diego had said—some stooped figures. The tops of wide-brimmed hats.

"I wish I could, amigo," James said. "But Molly and I have work to do."

[43]

MOLLY

It took James and Molly all of twenty minutes driving around to find out there was only one restaurant in town. So they went to Lala's Café, and Molly ate the best enchiladas she had ever had in her life. The place was small with mismatched tables and chairs and all kinds of Texas-themed collectibles hanging on the walls. She and James sat in a corner next to a refrigerator.

She couldn't help but look up every time the door opened, like maybe Joey would come walking in. She assumed he was staying with Byron at Mrs. Cardenas's house in one of the tents or maybe in the teepee. She imagined him sitting at Mrs. Cardenas's kitchen table eating a home-cooked meal. Her dad was right. She *was* distracted. She swallowed and then shook her head, trying to clear it.

While he ate, James stared at the map he had spread across the table. "What did you think of Diego?" he asked Molly in between bites.

"He seems legit. It was nice of him to bring us around and show us all of that. But . . ." She paused. "It almost seemed like he was trying too hard? Like he was showing us what he wanted us to see so we wouldn't ask about what he *didn't* want us to see? Plus, he didn't seem to care much about Robin's death. I know he only met her that once, but still."

James nodded. "I'm not sure I trust him, either. And I'm not sure he dislikes the Codys as much as he claims." He flipped the map around so Molly could see it.

"This road right here." He pointed to it. "Backs up to the edge of the area we were at today. We're doin' a stakeout tonight right there. The exciting stuff is gonna happen at night if it's happenin' at all."

"Why not at his house?" Molly asked.

"You see those little chihuahuas in the corner of his kitchen?"

Molly's eyebrows furrowed. "No."

"Probably because they were sleepin' in bird cages."

Molly giggled. "Really?"

"Yup. They're there to wake him up—and the rest of the family—if bad news comes knockin'. If Diego has shady business in the middle of the night, he isn't conducting it at his house."

"What will we be watching for?" Molly asked.

"Anything."

"Are we gonna spy on Mrs. Cardenas, too?"

James grinned. "Maybe. Haven't put together a strategy for her yet."

Molly sipped her iced tea and scooped the last of the beans and lettuce and guacamole into her mouth.

James pushed his plate away and folded up the map.

"You ready for a long night?" he asked. Molly was not

ready for a long night. She was tired but knew there was no getting out of it. She gave him a little salute as she swallowed her food, and by the time they left the café, the night sky was already pitch-black.

—

Molly yawned and stretched and cracked one eye open. Shit. She had fallen asleep. She had tried so hard not to, and James had nudged her multiple times during the night to keep her up. But now, in the early twilight, she could finally see the road ahead of them again. They had parked partially hidden by a tree. James held his binoculars in his lap and was pretty still, but Molly could see he was awake.

"Dad, you let me fall asleep," she groaned. Her mouth was dry and sticky. She opened her eyes real wide for a moment and then rubbed at the corners of them.

"I would've woken you up if somethin' happened," James said.

"So nothing happened?"

"Saw a javelina."

"But no humans?" Molly asked.

"No humans."

Molly rummaged around at her feet for a bottle of water and chugged a bunch of it. "So what's . . ." Molly started to say, but was interrupted by a tap on James's window. She leaned forward to see the face of an older woman. James rolled his window down.

"You're the investigator," she said. Her voice was smooth and surprisingly deep.

"Mrs. Cardenas," James said. Molly turned around to

look behind them. Had the old woman been driving? There were no cars in the area. Could she have walked from her house? Molly didn't think they were that close. How had Mrs. Cardenas even known they were here?

"My home and my land are sacred," the old lady said. "I refuse to welcome any sort of trouble from you or from anyone else."

"I understand . . ." James started to say, but Mrs. Cardenas raised a hand and cut him off.

"Please, listen. I will only say what I am about to say one time."

"Yes, ma'am," James said.

"My heart aches for the poor, young mother who passed. So it is for this reason I am telling you. When Mrs. Kinsel was visiting, I saw her speaking with an Oriental man who is not from here. They went somewhere together. Alone. His name is Zhang. I have seen him speaking to other Indians, too —even to Byron once or twice—but he has not ever spoken to me. I do not trust him."

Molly wanted to suggest that maybe the Codys had warned him against it or threatened him, as they were known to do, but she was a little afraid to say anything to this woman. She certainly didn't want to interrupt her. Her dad seemed to feel the same, because he only nodded.

"Trust that this is all the information I have for you. I will not abide you stomping all over my land and picking through my peyote like Mr. Reyes did yesterday. It is disrespectful."

"Yes, ma'am," James said again. "I appreciate this information. I truly do."

Mrs. Cardenas nodded once. "I hope you will leave town soon, and I hope you will learn what happened to the girl so she can rest peacefully." The old woman made the sign of the cross.

"I hope so too, ma'am," James said.

Mrs. Cardenas swiveled her bag around her body and opened it. She reached in and pulled out a large paper bag. "Empanadas," she said. "We never spoke of this."

James took the paper bag. "Thank you."

She was turning to leave when she stopped herself. She pointed a finger at them.

"Joey is a nice young man. You should both be kind to him."

"Yes, ma'am," James said once more. Then, Mrs. Cardenas turned, ducked under the tree that was hiding their car, and disappeared around the corner.

James opened the brown bag, peeked in, and took a sniff. "Mmmm," he said. "Well, isn't this a nice gift?"

[44]

CECIL

CECIL WAS IRONING a shirt when Dawn knocked. He placed the iron nose up at the end of the board and walked to the door. When he opened it and let her in, he noticed she was nervous. She was good at hiding it, but Cecil could tell.

"Please, sit," he said to her, and she perched on the edge of an upholstered chair at the threshold of the living room. Cecil sat on a couch across from her. Here, he could see out the big front window comfortably. Could see her dark-blue car with bird shit on the trunk.

"How can I help you?" he asked.

"I've been thinking." She clasped her hands together and then separated them again. "I really, really want to find out whether there is something actually wrong with the peyote. The women are getting a little freaked out. If the peyote is fine, I want the women to know that."

"I would like to know myself what's happening to the peyote," Cecil said.

"It's a little late for a tox screen. I know these women's families didn't want one done at the time, but I think I could still get tissue samples. They've probably been embalmed, so that presents a challenge, but drugs are still detectable in the tissue . . ."

A laugh escaped Cecil's lips. He'd had some guesses as to why the woman was here, but this had not been one of them. She truly had taken him by surprise.

Dawn had trailed off, stopped speaking entirely when he laughed at her.

"You are suggesting we illegally dig up these women's bodies to take a tissue sample on the off chance that any drugs in their bodies may still be detectable?"

Dawn flushed. "I was hoping that you might talk to the families. Convince them to let someone do it—us, if they don't trust the police."

Cecil studied the woman. "What makes you believe the families would listen to me?"

She swallowed. Chose her words carefully. "Because you are respected. They will take you seriously."

Cecil raised an eyebrow. "Unfortunately, our results would mean nothing. We are not trained professionals. My personal beliefs also prevent me from disturbing those women. They are at rest now."

"But don't you want women to feel comfortable taking the peyote?" Dawn asked.

"It is out of our hands."

She looked frustrated. Annoyed. "What else can I do?"

"Come to the community center tonight. I'll be making a statement. Byron has assured me of the quality and purity of the peyote he will be bringing home."

"Will it be enough for the community?"

"It will have to be," Cecil said.

Dawn was not satisfied, but that was neither Cecil's problem nor responsibility.

"Will I see you at this evening's meeting?" he asked.

"Sure." She stood. "Thank you for your time, Mr. Cody."

"You are welcome in my home any time."

She gave Cecil a tight smile. "Thank you."

―――――――――

Cecil sat behind the podium on the community center auditorium's raised stage, watching people shuffle in. He knew some of them were concerned. Worried sick, even. It might be keeping them up at night, this disturbance to their spiritual well-being. Others, he knew, were only there for the spectacle. To report back to their family and friends because they already thought of themselves as the one who knew things. He was familiar with their type and could picture the way their eyes would gleam as they pushed their way into the center of every conversation. These were the people he often relied upon.

When the seats were full and the noise at a steady hum, Cecil stood. He walked slowly to the podium, giving people time to take note. He would not shout over them, and he would not need to. The quiet spread in ripples, and when he could finally hear nothing but coughs and bodies shifting in seats, Cecil spoke.

"Thank you all for being here this evening. I want to start by apologizing." Cecil looked into the eyes of some of the audience members. "There is no excuse for the panic and worry you have all had to endure over the past few weeks. As one of your councilmen, it is my responsibility to prevent any harm to my people."

Cecil could see Barbara and Wayne Tully leaning against the back wall next to the double doors. Wayne was in uniform.

"I am sorry that I was not more vigilant. What my son Byron has discovered on his trip to Mirando City is that it is possible that any peyote purchased from a man named Diego Reyes could be contaminated."

He paused to let people whisper and mutter. He spotted Dawn chewing on her thumbnail at the end of one row.

"We do not and cannot know this for certain, but Byron has his suspicions. So what does this mean for you all?"

The room fell quiet again.

"When we were last in Mirando City in May, our beloved Mrs. Cardenas was sick. She was not able to sell any peyote then, though we held healing ceremonies on her land where we prayed for her health. At that time, we purchased peyote from Mr. Reyes, who, we were assured by the other Indians, was a professional. This was the first time we purchased from Mr. Reyes, and I promise it will be the last."

Cecil saw Russel Kinsel in the middle of the back row, shaking his head, arms crossed. There would be damage to attend to there, Cecil noted.

"If you purchased peyote from us in May, please dispose of what you have, or if you would prefer, you are welcome to bring it to me. Byron will return in two days with new peyote purchased from Mrs. Cardenas, who I am happy to report has made a full recovery from her illness."

People still gave one another worried looks.

"If you intend to make the trip to Mirando City yourself,

or if you intend to join us in February, please purchase only from Mrs. Cardenas. I assure you, she is to be trusted. If there is anything else you would like to ask me, or if there is any way I can further put your mind at ease, please see me after. I will stick around in the front lobby. Thank you all and have a good evening."

Cecil turned and left behind the curtain.

WAYNE

RUSSEL GOT HOME from work at about 18:10 every day. Wayne watched from his pickup as Russel took a right off the main road toward his trailer. Russel's trailer was at the very end of that road, and Wayne waited right where he was for a minute before following. He parked in the dirt about thirty yards from the trailer, partially hidden by someone's shed but with a good enough view.

Wayne watched Russel go inside and knew it would be a little while before he came back out again. Russel would probably eat some food, kiss his son, give his mother-in-law some money since it was Friday—payday—change his clothes, and then do something. Wayne was there to find out what that something would be.

He had brought the latest issue of the *Navajo Times* and propped it against his steering wheel, stuck his hand into the bag of beef jerky sitting in the passenger's seat, and ate a piece.

Just as Wayne had guessed, when Russel reemerged

about an hour later, he had changed out of his work clothes and brushed his hair and pulled it into a low ponytail.

Wayne followed him at a considerable distance as he drove farther away from Sanostee and toward Gallup. Eventually, Russel pulled into a ranch with a corral and probably a dozen or so cars and trucks. Wayne kept driving. He'd have to circle back, park off the main road, use his binoculars. This was a private gathering. Bull riding practice.

Once Wayne was settled and in place, he watched the men shoot the shit for a while. Smoke cigarettes. Cough. Nudge one another. Finally, they got serious. Got the bull ready. One of the men—not Russel—hopped on, and they released the gate. The man lasted longer than Wayne had expected. Maybe they practiced on the easier bulls. A few more men—still none of them Russel—rode the easy bull before they switched him out for a bull that even Wayne, in his bull riding ignorance, could see was angrier, difficult to handle. Russel did ride this one and lasted the longest. Wayne watched a few more rounds of this until the sun started to set and the men began to put the animals away.

Some of the men said goodbye, then jumped into their cars or trucks and sped off. But Russel and some others stayed for a little longer. Smoked cigarettes until it was probably difficult to see much more than the lit end sticking out in front of them.

Finally, Wayne followed Russel's pickup again. Down the highway, back toward Sanostee. But Russel didn't turn off where he should have to go home. Wayne noticed the other bull riders' cars and trucks hadn't turned off, either. They were all headed to Shiprock.

Everything was closing at this hour. All the calls Wayne

got after dark were to houses or parking lots or places along the banks of the river where teenagers and sometimes adults were known to escape to.

Sure enough, after a stop at the gas station for what looked like snacks and sodas, the fleet of cars and trucks pulled into an empty parking lot. Wayne drove past again. Circled back to the gas station, which was close enough, and parked in the corner, as far away from the lights as he could so he could get a good look without the glare.

He knew what he would see next. Alcohol or drugs. Both illegal on the reservation, though he knew most Diné had one or the other locked away at home. Including Wayne. Who didn't need a drink in their own living room sometimes? But on summer nights, when the young people felt bold, a parking lot was as good a place as any. Wayne wasn't here to arrest anyone, though. Some reservation cops did this frequently. Waited for an easy possession arrest. But Wayne only wanted confirmation tonight. That it was, in fact, drugs, and they were, in fact, coming from Russel.

He picked up his binoculars and watched the five young men hand Russel money. Not for the snacks, Wayne was sure of that. He had watched them all pay for their own snacks, though he imagined that's what they would claim if he were to question them right then. A few of them glanced around before Russel tapped some pills from a bottle into their outstretched palms. Made sense for these athletes. Aches and pains from getting thrown from the back of a bull and crashing into the ground, time and time again.

So, Russel had gotten more pills. Had they come from the hospital or from the Codys? It seemed unlikely the hospital would write another prescription so soon after Wayne had confiscated nearly a full bottle. It wasn't as if Wayne would ever get confirmation that Russel got his pills from the Codys. But he could and would confirm whether Russel had gotten a prescription filled legitimately. A phone call to the pharmacy would be easy enough. Wayne started up his truck and pulled out of the gas station parking lot.

There was something else Wayne knew after Cecil's little meeting the other night. If Cecil was blaming the contaminated peyote on the peyotero down in Texas, that meant he wasn't taking the opportunity to blame Dawn. Not that that was something Cecil would do publicly. But by making this statement, it seemed the Codys were protecting Dawn for whatever reason.

Wayne ate another piece of beef jerky and made his way home.

JAMES

"Ranger Demick! Glad I caught ya." James sat in the plastic chair sandwiched between the hotel bed and the window that looked out onto the hallway and ice machine. He held the phone in one hand and a pen in the other. Molly sat on the bed, legs crisscrossed, staring at James.

"Mr. Pinter," Ralph said on the other end of the line. "How's the investigation going?"

"I learned something interesting yesterday. Do you have a minute?"

"Sure. Let's hear it."

"I was told that there's an Asian man by the name of Zhang who was seen speaking to Robin, the woman whose peyote was most definitely contaminated. Apparently, he's been around, talkin' to some of the Indians who are buying peyote. He and Robin went off together one day, it seems."

"Zhang," Ralph repeated.

"That ring any bells?" James asked.

"It's a common name. Chinese," Ralph said.

"Don't know his first name, unfortunately," James said.

"China. Huh," Ralph said.

"What are you thinkin'?"

"So, I've got some friends in California that I keep in touch with. Army friends. Law enforcement now, too. They told me about this new drug. A narcotic. They've only come across it a handful of times, but it's been connected to two deaths. They call it China White and say it's about fifty times deadlier than heroin."

"Holy hell," James said.

"Yeah. It's serious. They told me to keep an eye out, but we haven't seen any in Texas. Not yet."

James put his pen down. Then picked it back up and wrote down what Ralph had said.

"If you have a minute," James said, "would you mind seeing if y'all have any Zhangs with a record?"

"Sure thing. I'll have a guy look into it. Might not be able to get it to you until tomorrow, though."

"No problem," James said. "Thanks, Ranger."

"My pleasure. Let me know if you need anything else."

"You got it."

Molly leaned forward as he hung up. "Well?" she asked, and he told her.

"So we really need to find this Zhang," Molly said.

"If he's been around town, other people will have seen him, too. Probably talked to him."

"So we ask around," Molly said.

"We'll start with Diego," James said. "After what Wayne told me this morning, I have a feeling he'll be eager to help."

Deigo's chihuahuas were awake this time and barking and circling Molly like she had Milk-Bones in her pockets.

"Aquí! Ven aquí!" Diego called. The dogs reluctantly left Molly's side but did not take their eyes off her.

"Friends!" Diego greeted them. "Come in, come in. We are about to have some food. Please, sit."

There were two tables full of food and people—one inside and a smaller one on the patio. Diego led them out through the sliding glass doors, and they sat at the round patio table with him and a young woman who kept putting her hand on his forearm. Diego didn't introduce her.

"How is your work coming along?" he asked.

An older woman came out and set drinks down in front of James and Molly.

"Gracias," James said. "No alcohol in hers, right?"

"No," Diego answered him. "No alcohol."

"I have a question for you," James said. "But first, there's something you need to know."

"You look worried." Diego popped a chip into his mouth.

"The Codys. They're blamin' you for this suspicious peyote. Told the whole reservation it came from you and it might be contaminated."

Diego leaned back. Nodded a few times, slowly. Then he scoffed to himself.

"Did you sell them any back in May?" James asked.

"I haven't sold to any of the Codys in years. I sold to them one time. About four years ago when I was just starting out. I didn't like their attitudes. Like I should be afraid of them or something. I didn't even know them. I've been dealing with criminals my whole life. They're nothing to me."

"What criminals?" James asked.

"This close to the border, smugglers of all kinds. Used to be weapons. Drugs now. Drugs all the time. I've been approached on many occasions. And I've worked too damn hard to stay away from it to be accused now by Cody scum."

"I didn't realize the cartels gave people much of a choice," James said.

Diego smiled. "We are on the right side of the border for resisting, yes?"

"I suppose that's true," James said.

Diego took a sip of his beer. "I thank you for this information. Now what do you need from me?"

"Chinese man. Zhang. You happen to know of him?"

"Of course," Diego said. He sucked on a lime for a moment. "He comes around sometimes. Always asking the Indians questions."

"Questions about what?" James asked.

"All kinds of things. Strange things. Personal."

"Huh. Why?"

"He says for research." Diego shrugged. "I try to mind my own business, but I can think of a few of the Indians he's talked to lately. I have their phone numbers. You can call them."

"Thanks, Diego. I appreciate that. He talked to Robin, too, you know."

"I didn't know." Diego leaned forward. Stared at James very seriously. "Listen, if these Cody fuckers are doing something shady and blaming it on me, I need you to find out. I need you to tell me."

"I will," James said. "I will."

Diego stood abruptly. "Come. To my office."

James glanced at Molly, who was slightly distracted by

the dogs still panting at her feet. "You comin'?" She nodded and the two of them stood and followed Diego inside to a very large, very white, very clean office.

"These calls are gonna be quite the long-distance bill. You sure you want me to call them from your phone?" James asked.

Diego flipped through the Rolodex and handed James three cards. "I'm sure. I remember Zhang talking to all these men."

Diego picked up the phone and dialed for James. A man picked up on the first ring and James had to look at the card in front of him for a name.

"Hello, Mr. uh, Reed. I'm James Pinter here with Mr. Diego Reyes down in Mirando City. How are you?"

"I'm fine. Is Mr. Reyes okay?"

"Oh, yes. Mr. Reyes is great. He gave me your number because he tells me you spoke with Mr. Zhang last time you were down here. Is that correct?"

"Yes. What's this about?"

James looked at Diego, who had made himself comfortable in a chair in the corner, his arm draped over the back. Molly sat closer to James, on a lime-green love seat.

"I'm a private investigator, and Mr. Zhang's work is of interest to my case. Mr. Reyes tells me that Mr. Zhang asks a lot of questions. Some strange questions, even. And that it's for research. Do you have any idea what sort of research Mr. Zhang is doin'? Did he ever tell you?"

"I know it's for the university," Mr. Reed said. "He does research for the university. They have a lab there, he said."

"Do you know which university, Mr. Reed?"

"A medical university. In San Antonio."

"Texas Medical College?" James asked.

"That sounds right."

"Do you happen to know Mr. Zhang's first name?"

"William. William Zhang."

"What sort of questions did William Zhang ask you?"

"He spoke to me and my wife. Asked us if we'd ever been in a car accident or a victim of a violent crime. He asked my wife if she'd ever had a miscarriage."

"That seems pretty damn personal," James said.

"It was, but he paid us."

"How much?" James asked.

"Ten dollars each."

"He ask anything else?"

"He asked us how frequently we took peyote. He also wanted us to rate how happy or sad or worried we felt on days we took the peyote versus the days we didn't. He asked us if we had any mental or emotional struggles." Mr. Reed paused. "That's all I can really remember right now."

"That's good. Real good. Real helpful," James said. "Anything else you want to tell me about him? Anything else you think I should know?"

"Not really. He seemed like a nice guy, actually. Friendly. Smiled a lot."

"All right, then, Mr. Reed. Well, thank you for your time. I appreciate it."

"All right. Goodbye."

James hung up the phone. "Looks like we're off to San Antonio," he said to Molly.

"You got what you needed?" Diego asked.

"We'll see," James said. "We'll check out Mr. Zhang and see what business he had with Robin and with the Codys. I don't think any of them were participatin' in his ten-dollar study."

"Perfect." Diego slapped his knees and stood up. "You'll stay for lunch and then you'll go to San Antonio."

"Please and thank you," Molly said. "I am starving."

Diego held open the office door for them. The dogs ran at Molly's feet, tails wagging, and Diego laughed.

"My dogs," he said. "I trust them. They only like good people."

[47]

MOLLY

THE WHOLE TIME James spoke to the administrative assistant at the university, Molly was watching the woman's eyebrows. She couldn't look away. They had clearly been overplucked—maybe for the woman's whole life—and now they were growing back in lone patches here and there and it looked awful.

Molly felt like she sometimes got sidetracked by small, insignificant things—like this woman's eyebrows—but James had told her it was a good thing. Or it could be, at least. Those little things, James had said, could sometimes tell you a whole lot about someone. Or lead you down a path of questioning you would never have thought to consider otherwise. But Molly wasn't sure that this woman's ugly eyebrows could tell her anything useful.

Luckily, James had been paying close attention to the woman's directions and was able to lead them through the campus maze to the correct building number, floor, and office.

Dr. William Zhang, PhD, neuropharmacologist, was not

in his office, but they did find him down the hall in his laboratory. He was just hanging up his lab coat, ready to leave for the day—Molly could see him through the door's window—when James knocked.

William Zhang turned around, visibly surprised. He was thin, about average height, and had a thick, healthy tuft of black hair sticking out in all directions. He was younger than Molly had expected. He walked over to the door and swung it open.

"Can I help you?"

"Hello, Dr. Zhang. My name is James Pinter. I was hoping to grab just a few minutes of your time."

William Zhang looked at his watch. "All right. I was on my way out. I'm just going to get my things. We can walk together."

William walked back into the laboratory but left the door open. He picked up a lunchbox and a briefcase from the corner before joining them in the hall and locking the door behind him.

"I'm sorry, Mr. Pinter," William said. "Where did you say you were from?"

"I'm a private investigator and consultant to the tribal police up on the Navajo reservation," James said.

William's lips had been slightly parted and his eyebrows furrowed, but he closed his mouth now.

"Is this about my peyote research?" William asked.

"Yes," James said. "Can you tell me a little about it?"

William sighed. "I'm not supposed to talk much about it. At least not to the press." He glanced sidelong at Molly. "You're not the press, are you?"

"No," Molly said. "James is my dad. I'm his assistant."

William acknowledged that with a single nod. "Even our funders don't know much about the peyote aspect of my research. Not yet."

"Who are your funders?" James asked.

"Brown and Bull."

"The pharmaceutical company?" James asked.

"Yes."

"Well, we aren't the press, but it would sure help our investigation if you could tell us a little about it."

"What are you investigating?"

"An incident that occurred on the reservation," James said, clearly offering up as little information as possible.

"Does it have to do with peyote?" William looked intrigued, curious. Not at all worried.

"It might," James said. "I heard you make visits down to Mirando City sometimes. Ask the Indians who are there purchasing peyote some interesting questions."

William nodded. He squinted up at the sky. "Let's find a place to sit down. Do you drink coffee in the afternoon?"

"I drink coffee at all times."

William brought them to a pizza place. One he promised had incredibly good coffee. The best on campus. They all ordered coffee and a slice or two, even though it wasn't quite dinnertime yet.

They slid into a booth—James and Molly on one side, William on the other—and sipped their coffees and waited on their pizza. The coffee *was* pretty good but Molly had had better.

"I appreciate you helpin' us out with this," James started. "Your association with the peyote has raised a lot of eyebrows, but I'm sure there's a reasonable explanation."

William took a deep breath. "I guess I'll start with what originally funded my research in the first place. B&B had a specific goal. You see, just this year, the American Psychiatric Association introduced a new anxiety disorder. They call it Post-Traumatic Stress Disorder, or PTSD, but you've probably heard of it referred to as 'shellshock' or 'combat fatigue.'"

"Sure," James said. Molly waited for him to acknowledge that he'd served in the Army and worked with some pretty messed-up soldiers. But he didn't.

William went on. "It isn't exclusive to soldiers, though. Anyone who survives a traumatic event can suffer from it."

"Like a car accident or a violent crime?" James asked.

"That's right." William was clearly pleased that James was following, but Molly remembered her dad had gotten that from Mr. Reed, the Cherokee man he'd spoken to on the phone.

"But in this case, soldiers are our main focus, because the Army is a big client for B&B. And this PTSD is a significant problem after Vietnam. I know it's been five years since the war ended, but that kind of stress—killing, watching men be killed in gruesome ways—it sticks with people for a long time."

"No kidding," James said. Molly couldn't tell if he was extremely focused and interested or if he was zoning out—something she had rarely seen him do. His expression was strange. She hoped *he* didn't have a PTSD episode right in the middle of the pizza place.

"So, I spent some time interviewing former soldiers who

have officially been diagnosed with PTSD," William went on. "And I noticed a pattern when they would answer about what—if anything—helped ease their symptoms. A lot of them reported that hallucinogens helped. Whether it was magic mushrooms or ketamine. Which is interesting, because mushrooms and ketamine do different things inside a person's brain, and yet they both seem to have the same effect on persons suffering from post-traumatic stress."

"And so you want to see if the mescaline in peyote produces the same results," James said.

"Yes! Exactly."

"So what's your theory?" James asked.

"Order up!" the woman behind the counter yelled. The three stood to get their pizzas, but when they sat back down, Molly didn't start eating hers right away. Instead, she got out her notebook. This was already confusing, and based on her dad's strange expression, she couldn't tell how much of it he was retaining.

"I have a few theories," William said after his first bite. "Complex theories. I'll try to boil them down to this: I think it has to do with either dopamine production or dopamine receptors. Which would be good news. A different way to treat a dysfunctional brain from the way B&B's competitor is doing it."

"Who is B&B's competitor?" James asked.

Molly wrote down, *dopamine*.

"Abe Carey. Another big pharmaceutical company. Larger than B&B. More money, too."

"And how are they treating a dysfunctional brain?" Molly asked. William smiled at her.

"Serotonin. They're about to come out with a drug that

prevents the reabsorption of serotonin so that serotonin levels in the brain stay high. They'll use it to treat depression. I have no idea if it will work for PTSD patients, but it's a concern for B&B."

Molly wrote, *Abe Carey = serotonin.*

"So you want to use mescaline to treat PTSD in soldiers?" James asked.

"Well, no. First of all, I can't. Only Indians are allowed to take peyote. It would be a legal headache for B&B. But their answers to my questions will help with my research. Frankly, I don't think B&B cares or even wants to know about the effectiveness of mushrooms or peyote. Ketamine, though . . ." William held up an index finger. "Ketamine they are very interested in."

Molly wrote, *ketamine.*

"Because they're already producing it?" James asked.

"Exactly. During the war, doctors used it as a general anesthetic for surgery. It's still commonly used in certain types of surgeries. But B&B is worried about getting forced out of that market, too. Abe Carey is currently trying to get a different anesthetic approved by the FDA. It has hit some snags, but they're still working on it. I believe they'll eventually get it approved. It's similar to morphine but about one hundred times stronger. Because of that, some doctors are concerned about its potential for abuse. So right now, they're mixing it with a different drug that causes a 'bad high.' But they're trying to get it approved on its own. It's called fentanyl."

"You said it's one hundred times stronger than morphine. Would that make it about fifty times stronger than heroin?"

William shrugged. "Sounds about right."

"You ever heard the term 'China White'?" James asked.

"No."

"You sure? That's not what the Codys ask for when they sell you peyote?"

William's face flushed. He cleared his throat.

"I'm not supposed to purchase peyote. But it's vital for my research. It's not for me. It's not like I'm taking it myself."

Molly froze. She thought about writing *buying peyote*, but she couldn't look away from her dad and William.

"The Codys have plenty of cash," James said. "What they could really use is a new drug that hardly anyone has seen yet or used before. You have access to that."

"Actually, I don't," William said. He lifted his chin a little. Cleared his throat. "B&B's competitor, Abe Carey, works with the fentanyl. I've never worked with it, never even seen it. My lab has nothing to do with that."

"Where is Abe Carey's lab?" James asked.

"I have no idea. I assume they fund a university lab like B&B does. But I don't know where that might be."

Molly looked down at her notes again. She wrote, *Abe Carey = Fentanyl = China White ??*

"Hm," James grunted. They had barely touched their pizza. Molly looked at hers. It was cold now. She could tell without even touching it.

"Robin Kinsel," James went on. "You two were seen together last time she was down here. Was she participating in your research?"

Zhang swallowed a few times. Furrowed his eyebrows. "Robin Kinsel . . . I don't know if I remember who that is."

"You two went off alone. Somewhere."

"Oh!" Zhang coughed like he'd almost choked on his

pizza. It took him a moment to recover. "Robin, yes. She wanted to know about my study. She had heard about me, I guess, from other Indians on her reservation. That I was researching peyote. She had a proposal for me, actually." His face turned a little red. "I felt bad that I couldn't help her more. She didn't understand that this isn't a personal project of mine. That I couldn't just give away my time and my expertise in exchange for nothing."

"What did she want your time and expertise for?" James asked.

"She wanted to do a scientific study on the effectiveness of using peyote to treat addiction. I told her that her theory was intriguing, but I just didn't have the time or the space or the resources to help her. She was disappointed, but I gave her the phone numbers for a few of my colleagues who might've been able to connect her with someone who could find funding for a project like that. I didn't think she would get very far, but I told her it couldn't hurt to try."

"Did she contact them?" James asked.

"I have no idea."

"And that's all Robin wanted from you?"

Zhang shrugged. "I guess."

"Well, I do appreciate your time, Mr. Zhang. And thank you for explaining your research," James said.

"Are you going to report me for buying peyote?" William looked curious again, as if the threat were abstract, part of his research.

"No. I'm not gonna report you for that. I respect what you're tryin' to do. Those soldiers need help. They need to be able to put that war behind them. I wish you all the best."

James stood, reached over the table, and shook William's hand.

"Good luck with your investigation," William said.

James and Molly gathered their trash, threw it away, and left.

"Talkative guy for someone who's supposed to say quiet about his work," Molly said as soon as they were back in the car. "Do you believe him?"

"About which part? That he doesn't have access to fentanyl? Absolutely not," James said. "He was a little too confident in his answer there. A little too smug."

"And what about Robin?" Molly asked.

"Sounds reasonable enough. And in line with what we know," James said.

"Do you think Clarence knew?" Molly asked. "He doesn't like outsiders, right? So, maybe not?"

"Very good," he said. "That could be their rift right there. He found out Robin was goin' behind his back to work with outsiders on *his* project? *His* brainchild?" James shook his head. "I can't imagine he would've been too keen on that. Not too keen at all."

48

PAULA

G RANDMA B EANS BROUGHT sage to Robin's memorial. She'd told Paula that she believed Robin had already moved on to the next world, that her spirit was long gone and no longer posed a threat. Still, she believed it was best not to speak Robin's name, but at this ceremony held by the Native American Church, they would probably do just that. The sage would protect Grandma Beans and Paula. Paula was just glad to have company.

They stood a ways apart from the majority of the people gathered, but close enough so Paula could still note who'd showed up to this thing. Clarence and Patricia were both at the very front beside the teepee. There were clusters of young women—some of whom Paula recognized from the WARN meeting—and some elders that Paula assumed were family members. Of course, Cecil Cody was there, too. Paula had never talked to any of the Codys. They scared her, and Paula wasn't often scared. She guessed it had to do with the way they were revered on the reservation. Their lore. It was stupid, but she didn't feel authentic enough for the Codys. Not that they were good people. Molly, James, and Wayne had told her enough to know that.

Patricia started by saying a few words about Robin and her life and her contribution to the Navajo people as Grandma Beans gripped the other end of the burning sage in her hands. Paula liked the smell. After Patricia spoke, Clarence sang songs in both Diné and other languages Paula didn't know.

She tried to see who the elders with Cecil were, but she didn't recognize them from bingo. Just then, someone approached Paula's other side and put a hand on her shoulder. It was Wayne. He stood beside her like that until Clarence was finished and some of the people around them began leaving flowers and beads and pouches of corn pollen and tobacco next to a giant peyote cactus at the front before quietly drifting away.

"Some people aren't leaving," Paula observed.

"Those are Native American Church members," Wayne said, lowering his hand. "They'll hold their own meeting tonight for Robin. This part was for the rest of us."

Paula turned to him. He was dressed in plain clothes, his hair braided. "The woman's own husband never showed up," she said.

"It seems strange," Wayne agreed. "But there could be plenty of reasons why."

"Yeah, like he's a jerk who killed his wife so he can ride bulls all the time without being nagged about it."

Wayne raised an eyebrow. "The memorial got you emotional."

Paula huffed. "I guess. It's just, Robin seemed like a

pretty rad chick, you know? It makes no sense that she had to die."

"No, it doesn't."

Grandma Beans extinguished the sage and put her arm around Paula. She pulled her in close, and Paula rested her head on her grandmother's shoulder.

"It's all right to be angry or to grieve," Wayne said. "It took me a while to learn that. I thought as a cop I had to separate myself. Be professional and distant at all times. But some cases are harder than others. They can hit you in ways you don't expect. If this feels personal, let yourself be sad."

Paula gazed at Wayne. His strong and commanding presence comforted her, and for the first time, Paula really noticed the wisdom behind those eyes. She nodded. "Thanks."

"I'll need you in the coming weeks. Rest up." He squeezed her shoulder one more time and then headed for his truck.

Grandma Beans kissed Paula's forehead. "Let's get some ice cream."

49

KAY

VICTOR HAD AGREED TO A CEREMONY, but first he needed to determine why Kay was struggling so much to get pregnant. Medicine men were not typically diagnosticians. It was so rare it was almost unheard of. But Victor Black was both. He'd given Kay the choice of seeing a different diagnostician, but she was comfortable with Victor now. He asked her to keep track of her dreams, to write them down for a week or so and then to come see him.

When she sat down in his hogan with his ceremonial objects surrounding them, she felt at peace. Maybe he could give her answers. Maybe he could heal her.

Victor placed his hand on hers and told her a story she had heard many times before about how First Man and First Woman were given a child by the Holy People in an unusual way. Changing Woman was made from turquoise, not birthed. And Changing Woman gave the Navajos everything they had. She was the mother to them all.

"So," Victor said to her, "not everything powerful and worthy must come from the birthing process. Now, let us try to see what is happening to you. Before we address your dreams, please tell me any aches, pains, or anything strange you have noticed about your body lately."

Kay tried to think. "Every year it gets harder to sleep through the whole night. My back and my neck, they bother me."

Victor smiled. "Try more pillows. I sleep with five! This is good to know, but it could be a natural part of aging. What else can you think of?"

Kay smiled, too. She took her time now. Thought about things that could be relevant. "Ever since I lost my first baby, I cramp much worse during my monthly bleeding."

Victor nodded slowly. "And your blood? Is it heavier or lighter?"

"Heavier," Kay said. "At first I thought it was just because of everything I went through, but they never got lighter again."

"Hmmm," Victor said. "Now, tell me about your dreams."

Kay looked down at the notebook open on her lap and scanned through her notes, even though she had pretty much memorized them.

"I dreamed of fire," Kay said, staring at the page. "At first it was a good fire. A comforting fire. It was bringing me warmth. But as I walked closer, it got bigger and bigger. But I couldn't stop walking toward it. I kept walking even though I was afraid. It was as if something pushed me." Kay paused here. She knew enough to know the next part was bad. "And then, just before I was close enough to touch it, to be burned by it, a snake appeared at my feet and bit me."

She hesitated, and at first Victor said nothing, did nothing. Then, his hand on top of hers began to tremble. Only a little at first, but then it shook violently. Victor's good eye that had, just a moment ago, been soft, turned hard and dark. His jaw clenched. And then, his eyes closed. It felt to Kay like the air had been sucked out of the hogan. There was a painful silence before Victor spoke again. It was then that he told Kay she would never have children. Ever.

———

Kay lay on Barbara's couch, her eyes red and puffy, her nose raw. She had begged Victor to tell her something else, anything else. She would do anything, any ceremony, any type of healing he wanted.

He'd said she would need a ceremony still. That was necessary if she wanted to assure the well-being of her family and the protection of her own life. But it would not help her to have children.

"The snake," Victor had said. "He has done something to you. Something terrible. It cannot be undone."

She wanted to scream at him. To call him a fraud. But he was the best medicine man on the reservation. If he could not help her, she could not be helped, so instead she'd sobbed and pleaded. He told her to come back the next day for an Enemyway rite, and then she drove straight to Barbara's. Through her tears, she told Barbara all of it, and now, after having soaked Barbara's pillow, Kay listened to her making tea. Suddenly, she felt very tired. She closed her eyes. She missed James. She wished he were there. She wished she hadn't kept all this from him.

[50]
JAMES

BARBARA'S MESSAGE had sounded urgent, but when James called her back, she didn't answer. He would try again after going to Demick's office, he thought. But when he got there, Demick was out on some urgent call, and all James got out of the visit was confirmation from Demick's underling that there were no Zhangs with criminal records in Texas. If William Zhang was dipping his toes into a life of crime, it was new.

James's second phone call to Barbara went unanswered, too, so he decided to call Wayne.

"How is it going down there?" Wayne asked him.

"Gettin' some good stuff. How's it goin' up there?"

"Do you . . . uh . . . do you think you're in a place to come home? Could you leave what you've got with that Texas Ranger?"

"What's goin' on, Wayne? Is everyone okay?"

Wayne sighed. "Kay is okay. But she needs you."

"What happened?"

"I don't know the whole story myself. I'll let Barb and Kay tell you. But if you can come home, you should."

"I can come home." James looked around the hotel room, trying to figure out what it would mean for the investigation. He'd have Molly pack up. He'd visit Diego one last time. Leave their notes for Demick. "We'll leave in the morning before the sun is up. Be home by tomorrow night."

"All right. I'll tell Kay. We can catch up when you get back."

"Thanks, LT."

Molly was passed out in the passenger's seat by the time James pulled into their driveway. It was pitch-black outside, past midnight. He left her undisturbed and shut the car door quietly behind him. Before he could make it to the front door, Barbara stepped out onto the porch.

"Kay's asleep," she said. "She's had a long couple of days."

"What's goin' on, Barb?"

"There are some things I'm going to tell you and then Kay will tell you again. I'm telling you them now, so that you don't get angry with her later."

"Fine. What?" James's patience was waning. Barbara sat down on the porch step.

"Kay has been seeing a medicine man. She was hoping it would help her to get pregnant."

"All right," James said. "So, she's been . . . what? Taking herbs and tea and things?"

"That's right," Barbara said. "But she felt like she needed

to do more. She decided to have . . . the medicine man hold a ceremony."

She paused. Folded her hands together in her lap. "Sit down," she said. James sat next to her.

"She didn't tell me about any of this, either," Barbara went on. "But she did tell me the two of you were trying for a baby. And that she had lost her baby before." James looked at Molly through the window of the car. Her head rested against the window, her mouth slightly open.

"It's such a lonely thing," Barbara finally said. "Losing babies. Not being able to have more. I want you to remember that. To understand that. You had one without even trying, but that's not how it works for some of us."

"I know, Barb." James's voice was softer now. "So she saw a medicine man and he held a ceremony for her. Why would that bother me?"

"It wasn't any medicine man," Barbara said. "It was Victor Black. And the ceremony, it wasn't the one Kay had hoped for. It didn't go the way she had planned."

James's head snapped toward Barbara. His heart pounded in his chest. "Victor Black? Victor fucking Black? That's who she was seein'? Hell, Barb. What'd he do to her?"

"Like Wayne told you, Kay is fine, physically. But Victor told her she wouldn't ever be able to have kids. He said she was barren."

"How would he—" James started, but Barbara put up a hand to stop him.

"I know what you're going to say. But Kay believes that Victor knows with every ounce of her broken heart. Do not belittle her."

James huffed. "Damn it. You know Cecil is behind this."

"Why?" Barbara asked.

"I don't know and it pisses me off that I don't. To make Kay desperate? What's Kay got to do with any of this? She isn't in WARN. Why's he goin' after her?"

"A relationship between a medicine man and his patient is supposed to be discreet," Barbara said.

"And you trust that anyone with a relationship with Cecil Cody is discreet? Because I sure as hell don't."

"Well, I don't know. I don't know the man," Barbara said. "But if he *is* going after Kay, it's probably to rile you up. Just like he's doing right now."

James yanked his cigarettes out of his shirt pocket and lit one. He took a long, deep drag.

"I've just got to prove to her that he's wrong," James said. "We'll go to a *real* doctor tomorrow."

"I gave her the card to my fertility specialist in Albuquerque," Barbara said. "You can go there. He's not cheap, but he's good. But don't you *dare* call him a 'real' doctor. Not to Kay."

"All right, all right. I'm just angry, Barb."

"I knew you would be."

"You were right to tell me first," James admitted before putting the cigarette back up to his lips.

Barbara chuckled. "I know."

James exhaled and watched Molly stir. He'd better get her into the house. Her neck would get sore sleeping like that. He finished his cigarette and got their bags. Barbara slept on the couch that night and made them all breakfast in the morning. And James. James was gentle and loving with Kay. But he made sure she knew that they would be getting a second opinion.

MOLLY

JAMES THOUGHT he was keeping a secret from Molly. That she didn't know that he and Kay were trying to have a baby. But Molly had seen the pregnancy test box in the trash weeks ago and said something to Kay, who then confided in Molly. She told her to wait to say something to James until he was ready. Molly liked that. That Kay knew Molly could handle that sort of information. Sometimes, when James was out, the two of them would talk about baby names and what color they would paint the nursery. Sometimes Kay would stop abruptly. Say it was bad luck to get too ahead of herself. But Molly was excited now, too. A baby brother or sister. The idea made her smile.

So of course she was sad when Kay told her what had happened with Victor. James stumbled over an explanation, and Molly could see he was both a little embarrassed and a little irritated that this was how he was breaking the news to her. She almost told him that she already knew, but she didn't. The three of them were going to take a trip to Albuquerque together to see this new doctor. Somehow, James had been able to make an appointment for the very next day.

Before they left, though, Molly and James had to debrief with Wayne, and so they met at the station that afternoon.

James had already told Wayne about Diego and Byron and Mrs. Cardenas over the phone while they were still in Texas, and he now told Wayne about Zhang and what Robin had wanted from him.

"So this Zhang has access to a deadly new narcotic," Wayne said.

"He claims he does not, but I'm not sure I buy that," James said.

"And Robin did not tell Clarence that she was going to seek out this Zhang for research help," Wayne went on.

"That's right. Help from an outsider."

"If Clarence found out, I wonder how?" Wayne asked.

"The Codys?" Molly guessed.

James nodded. "I'm sure the Codys would be eager to rat her out. Especially if they knew that would weaken Robin and Clarence's addiction project."

"I'm looking into a possible Cody connection to Russel, too. I followed him the other night and found out he's already got more pain medication and it's not from the hospital's pharmacy. I gave them a call and they said they've got nothing filled for or picked up by Russel Kinsel over the last few weeks."

"And who else would he get the pills from," James said. It was not a question.

"Exactly. If Russel has a relationship with the Codys, the Codys could have had plenty of access to their home and plenty of information about when Robin and Russel would or would not be there." Wayne paused to open a filing cabinet. He pulled out some papers.

"I also got these from the hospital. Finally. The women's records. They seem slim, but what do I know about medical records? They were all somewhat healthy women, I suppose, which is why this is strange in the first place." He plopped them down in front of James, who leafed through them for a minute.

"I'd like to ask a medical professional to look through these," James said.

"You want me to call Raymond?"

"I'm thinkin' a fellow doctor. Not that I don't appreciate Raymond's help."

"A fellow doctor? You got someone in mind?" Wayne asked.

"I do," James said. He scooped the papers off the desk. "I'll give him a call when we get back."

"How long will you guys be gone?" Wayne asked.

"A couple of days. We've got a hotel room for a night. Molly and I have another appointment while we're there."

"Is that right?" Wayne asked.

"Remember my friend Charles with the FBI? I've sent him some labs to run in the past."

"Sure," Wayne said.

"Well, when Molly and I found out about Dawn's brother in federal prison, I gave Charles a call. Asked him to send me the case files, which he did and which I read. But he called me again while Molly and I were in Texas. I just got the message this morning. Seems like there was more to the case. The Albuquerque office let him know that they only sent about half of it. Some of it is considered sensitive, kept somewhere else. It was overlooked. But they found their error and wanted to let him know that we only received the half of it. He told me the rest is pretty damn interesting. He thinks I ought to take a look, so he let the Albuquerque office know we'd be stopping by."

"Interesting how?"

"I'm not exactly sure, but he said I'll know more about it than he does. Whatever that means. Piqued my interest enough to take him up on it, though."

Wayne nodded. "Well, good luck down there. With the FBI office and with the doctor."

"Thanks, LT," James said. Wayne passed Molly a handful of Starbursts. Pink and orange ones only. Her favorites.

[52]

WAYNE

PAULA SAT with her legs dangling off the San Juan River Bridge. She was tossing rocks through the railing into the very low and slow-moving river below when Wayne pulled up next to her.

"Aren't you supposed to be in school?" he shouted through the open window of his cruiser.

Paula spun around and grinned at Wayne. "It's summer still. And believe it or not, I did not fail one class last year and I don't have to do squat right now. They promoted me all the way to the eleventh grade."

"Hm. Sounds suspicious."

"Not suspicious at all! I'm an upstanding member of the Navajo Nation."

"That doesn't sound like something an upstanding member of the Navajo Nation would say. With your sidekick gone yet again, it's probably only a matter of time before you get into all sorts of trouble. Do us both a favor and get in." He leaned over the passenger's seat and swung open the door. Paula got to her feet and slid into the car.

"Is this an arrest? I feel like I have rights, but I don't know what they are." She closed the door behind her.

"If it were an arrest, you'd be in the back. Actually, I need your help again. With real, bona fide police work."

Paula raised her eyebrows and then gave him a silly salute. "Aye, aye, Captain!"

"Lieutenant, actually."

"Do they give you a sense of humor when you make captain?"

"I doubt it," Wayne said.

"Will I get paid this time?"

"Absolutely not," Wayne said.

"All right, all right. I'm in," Paula said. "You don't have to beg."

"We're going to follow Clarence Draper after he closes up his trading post for the day."

"Why? Is Clarence a prime suspect now?"

"Yes. I'll tell you all about it on the drive."

"What do you need my help for?" Paula asked.

"Well, Clarence knows me. We're going to follow him because I believe he has a support group tonight at the hospital. The ladies at the front desk couldn't seem to tell me who headed the addiction meeting in the basement there on Friday nights, but I suspect it might be Clarence. I can't imagine ONEO would give him community space. Anyway, if I'm right, I'd like someone to be able to follow him in, maybe even listen in on the meeting. It would be better if that person were . . . not me."

"I'm definitely not you," Paula said. "For one, *I* have a sense of humor."

Wayne smiled. He couldn't help it. The kid was great

company. And was, apparently, feeling much better than the last time he'd seen her. "Perfect. Just what I was looking for. In case I need my undercover agent to crack a joke."

Paula shrugged. "You said yourself cops aren't very funny. He'll never suspect a thing."

"Did I say that?"

"I think so," Paula said. "I heard it."

"All right, wise gal. To the trading post, then."

Paula had Wayne's binoculars pressed up against her eyes. Clarence hadn't left the trading post yet, so she was watching him through the window of the cruiser. Wayne was parked across the street, on the side of the road, as if he had set up a speed radar.

"Seems to be doing normal things," Paula muttered. "But it's hard to tell since he keeps moving out of view." Paula set the binoculars down in her lap. "Are all those rugs from the WARN ladies?"

"Not all of them," Wayne said. "Some are from tribal elders. But a good amount of them come from WARN."

Paula raised the binoculars again. "And because Clarence doesn't like outsiders, and because Robin was trying to work with outsiders on the down-low, you think Clarence found out and poisoned Robin?"

"It's possible," Wayne said.

"Oh! Oh, he might be leaving!" Paula exclaimed. "What time is it?"

Wayne looked at his watch. "18:02."

"All right, Colonel Potter. What time is that really?"

"Closing time. Six p.m."

Paula tapped the dashboard with her palm a few times. "Let's go, let's go."

Wayne watched the lights inside go off. He imagined—since Paula still had the binoculars—Clarence flipping the sign from Open to Closed. When Clarence stepped outside, he didn't look around at the empty parking lot or take a moment to watch the vultures gliding overhead. He walked to his car like a man with a purpose.

Wayne kept his distance as he followed Clarence's car down the highway toward Shiprock. They followed him past the police station and into the hospital's parking lot.

When Clarence pulled into a parking spot, Wayne drove past slowly. He would've waved if Clarence had looked up—it was normal enough for a cop to be at a hospital—but Clarence didn't seem to notice the cruiser inching past the rear of his car. By the time Clarence got out, Wayne was backing into a spot in the back of the lot.

"Guess I'll have to catch up," Paula said, swinging open the car door.

"Remember what we talked about! Be normal!" Wayne called after her. She slammed the door, and Wayne watched her jog toward the front door until she was close enough to Clarence. He didn't turn around. Then, they were both inside and Wayne couldn't see anything else.

Wayne knew Paula might be awkward and strange but she would never admit to doing what she was doing. He trusted her. She had done just fine at the WARN meeting.

Wayne kept telling himself this as the minutes ticked by. Twenty minutes. Thirty. He seriously considered going in after her when he finally saw her come out, half-walking, half-jogging toward his cruiser.

"What happened?" he asked when she finally got in.

"It was the addict meeting," Paula said, popping a stick of gum in her mouth. "I told him my aunt was an addict and I wanted to see what the fuss was about. I told him I had heard *great things* about his program."

"Did he ask you questions about her?" Wayne asked.

"A few."

"And you answered them . . . normally?"

Paula smirked. "I know some addicts, Wayne. I didn't have to make that much up."

Wayne thought about Paula's relationship with her mother and wondered if that was who she meant. He had never pried.

"All right, so what did Clarence say to the group? Anything interesting?"

"He was a little scatterbrained. Upset about that bombshell Cecil dropped on the community that the peyote was probably contaminated. The people there were worried about it. He basically spent the whole time telling them the peyote *wasn't* contaminated."

"What exactly did he say?" Wayne asked.

Paula paused. "He said, 'I can promise you the peyote you receive in my teepee is safe. It has never not been safe. It has never been contaminated.'" Paula stopped again. Tilted her head like she was listening for something. "He said, 'I eat it myself at every meeting. You see me. If I was concerned, would I still be eating it?'"

"Did he mention Cecil directly at all?" Wayne asked.

"No. He said, 'Claims have been made.' I noticed he was careful about that."

"And did he try to explain why he was so sure his peyote is safe?" Wayne asked.

"No," Paula said. "Just that he was confident in the peyote he had in his possession."

"I wonder how much he has left from Robin. If his story is true, he must be in a bind now or will be soon."

"He has enough for another meeting next week," Paula said. "He told me to come and bring my aunt."

"Huh," Wayne said. "Well, bring your aunt then, I guess."

Paula snorted. "Do I get witness protection or something for being your little spy?"

Wayne shook his head. "You've been watching too much TV."

KAY

Kay knew James was being reasonable about all of this, considering she hadn't been honest with him. But she also knew he thought Victor was a fraud, and that knowledge hurt. She didn't know what she had hoped to get out of all of this—besides a baby, of course—but pushing James further away from her traditions and beliefs wasn't it. He was keeping his opinions to himself, though, and Kay was grateful for that.

Barbara's doctor was understanding about expenses. As Kay and James sat in the shiny, sterile room—Kay in a hospital gown, James with his hat in his hands—the doctor explained that they would do some preliminary tests first. Bloodwork for Kay and sperm counts for James. Kay was glad Molly had stayed in the waiting room. She probably would have been horrified to hear the doctor talk about her father's sperm.

They didn't have to do anything else yet, the doctor said. No imaging or anything. The imaging would be much more expensive, and they wouldn't resort to that until they ruled out other possibilities. Kay smiled and nodded and said, "Thank you," but she was sure of what they would find. Victor was right. She tried not to feel guilty about the money James was wasting. She tried to process—silently and alone—the fact that she would never have children. She tried not to sob every time she thought of the baby she would never have. She knew James and Molly would only try to reassure her, try to change her mind, try to give her hope.

But Kay knew. She had always known on some level. Something was wrong with her.

54

CECIL

THE SMELL of the burning cedar calmed Cecil's mind and spirit. Victor sat next to the fire, but Cecil stood. From the pouch around his neck, Cecil retrieved a pinch of corn pollen and set it in his wrinkled palm. First, he sprinkled some on the crown of his head. Next, a dab on his tongue. And finally, the rest was let go in the wind in the direction of the east. He muttered quietly enough that his prayer reached only the ears of the Holy People, not his friend seated beside him. Then, Cecil sat.

The two men were silent for a minute or so before Victor sighed. "I had a vision the other day while diagnosing a patient. Something ugly."

"Something I need to be aware of?" Cecil asked.

Victor nodded. "It could be . . . that the future of the Diné people is under attack. Or will be soon."

"It always is," Cecil replied.

"There will be repercussions," Victor said.

"What are you saying?"

"These women, their deaths. It's leading to something big. We have not seen the worst of what is to come."

Cecil breathed deeply. "Who?"

"I cannot tell," Victor said. "It could be someone close, a friend. They may use witchcraft. But it could be an outsider, too. A person who has been deceitful, who has gained the trust of our people but who intends to destroy us. I am certain there will be betrayal."

Cecil squinted into the fire. Watched the sparks hop and dart into the night air. "And what should I do? What is my role in this?"

"You will need to protect yourself. By any means necessary."

"I always do."

Victor leaned back in his seat. It creaked under his moving weight. "We will perform a ceremony for you. Soon."

Cecil closed his eyes. Let the heat of the fire burn the insides of his eyelids. "If it will ease your mind," he said.

"It will do more than that," Victor said.

"I trust you," Cecil said. And it was true. There might be no one Cecil trusted more than the man seated next to him.

"Are you aware that Doug Ahasteen might be involved in this investigation?" Victor asked.

"Ahasteen? Why?"

"Who knows? But he was over recently to whine at me about not joining the Medicine Man Association. He stole the contract between ourselves and Dawn Harvey. I assume by request."

"Tully's request?" Cecil asked.

"Yes. Tully came to speak to me about Mr. Chee's missing horse. He was the distraction."

Cecil smirked. "Why use Ahasteen? That man would trip over the wind."

"Because Ahasteen is angry with me. That's why."

"Hmmm. They are worried about Dawn Harvey," Cecil said.

"It appears so."

Cecil reached into his shirt pocket for a hand-rolled cigarette. He brought it to his lips. Lit the end. Inhaled. "It is good you told me."

55

MOLLY

THE FBI's Albuquerque office was no fancier or more impressive than any other detectives' offices Molly had been to. Though she understood she and James were only there to look at files and she wouldn't be given a tour of their newest, most cutting-edge investigation techniques. The coffee was good, though, and Molly had two cups while she and James combed through the files.

"How did Charles read all this?" Molly asked. "I thought he was in the Denver office."

"They faxed it over," James said.

Molly waited for her dad to read what was in front of him. His eyebrows were knitted together and his mouth turned down.

James muttered something under his breath. He flipped through to the next folder, which was full of photos. "Well, I'll be damned," he said, loudly this time. He slid a photo across the table to Molly. It was of the side of a building. Hanging out the window was a sign that read—like Barbara had told them already—Native American Embassy. But below the windows and the sign, on the concrete part near the street, there were spray-painted words. Molly gasped.

"It says the same thing! Except for the 'watch your back' part. But the Diné words are the same! What did Wayne say they meant? Enemy or outsider? Liar?"

"That's right. I would imagine more like enemy in this context. Looks like the same writer to me, too. Same handwriting and all. What do you think?"

Molly nodded. It looked exactly the same. Except for the color. The paint in the photo was red. "Not avocado."

"No, not avocado."

"So, who was there?" Molly asked.

"That's the thing," James said. "Most of these people are in prison now. But someone is obviously not." He squinted at another photo, and Molly grabbed the last folder, sitting unopened on James's other side.

"There are more files in here, Dad," she said. "Here, you look at these. I'll look at those."

They switched. Molly studied a photo of a man holding two halves of a torn document, grinning. He looked a lot like Dawn Harvey. The next photo was of an older man clutching a painted pot with tears in his eyes. Molly didn't know what significance the pot held, but the photo was touching. It felt like it ought to be in *Life* magazine or something.

Suddenly, James started to laugh. Quietly at first and then louder, and then so quiet again that Molly realized he had tears in his eyes from whatever he found so hilarious.

"What?" Molly asked, grinning herself.

"It's a fuckin' early Christmas present, is what it is."

"What do you mean?" Molly asked.

James shook his head. He took a deep breath. "Let me see those photos. We're going to make some copies."

[56]

JAMES

JAMES WAS in a damn good mood after the Albuquerque visit. He had started the process of proving to Kay that any friend of Cecil Cody's wasn't to be trusted, and he was looking forward to her mood improving again—though he knew he would need to be patient. She would want every test run, every possibility exhausted. James didn't care about the money. It would be worth it.

He had a meeting now, at the Shiprock hospital, and had the four women's medical records tucked under his arm. He was not meeting with Dr. Ciccone, though. James wanted a fresh pair of eyes.

He knocked on Dr. Bettis's door. A moment later, the door opened and in front of him stood a man shorter and a few years younger than James. He was trim, with his hair braided down his back. A good-looking fella. James was secure enough to admit as much. He stuck his hand out.

"It's good to finally meet you, Dr. Bettis."

The man smiled. "You can call me Al. I'm not sure you've heard about my greatest attributes."

"Kay doesn't talk bad about you. She's a classy woman."

Al laughed. "I know Kay has a talent for holding grudges."

James shook his head. "She's moved on."

"I'm glad for the two of you. Truly. We were never a good fit, but she deserves happiness."

"I appreciate that," James said. "And I appreciate you takin' the time to meet with me today. I need a fresh pair of eyes on these records. An expert." James set the records down on Al's desk.

"And why these women?" Al asked.

"They're all possibly connected to a case I'm investigating. All young, seemed by all accounts to be fairly healthy, and died suddenly in the hospital. I don't want to give you much more context, because I don't want to skew your perspective."

Al nodded and picked up the first record. He moved his lips silently while he read. Then he moved on to the next and didn't speak until he had finished reading through all four women's files.

"This all?" he asked.

"Should there be more?" James asked.

"These are official hospital records but there are no doctor notes. Basically, this is just telling what the patients were diagnosed with, prescribed, or what sort of operations were performed."

"That's right. We do have some notes on Robin Kinsel somewhere. Not exactly legible, though. Where would we find the rest?" James asked.

"Depends on the doctor. I want the nurses and the next doctor my patients might see to have access to my notes. Not all doctors feel this way, though. It could be in the doctor's personal files."

"All right, so with what little we have here, you see anything that sticks out to you?" James asked.

"Sure. They've all had monopolar electrocautery tubal ligations. Dr. Ciccone is the expert on tubal ligations here. We have residents from all over who come to learn from him."

"Can you explain what that is?" James asked.

"A tubal ligation is permanent birth control. In this case, a woman's fallopian tubes are basically seared shut by an electric current. Though it's interesting the doctor hasn't switched to the bipolar method. Maybe we just don't have the money for the equipment." Al shrugged. "Like I said, he's the expert. He might have better insight."

"And all four women underwent the procedure?" James asked.

Al nodded. "They've been offering it more and more for women who are done having children. It's very effective, and it's a one-time procedure."

"Is it relatively safe?" James asked.

"Yes, usually quite safe. Dr. Ciccone has probably done thousands of these procedures in his career."

"Interesting. You have any idea how the community at large feels about these?"

Al smirked. "There are plenty of men who are not too happy about it. You can imagine why. It puts a lot of power in the hands of these women. Some object for personal reasons, some for tribal reasons."

"Tribal reasons?" James asked.

"They feel it's putting the future of the tribe at risk. A

large part of a woman's responsibility is to ensure our future as a people."

"You said 'done having kids,' so haven't they already done their part?"

"Who's to say how many is enough?" Al countered.

"What do you think about it all? Tubal ligations, I mean."

"I think it's up to the women. If they want to be done, they ought to be allowed to make that choice."

"And the other doctors feel that way too?" James asked.

"I suppose you'd have to ask them."

"What about husbands?" James asked. "They have a say in this?"

"I don't believe we require the husband's permission. Not on the reservation."

"I bet there are men who would like to see that changed."

"I'm sure there are plenty," Al said.

"How long have the reservation hospitals been performing these procedures?" James asked.

"As a form of birth control? About seven or eight years. Maybe ten at the most."

"Has it become more popular in that time?" James asked.

"Certainly. Word has gotten around. Women request it without anyone even asking them about it."

"This is good stuff, Al. Thank you."

The men stood and shook hands.

"I'll try to get some notes from Dr. Ciccone. See if we can't pick his brain a little more if you'd like."

"Sure," James said. "That'd be helpful. Although it might be better if I do the askin'. I don't want him thinkin' I'm goin' behind his back."

"Understood," Al said.

"But I might come back to you if he's willin' to hand them over. Like I said, a fresh pair of eyes."

"Of course. You're welcome anytime."

On the way out of the hospital, James stopped at Dr. Ciccone's office to see if he could catch him and ask for his notes, but the doctor wasn't there. James would have to come back or give him a call. That was fine. He had enough to chew on for now.

[57]

DAWN

"WHAT CAN you tell me about tubal ligations?"

Dawn had not been sleeping this time when James Pinter called her on the phone, but she still felt caught off guard and slow to answer.

"Tubal ligations? Like, what they are?" Dawn asked.

"I know what they are. Tell me about your patients. How do they feel about them?"

Dawn considered the question. "Some of my patients like that they have choices when it comes to planning their families. Others want nothing to do with the procedure."

"The ones who want nothing to do with it, why?" James asked.

"For pretty much the same reason. They don't want anyone telling them what to do with their own body and their own family."

"Telling them what to do? Isn't it their choice?" James asked.

Dawn thought carefully again and wondered why she had even picked up the phone.

"I think some of the hospital staff can be a little pushy," Dawn finally said. "Some of the nurses, in particular."

"Why?" James asked. "Why would the nurses care?"

"We're a teaching hospital, right? Which means we get a lot of residents. They're learning how to do surgeries, so we need surgeries to perform. There are incentives for us to fill elective surgery spots. Monetary incentives. And tubal ligations are Dr. Ciccone's specialty."

"So y'all get paid more the more tubal ligations women agree to have?" James asked.

"Yeah. I think it's a little gross to convince anyone to have any elective surgery. But tubal ligations are one of the more common and popular elective surgeries. Carole, for example, is known to throw a little shame and guilt into her spiels about why these women ought to have the procedure done. I guess it makes sense. She probably needs the money, since she sends her son to a private boarding school off the reservation."

"Who else knows about these incentives?" James asked.

"I have no idea. I can't imagine Carole goes around telling people where her bonuses come from."

"How about you?" James asked. "You mention it to anyone?"

Dawn knew she had complained about it on multiple occasions to multiple friends. But that was none of this investigator's business.

"Not that I can think of."

"I've got somethin' else to tell ya," James said. "Something a little more personal. I think we ought to meet in person. It's about your brother's case. I dug into the FBI's internal files and learned some things I think you'll want to know. Things you *should* know."

"Why are you picking at an old wound like this?" Dawn asked, annoyed. "What the hell can I do now about my brother being in federal prison? Not a damn thing."

"Trust me," James said. "This is important information. How about we meet somewhere off the reservation? I'll buy you a beer or two. Or a glass of wine if that's more your thing. Hell, even a shot of whiskey. Whatever you want."

Dawn did not need a night out. She didn't need to get drunk or even tipsy. She had too much to do all the time with all of the programs she was running now. Besides, she could tell she was being baited and she didn't like it.

"I'll think about it." She didn't wait to hear how he responded. She hung up.

[58]
MOLLY

IT WAS Molly's first time at a prison, and James said it was a good first prison to visit. It was a federal prison, which apparently meant that it was a little nicer than other prisons. But it was medium security, meaning some of the prisoners were pretty dangerous. James said it was bullshit for LeRoy to be sentenced there. He had no record of violence.

Usually, only family members or lawyers were allowed to visit federal prisoners, Molly had learned. But of course, her dad had connections.

Molly hadn't expected to sit directly across from LeRoy in a big, open room like this. She thought they would be alone or separated somehow from the violent prisoners. But they weren't. There was a big, tattooed man just feet away from her who'd been kissing a woman when she and James first walked in.

LeRoy looked calm and assured but also a little puzzled. He wasn't that big, just a little taller than Dawn and a little shorter than James. His hair was still long and well-groomed, his prison jumpsuit a little baggy.

"Nice to meet you, LeRoy," James said. "My name is James Pinter and this is my daughter, Molly."

LeRoy said nothing, just kept staring.

"We're here because we need your help figurin' somethin' out. We're investigating a case up on the reservation. Your sister's helpin' us out."

One side of LeRoy's mouth curled into a half smile. "That seems unlikely. Dawn doesn't like cops."

James smiled too. "She's doin' her best. Besides, I'm not a cop. I'm a private investigator."

"But you work with tribal police," LeRoy said. "A consultant."

"That's right," James said. Molly knew her dad had to be a little thrown off that LeRoy knew that, but he didn't show it.

"Dawn told me who you are. But none of that's got to do with me. So what is so important to bring you all the way down here?"

Molly glanced at her dad before pulling out some sketches she had done of Russel and Clarence.

"You recognize either of these men?" James asked him, handing him the drawings.

LeRoy looked at them for a long time. "What if I did? What'd they do?"

"They're suspects in a case involving a suspicious death and a threat to a woman," James said. "One is her husband. The other is her roadman."

LeRoy shrugged. "I don't think I know them."

"You see," James began, "we recently obtained access to the FBI's files on your case. We saw some photos that led us to believe that the man who threatened our current victim is the same man who spray-painted some words on the BIA building when y'all were in DC a few years ago."

LeRoy glanced down at the photo. "There were lots of people there. How the fuck would I know if these guys were two of them?"

"Maybe you have an excellent memory," James said. LeRoy raised an eyebrow. "Did you know that FBI informants generally receive immunity when they commit crimes in the process of obtaining information?"

"What the hell are you talking about? Snitches? Yeah, I know how that works. Why?"

"Well, I thought to myself, how strange that someone at this little rally, this little attempted BIA takeover, would find themselves walking free nowadays, not even three years after the rest of you had the hammer brought down on you, and nearly the whole American Indian Movement was dismantled."

LeRoy jerked his head at the drawings. "You sayin' one of these men was a snitch?"

"No, I'm wonderin' if one of these men is a copycat. If maybe he saw the spray-painted words and decided to replicate that same threat. Hell, even the Feds make mistakes sometimes. They could've missed him. Or decided he wasn't worth the effort." James paused for a moment. Folded his hands together on top of the table. "No, LeRoy. I know exactly who the snitch was."

LeRoy's eyes narrowed. "You gonna tell me or you tryin' to piss me off?"

"I'm gonna tell you," James said. "A man by the name of Byron Cody. You happen to know him?"

[59]

WAYNE

THERE WAS something about the way the pharmacist had asked Wayne to repeat himself when Wayne called to find out if Russel Kinsel had picked up any medication over the last couple of weeks that made him decide to pay the pharmacy a visit.

It was at the end of a long hallway on the north side of the Shiprock hospital. Wayne waited for two elderly women to fill their prescriptions and then he flashed his badge at the pharmacy technician.

"I'm going to need the full pharmacy records for a patient named Russel Kinsel," Wayne said.

The technician glanced over her shoulder. She looked nervous.

"You can tell your boss," Wayne said. "He or she can get it for me."

The young woman nodded and scurried away. Wayne watched another annoyed and clearly busy technician open the neighboring window and call to the next customer. The lighting down in this corner of the hospital was bad. A few bulbs had gone out, and both the pharmacists and customers squinted at words on bottles under the dull yellow light and nearly shouted to make themselves heard over the buzzing of the generator right outside the exit doors.

The technician was back again. "My boss wants you to write the name down. And address, please."

Wayne wrote it down and slid it under the glass. The technician disappeared again, and Wayne tried not to overhear the very loud conversation beside him about how the antibiotics had not cleared up the man's chlamydia infection.

Instead, Wayne thought about the visit he had made just before coming to the pharmacy. He'd gone to legal services to find out whether Russel had actually started to file a lawsuit against the hospital and, if so, what Wayne might be able to learn about it. He knew about client confidentiality, but he was also on good terms with the head of legal services, and Wayne was able to learn enough to convince himself to go back to the pharmacy. Something wasn't adding up. Russel was most likely lying, but what if he wasn't?

Finally, after trying to avoid listening to three more sensitive and private conversations at the next window, Wayne could see the technician returning with a single sheet of paper in her hands.

"This is all we have on that patient," she said, sliding it to Wayne.

The last date Russel Kinsel had picked up any prescription at the hospital was almost ten years ago when he was a teenager. And yet, the bottle sitting in Shiprock's evidence locker said otherwise. So who inside the hospital was slipping Russel oxycodone?

[60]

KAY

WHEN KAY GOT the call from the doctor, she didn't know what to feel. She'd been so certain it would be bad news. That whatever was wrong with her would show up immediately. But that's not what happened. The bloodwork was normal, sperm counts were normal. Everything looked fine so far. She scheduled the next visit, an ultrasound, for the following week and then sat silently, staring at a black, lifeless television screen.

Why hadn't Victor given her more information? Was it because he truly didn't know? Or did he see something so awful, so terrible, that he couldn't bear to relay it to her? She wanted to make peace with her reality. She tried to be accepting. She tried to grieve.

But the phone call did not help. As much as she wanted to suppress the hope, it rose inside her anyway. She had promised James she wouldn't see Victor again, but now, sitting at home alone with the news of her bloodwork, she felt like she could jump out of her skin. James was gone for the afternoon. Molly was with Paula. Kay didn't have a student to tutor until the following morning.

She only wanted to talk to Victor for a few minutes. She just needed to know what he'd seen. *Exactly* what he'd seen. Maybe she could make sense of it. She grabbed her truck's keys from the counter, laced up her boots, and left Molly a note.

[61]
JAMES

DAWN HAD CALLED James the day after his visit to the prison. James had known she would, and now he was driving to Farmington to meet her at a bar called the Tap.

It was a clear day. A day so hot the heat seemed to suck all the sweat from James's forehead the minute it appeared. A beer would be nice, he thought, as he parked on a side street.

He found Dawn by herself at the pool table, focused on racking up balls. A pool cue leaned against the table beside her. James said nothing as he approached. He listened to Aerosmith singing about dreams and lit himself a cigarette.

"This is a real fucked-up game you're playing," Dawn finally said, rubbing the chalk onto the tip of the pool cue.

"No game," James said. "I didn't know what I would learn when I went digging through those files."

Dawn finally looked up at him. "What do you want from me? No, *really*. What do you want? A confession? I have nothing to confess. Do I sometimes provide pregnant women with peyote to help ease their pain in labor? You bet your ass I do. Do you know what happens to them otherwise? We knock them out so they remember nothing. But their bodies? They have to be tied to the table because they thrash around. It takes them twice as long to labor. The babies can suffocate and the mothers tear open because the doctors have to use forceps. The risk of death for both mom and baby increases dramatically. Do you know what happens when they take peyote? Nothing. Not a damn thing other than the fact that their pain subsides."

James was quiet. He knew this part was cathartic for Dawn.

"My programs are good for my people. More Diné nurses mean better outcomes for Diné women and Diné babies. And now—" Dawn's voice shook. "Now you want to take that away from me." The next part she said quietly. "You fucking asshole."

James took a few steps back to tap his cigarette into a nearby ashtray. "That is not my intention."

Dawn laughed incredulously. "Oh, it *is* your intention. You know Byron helps with those programs. You know he gets me the classroom space through ONEO. You *know* this. And how the *fuck* am I supposed to work with him now? Huh?"

"My intention is to find out what happened to the Krylon spray paint can, the avocado green color that you purchased from Hammer Away."

Dawn's face screwed up into a look of bewilderment. "What?"

"Hammer Away. A hardware store. You purchased a can of Krylon spray paint. Avocado green. What happened to it?"

"I used it in my new classroom space," Dawn said. "It was

boring in there. I was getting it ready for my midwife students."

"And Byron was helping you. I'm guessing the paint can disappeared afterward."

Dawn's forehead was still wrinkled in confusion. Her nostrils flared. She was looking at the pool balls, still racked inside the triangle.

"It did," she finally said. "It did disappear. I didn't even notice. But yeah, I never brought it home with me. What does that have to do with anything?"

"So Byron set you up too, as well as your brother."

Dawn glared at James.

"You see, Byron threatened Robin Kinsel before she died," James went on. "He used your can of paint to write the same messages he wrote on the BIA building during the event that caused your brother's arrest. Byron had a vendetta against Robin for multiple reasons."

"Why me? Why set me up?" Dawn asked.

"Because you have an agreement with his father to obtain the peyote for these women. He could make it look like you were the one who poisoned Robin. I doubt it's personal, just convenient. Unless you know something I don't."

James took a drag of his cigarette, and Dawn slowly dropped onto a barstool. "But I didn't poison her. I never even gave Robin Kinsel peyote."

"Maybe not, but the evidence is stacked against you."

Dawn looked at James. She was no longer confused, no longer angry even. "And now there *is* something you want from me, isn't there?"

WAYNE

Wayne was at the station waiting for James and Kay's ex-husband, Al. Molly was in Officer Begaye's office, running some copies of the documents Wayne had picked up from legal services. Wayne wasn't sure how the medical history of these women could help them with the case now. It seemed they were pretty damn close to nailing the Codys, and whether Cecil and Byron had targeted the other three women or Robin had given the women peyote that she didn't know was contaminated, there wasn't a lot of doubt in Wayne's mind that the Codys were to blame for their deaths. What worried him was Byron's connection to the Feds.

He wondered when the Codys had been caught. What deal had been made. It worried Wayne. Would the Feds excuse murder? How far would they go to protect a valuable informant? Wayne imagined it wasn't easy to convince an Indian to do this work. To rat on their fellow tribal members.

He was lost in his thoughts when James and Al knocked on his office door.

"You ready, LT?" James asked.

"Sure," Wayne said, rubbing his eyes. "You two head to the conference room and I'll grab some coffee. Al, how do you like yours?"

"Just a little bit of milk, please," Al said.

"You got it."

Wayne got the coffees and headed to the conference room where Al had a fat folder sitting in front of him. Wayne walked around the table, handing out the coffees so they wouldn't spill.

"I've got to admit," James was saying, "I was surprised when I got your call. I never heard back from Dr. Ciccone, never got his notes for the rest of the patients."

Wayne sat next to James.

"Well, I've got them here, and I'll tell you how that came about," Al said. "You see I was curious about the bipolar versus monopolar methods and why Dr. Ciccone was using one over the other. I told you the procedure is relatively safe, which is true, but bipolar is safer. Plus, there are other tubal ligation methods that don't involve the use of electricity at all. Truly, it was just my curiosity as a doctor that led me to look. If we were still doing the monopolar surgeries because of funding reasons, I was willing to submit for a grant so we could change that. I was wondering if we were giving the women a choice in the matter and if that was why."

Al paused and blew on his coffee. He took a sip. "So, I went searching for the release forms, the consent forms." He took a deep breath. "Before I go any further, I want you both to know this is not going to be an easy conversation. Frankly, it's a little upsetting."

James nodded. "Go on."

"I noticed something on the consent forms. A faint line

right above the women's signatures. It was on all of the consent forms. It concerned me so much that I found the original form—with no line. And I started to think, are these consent forms being tampered with? I also noticed that it was the same nurse every time who signed the consent forms next to the patient signatures. Carole Sherborn. I had a theory forming about these women's deaths, and I needed to find out more information."

Al leaned forward, his forearms resting on his knees, his hands wrapped around his coffee cup.

"So I snuck into Dr. Ciccone's office and took his notes."

"Snuck in?" Wayne asked.

"It wasn't locked," Al explained. "But he wasn't there, nor was he aware that I was there."

"Can you actually read his notes?" James asked. "Looked like chicken scratch to me."

Al nodded. "I have practice reading Dr. Ciccone's handwriting."

Al sat back and took another sip of coffee. Then, he stared into his cup as if the notes were written there.

"I believe Dr. Ciccone is letting the residents perform the surgery on their own, without his supervision. I don't know why. It's obviously not allowed. But most of these notes were quite legible. Not in Dr. Ciccone's handwriting at all."

"Isn't it possible the residents simply recorded the notes?" James asked.

"They might have. There's nothing definitive in there. But I discovered something else. The first woman who died, I'm not sure if you remember her name. It was Sonya. The notes for her are more revealing than the others. They were all treated for sepsis when they were admitted to the hospital.

But Sonya's records explain that the doctor suspected she had suffered a bowel perforation during the tubal ligation surgery and had been leaking from her intestines ever since, which is why he treated her for sepsis. Bowel perforation can occur if the electrified forceps accidentally come in contact with the intestines."

"So you're saying that all of these women might have suffered from bowel perforations?" Wayne asked.

"Yes. And it would be strange to have an experienced doctor such as Dr. Ciccone make that many mistakes. It's even stranger that the women weren't told what sort of symptoms to look out for if they were to experience a bowel perforation. None of them made it to the hospital in time to be saved. Meaning they had no idea what was happening to them."

"You think the residents didn't know to tell them because they're inexperienced?" James asked.

"It's possible. But what I'm more worried about is that maybe no one told these women because these women had no idea they were actually undergoing this particular surgery. They were all admitted for other reasons—ruptured cyst, miscarriage, labor complications. And the consent forms seem suspicious to me."

Wayne leaned back, away from Al, and James let out a low whistle. "Holy shit. That's one heavy accusation."

"I know." Now, Al looked really uncomfortable. He set his coffee down and picked up the folder. He set it in his lap, rubbed the back of his neck, and took a deep breath. "I didn't know at first how we could find out whether this theory is true other than by finding more women who have had the procedure done and simply asking them. Which, as you can imagine, would be an extremely uncomfortable conversation, not to mention incredibly inappropriate if I turned out to be wrong."

Al cleared his throat. "But . . . I've found a patient who I know can confirm whether or not the procedure was done willingly."

The realization came crashing down on Wayne too late. This was not going to end well. He tried to lean forward and snatch the folder from Al, but James beat him to it. He was on his feet and across the room in only a few seconds.

"Give me the folder," Wayne said to James's back.

"I don't think so, LT." Wayne could see James's shoulders moving up and down quickly as his breathing intensified. "Is it who I think it is, Al?" James asked.

"Yes," Al said, quietly. "At first, when I saw it, I thought maybe she had kept it from me. Our relationship was in that rough a shape at the time of her miscarriage. But I knew you would know. She would tell you."

Wayne waited for an outburst, and when the room grew silent, he thought about fighting James for the folder. Restraining him. He didn't know what to expect. But James only turned and left the room.

Shit, Wayne thought as he raced after him. *Shit, shit, shit.*

[63]

JAMES

It was loud and quiet at the same time in James's head. Like the aftermath of an explosion. He went to Wayne's office where he had left his pistol. Dropped the folder on the desk. Picked up the gun. Loaded it. Thought about the last time he had killed a man. The soldier who went crazy while James was investigating a case. The man started shooting his fellow grunts. James stopped it. That had been hard. This would be easy.

"I'm gonna fix this," James muttered. He thought of Dr. Ciccone's face, and his vision went black. He blinked. He could see again, Wayne and Molly standing in the doorway.

He said it louder this time so they could hear him. "I'm gonna fix this."

[64]
MOLLY

Her dad was scary in that moment. Really, really scary. Molly's hands tingled. She knew she had to stop him. She might be the only one who could. She'd heard the whole thing. Al's entire explanation. She understood what had happened to Kay.

"Dad," Molly said. "Don't do this."

James's whole body shook.

"Put the gun down," Wayne tried next. "You can't undo this, James."

James didn't move.

"I know. This is so fucked up," Molly went on. "I love Kay, too. It's not fair. It's not fair to Kay or to you or to our family."

James was not looking at her. He was looking through her. But he still hadn't moved. Molly glanced at Wayne whose eyes didn't leave James. But he gave her a quick nod of encouragement.

"I know you missed my childhood, and I know you

wanted to experience that. To try again. But I. Am here. Now." She said that last part loudly, hoping to snap him back to the here and the now.

James was breathing heavily. She could see his chest rising and falling.

"I'm sorry you missed it when I lost my baby teeth. Or when I got my first haircut. I'm sorry you weren't at my first day of school or at my first dance recital. I'm sorry you never got to pretend to be Santa Claus. But there is still so much ahead of us. You're here. Right now. With me. You got to meet my first boyfriend."

James blinked rapidly. His eyebrows furrowed.

"You'll watch me graduate from high school. You'll walk me down the aisle at my wedding. You'll hold your grandchild in your arms someday."

James closed his eyes for a moment. Then opened them back up. It seemed he was trying to focus again.

"And then you can be the best granddad in the whole world. You can be there for everything. But only if you don't do this today. Only if you put that gun down and stay right here at the station with me and Wayne."

James's muscles went slack. He took in a deep, shaky breath and dropped the gun onto Wayne's desk. Wayne rushed forward, grabbed the gun, removed the magazine, and emptied the chamber. James fell into the chair beside the desk. Let his head slump onto his chest.

Molly walked to him. She crouched down, right in front of him. She grabbed his hands

"It's okay, Dad. I'm here. I'm right here."

He looked up and into her eyes. Searched them for a

moment. "Thank you, Molly. I love you. You know that? I love you."

"I love you, too, Dad."

[65]

KAY

WITH MOLLY'S HELP, James told Kay everything. It was the answer she had been looking for, the answer she had been waiting to hear, the answer Victor could not give her. Molly held her hand and rubbed her back because James was having trouble holding it together. Kay knew in that moment that had Molly been given a chance, she would've been an incredible big sister. Just like Linda had been for Kay.

Kay kept her ultrasound appointment, just to confirm. It would help with James's case anyway, and she wanted to help. Despite all the evidence, Kay still wondered if this was somehow her fault. What had she actually signed? Did it matter? She crawled into her bed and didn't come out for days. She heard James and Molly speak sometimes, heard Wayne come and go.

One day she heard Wayne say he intended to bring Carole in for questioning. Apparently, the other nurse, Dawn, had some incriminating evidence connected to Robin Kinsel's death. Wayne had spoken to her, had met with her. Kay didn't hear the rest because she couldn't listen anymore.

She rolled over and tried to think of nothing. She saw the snake from her dream over and over again. Biting her ankle, sinking his fangs into her skin.

Sometimes the rage welled up inside of her so quickly and so abundantly that it made her sick. Her head pounded constantly. Sometimes she cried, and sometimes she couldn't.

One night when James was holding her, he asked her, "What can I do?"

And Kay answered, "Don't let them get away with this. Please."

WAYNE

JAMES HAD TOLD Wayne that he hoped Dawn could get something out of Byron. If not a full confession, then at least something that would help. She could bring up Robin's death, or Clarence's addict program, or even the council's decision to deny WARN space at the capital. That night at the bar, Dawn had been skeptical but agreed to try.

When Wayne called her with a new mission, Dawn had been much more confident about her odds of success.

Now, Wayne drove to the station with Carole in his back seat. He had asked her to come with him because they had questions about Russel, who had named Carole as the one who'd kicked him out of the hospital. They wanted to know more about Russel's behavior, Wayne told her. Carole seemed fine with it. Not eager, exactly, but ready to help.

James would be at the station too and would join Wayne for questioning. At first, Wayne had thought it was a bad idea, but when he thought about what that hospital had done to those women, to Kay, he decided he didn't care much if

James was harsh with Carole. James would still be professional enough.

Wayne ushered Carole back into the interrogation room, and before James shut the door behind them, he offered Carole a coffee or water or soda. She accepted the soda, and James sent Molly to grab one. They would be recording the interrogation, and Molly would be listening in the whole time from the conference room.

After Molly returned with the soda and James closed the door to the windowless room, Carole started to look a little nervous.

"What did you need to ask me about?" she asked.

James looked at ease, which both reassured Wayne and frightened him a little.

"We've got some questions about Russel Kinsel," James said.

"All right," Carole said.

"We confiscated a bottle of pills from Russel's bathroom," James went on. He walked slowly across the room and back again as he spoke. "Prescription narcotics filled at the hospital's pharmacy."

"Yes," Carole said.

"We are fairly confident this was the same narcotic used to contaminate Robin's peyote. That it was crushed up and rubbed on the peyote chips."

"Gosh, that's awful," Carole said.

James's smile was so small that someone who didn't know him—someone like Carole—might not have seen it at all.

"Awful indeed. Now here's the interesting part. Russel Kinsel has never actually filled a narcotics prescription at the

Shiprock hospital. Not once. He receives his medical care from a doctor in Gallup."

"Hmm." Carole swallowed, nodded. "That is odd."

"Yesterday I decided to have a little chat with Russel," James went on. "And I learned some details about the night he brought Robin to the hospital."

Wayne flipped open the folder on the table in front of him and pulled out the medication sign-out chart from the evening of Robin's death that Dawn had copied for them.

"The first time I looked at this chart that Wayne is holding," James went on, "was with you. I was only looking for Robin's information on this chart and I found it. Since then, I've had some other folks look at it. Folks who know what they're talkin' about. You'll see your own signature farther down the sheet for that same evening. Carole Sherborn signed out oxycodone for a John Smith in room 550, a man who, of course, does not exist. We looked into the hospital's records. No such man was admitted that night, and room 550 was never used."

Wayne watched Carole's face lose color.

"This was past when your shift should've ended, but of course you were caught up with Russel Kinsel. Now, before you had the man escorted to his car, you had him 'cool off' with security and sign some forms. Basically, you held him illegally while you went to his home, poisoned Robin's peyote, and left a prescription bottle with Russel's name on it in their bathroom. The lock on the back door of his house being broken was pure luck, because I imagine you were willing to break in if need be."

Carole's gaze darted to the door, and Wayne worried for a moment she would run out of the station. But James stopped pacing just then and blocked her escape route. She looked up at him but still said nothing.

"I asked myself, why go to all this trouble because of Robin? At this point, the hospital had been negligent enough to be responsible for three other women's deaths. But then I realized. It was because of Russel. He'd made a stink about your incompetence and you couldn't have anyone looking into that. You were right to worry. He's filing a lawsuit against Indian Health Services as we speak. Unfortunately, your plan to frame him has failed miserably."

Carole took a deep breath and her bottom lip quivered. "You've got this all wrong." Her voice was quiet.

"Don't worry. You'll have a chance to set me straight," James said. "But we've got more. I'm gonna let Lieutenant Tully take this over for a minute, and I'll be right back. But I will say this first: I wouldn't think about leaving until we've said what we need to say. Because I know you didn't act alone in this, but if you leave this station, you'll be the one bearing sole responsibility and suffering all the consequences. You and you alone."

James stared at Carole for just a beat before turning to leave. Wayne knew he wasn't going far, but it would be foolish, maybe even dangerous, for James to be present for this next part.

When it was just Wayne and Carole, Wayne pulled up a chair and sat down.

"We also know that you've been signing fraudulent consent forms for tubal ligations. We are working on contacting all of the women who might have been affected by this, but we have one definite patient and victim who has attested to the fact that she never signed a consent form for a tubal ligation and yet one was performed on her anyway."

Carole would not look at Wayne. She stared at her hands in her lap instead.

"What we need from you is information about the residents performing these operations without supervision and Dr. Ciccone's role in all of this. As the head of surgery at Shiprock, he must be aware of what's going on. He has offered bonuses and you have been rewarded for bringing in tubal ligation patients."

Carole still said nothing.

"Like Detective Pinter already said, if you refuse to speak, you will bear the legal brunt of this case. On the other hand, if you help us out, we will show leniency." Wayne looked at the woman trying not to cry in front of him. "Come on, Carole. There's no reason to protect him. He's your boss, and you were most likely pressured into doing what he wanted. You've got a son who needs you to avoid as much prison time as you can."

Carole finally let out a small sob. "At first, I was really trying to convince the women it would be the best thing for them. I did want the bonuses. I wanted to send my son to a better school. I already felt like a terrible mom for making him live . . . here. But I didn't have a lot of options after his father left."

Wayne handed her a tissue and she dabbed her eyes.

"Some of the women were easily convinced. Others weren't. I got tired of trying to talk sense into them. I asked Dr. Ciccone if there wasn't some other elective surgery I could focus on. But he said the tubal ligations were the most important."

"Why?" Wayne asked.

"He was always saying things like, 'Look around. There already aren't enough resources here to help these people. They need more and more government assistance every year.' Sometimes he even talked about China's new one-child policy and how we might have to do that here soon."

Wayne was glad James was not in the room for this. He hoped Molly could keep him calm.

"So, Dr. Ciccone is worried about overpopulation," Wayne said.

"I guess. He's had to take on more and more responsibility over the last couple of years and he's been able to do fewer and fewer surgeries. But he didn't want them to stop. He said we were making progress. That's why he started having the residents do the surgeries without him."

"And you're the only one at the hospital who knows about this?"

Carole nodded. "I got paid extra for not saying anything. And the residents don't ask a lot of questions. They might know it's wrong for them to be unsupervised, but they need the hours. And Dr. Ciccone is the one in charge. I think they might think there's a good reason for it."

"Do the residents know these women have not consented?" Wayne asked.

"No."

"But Dr. Ciccone knows," Wayne said.

"He caught me messing with a consent form. It was the first time I had done it. I was so desperate. I couldn't just pull my son out of school." Carole paused and began to sob more violently. Wayne waited a minute.

"Have a drink," he said, gesturing to her soda. She did and Wayne waited for her to be able to speak again.

"I was surprised he wasn't angrier. He said we could help each other and that's when he started putting me on the surgeries with the unsupervised residents. He said I understood the situation and the direness and the needs of the reservation, but really he was just blackmailing me. But he told me to keep doing what I was doing with the consent forms and he would pay me double."

"That's a very difficult situation to be put in, Carole," Wayne said. "I'm guessing he put you in another difficult situation when he directed you to poison Robin Kinsel's peyote and make it look like Russel had done it."

"He was there for the whole thing. For Russel's outburst, I mean. He told me what to do."

"It was smart of you to tell me about all of this," Wayne said. Carole let out a long breath.

"We'll question the residents too to support your statement. Any in particular you believe would tell the truth?"

"There's one who left the hospital. I can give you his name. He was paid off, too. He didn't like what was happening."

"Thank you, Carole."

"It seems like a lot of money for a reservation doctor to be throwing around, doesn't it?" she asked with a desperate sort of laugh. "I kind of always thought he was getting paid by someone else, too. Not just Indian Health Services."

"That's an interesting theory and one I'll certainly look into," Wayne said. Carole nodded and looked down at her hands again.

"Look, I can't promise you'll get out of this completely

unscathed. But I will do my best to limit the crimes you're charged with, and I will speak to the judge to try to get you the shortest sentence possible."

Carole let out another sob, and Wayne knew James was not coming back in. That was fine. The sympathetic angle had worked on Carole and James had no sympathy to offer.

"I'll be the one coming to get you," Wayne said. "You're not to go back to work. You'll take leave. You're not to contact the doctor or else this deal will no longer hold up. Do you understand?"

She dabbed her eyes again. "I understand."

[67]

JAMES

OVER THE NEXT FEW DAYS, the remaining pieces of the puzzle fell into place. They found the resident who supported Carole's claims that the surgeries were being performed unsupervised. In fact, this resident also claimed that he had brought up the exact issue Al was concerned with —bipolar versus monopolar methods. Dr. Ciccone had told him that the bipolar method just wasn't effective enough and despite the additional risks that monopolar presented, they would continue to perform that method.

Wayne was able to track down wire transfers to Dr. Ciccone's bank account from an organization called Over the Limit. They were a national group dedicated to controlling the population by specifically targeting immigrant populations and anyone else they felt was a "burden" to the tax system—including American Indians. This was how the doctor was paying Carole.

It was finally the day of Dr. Ciccone's arrest, and James had decided that he wanted to bring Kay along. She needed to see justice in action. She needed to look the man in the face—the man who was responsible for all her pain. To finally understand that it wasn't her fault.

Molly and Kay drove together and sat in the waiting room while Wayne and James alerted first Dawn and then Al to what was about to happen.

Dr. Ciccone was finishing up in surgery, and when he left the operating room, he had a party waiting for him in the hallway.

"Dr. Ciccone," Wayne said. "I have a warrant for your arrest. You are being charged with negligence in the death of four patients under your treatment. Put your hands behind your back."

The doctor looked at each person in front of him— Wayne in uniform, James in plain clothes, Molly and Kay, a fellow doctor and one of his nurses—but his expression betrayed nothing. Neither shock nor anger.

"Where is Carole Sherborn?" the doctor finally asked.

"In a holding cell," James answered. Wayne moved toward the doctor and started to cuff him as James read him his rights.

Just then, James noticed movement from the corner of his eye, and before he could even register what was happening, Al had brushed past them all and punched the doctor right in his crooked nose.

Molly gasped. Al shook his hand out. "Son of a bitch."

The doctor stumbled, tried to catch himself, but with his hands trapped behind his back, wasn't able to. He fell hard, and at first, he didn't move. *Shit*, James thought. But then the doctor groaned and rolled over, blood leaking from his eyebrow.

"That was quite the trip and fall, Doctor," James said as he walked over to help the man to his feet.

"Trip . . . trip and fall?"

"That's right."

"I was just a-a-assaulted! In your custody!"

James grabbed one arm and Wayne the other. "Assaulted? You must've hit that head real hard."

James and Al exchanged smiles and Kay let out a laugh. "That might be the nicest thing you've ever done for me, Al," she said.

"See!" the doctor shouted as James and Wayne nearly dragged him to the elevators, leaving the group behind. "She saw!"

"We all saw you fall over, Doc. Looked like it hurt like hell." Blood streamed down the doctor's face now, and before the elevator doors closed, James heard Dawn laugh and say, "That was awesome. High five, Dr. Bettis."

DAWN

Dawn had to admit that Detective Pinter had been pretty helpful after completely upending her life. He had set up a meeting with her and the head of WARN, an organization that Dawn wouldn't have dreamed of being associated with a year ago. But James claimed they were already big on job training for high school girls and that they would probably be very open to adding Dawn's nursing program to their offerings. They didn't have the community center space like ONEO did, but they promised to share the high school basement where they held their own meetings. Besides, James's wife had also agreed to share her actual classroom, too, for any evening classes Dawn would be holding, which would probably be all of them now. Dawn was willing to do anything to cut ties with the Codys. Which led her to her next meeting.

She had felt guilty for days after the arrests. How could she not have known what was happening to the women on the reservation? Her patients? The people she cared about the most? But that guilt quickly turned to resolve. Dawn had always known Carole was a piece of shit, and Dr. Bettis had been the one to discover exactly what was going on. Another Diné medical provider. That was no coincidence. They needed more nurses, more doctors like them.

And they needed to be wary of these hospital programs. Dawn had never liked the twilight birth, but she trusted it even less now that she had seen the terrible things happening right under her own nose. They needed alternative methods. The option of natural remedies in tandem with Western medicine. They needed to listen to their patients, to work with them. They needed to keep them safe.

The trading post was empty when Dawn arrived. It was after her shift, early in the morning. She could smell the coffee brewing as soon as she opened the door and inhaled its nutty fragrance. She found Clarence Draper hanging a new rug on the wall. He looked over his shoulder.

"Welcome to the trading post," he said before going back to his work. Dawn walked over. The rug he was hanging looked different from the black and white and brown rugs surrounding it. This one was rich in greens and blues. It had a calming effect.

"That's a beautiful rug," she said.

"It is." He got up from his knees and took a few steps back to admire it. "Are you interested in purchasing one?"

"I'm actually here to speak with you."

Clarence turned to face her, and she reached out a hand to shake. "My name is Dawn Harvey. I'm a nurse over at the hospital in Shiprock, and I've been working with investigators on Robin Kinsel's case."

Clarence shook her hand. "I still can't believe what happened to those women."

"I know. And I'm sorry. I should've done more. I should've known." Dawn paused to stop herself from choking up. She swallowed a few times before continuing. "You and Robin were close, weren't you?"

"We were business associates. She was a church member. A good woman. I miss her."

"You two had a program to help addicts, didn't you?" she asked.

Clarence eyed her carefully, so she went on. "I'm asking because I understand that Robin was making her own connections in Texas. She was purchasing peyote for the two of you without having to go through the Codys. I'm looking to do the same. I can't associate with that family any longer, but my patients in labor rely on the peyote for pain management."

Clarence nodded slowly. "I see. Unfortunately, I can't encourage that. I know now that Robin wasn't murdered, but the Codys did threaten her. They still might have harmed her in some way if they had gotten the chance. I can't ask you to put yourself in the same situation."

"I won't be harmed," Dawn said, smirking. "I might be the one person on the reservation the Codys are afraid of."

Clarence's eyebrows went up. "And why is that? Perhaps I ought to be afraid then, too."

Dawn laughed. "My brother isn't too happy with them. And that's putting it mildly. He's in federal prison, and he's got some pretty dangerous connections. He has sent a message. The Codys know not to mess with me."

Clarence seemed to find this amusing. His face lifted, and he grinned. "Well then, when do we leave for Texas?"

MOLLY

MOLLY AND JOEY sat on the hood of Joey's Jeep parked on the banks of the river. Molly picked at the friendship bracelet on her wrist. She and Paula had made them together days ago. She had admitted to Paula that she'd been jealous of her earlier on in the case and then Paula said that she was a little jealous of Molly and Joey and then they made a pact that they would never again get jealous of each other. For any reason. Ever.

Molly took a deep breath. "My dad doesn't think I should tell you this. He doesn't think you'll believe me, but I'm going to anyway."

"Is it about Byron Cody?" Joey asked.

"Yes." Molly was surprised he knew.

"I'm not going to start hanging around with him and selling drugs, you know." He nudged Molly with his elbow and cracked a smile.

She laughed. "Well, that's good to hear. It's just . . . be careful."

"I know."

"My dad said he can be really charming. But I think you should know that he was the one who threatened Robin Kinsel. He didn't like that she was helping Clarence with his addict program. He *wants* people to be addicts, you know?"

Joey was quiet. Squinting at something in the distance.

"I guess that makes sense," he finally said.

"Are you mad now?" Molly asked in a quiet voice.

"At you?"

She nodded.

Joey grinned. "Of course not. I sort of like you, actually. And I have a feeling you sort of like me, too."

Molly blushed.

"Plus, you totally saved my life that night at the NAC meeting," Joey went on.

Molly giggled and shoved Joey just a little. He scooched closer to her and looked her in the eyes.

"So, we're probably already past this. But what do you say, Molly Pinter? Are you my girlfriend or what?"

"Yeah," Molly said. "I'm your girlfriend."

Joey looked at her again with a sly smile on his lips. "Do I have to ask?"

"Nope," she said. "You don't." And then, Joey kissed her.

When Molly got home, she found Kay under a big blanket on the couch watching some horror movie. Molly crawled under the blanket beside her, her legs touching Kay's.

"I'm officially Joey's girlfriend," Molly said after a few minutes.

Kay looked down at her and smiled. It was nice to see Kay smile. "That's awesome," she said.

"And I told him that Byron was the one to threaten Robin."

"How did he take that?" Kay asked.

"Good. He believed me, I'm pretty sure."

"Molly's first boyfriend." Kay's smile faded. She closed her eyes. "Wayne told me what you said to your dad when he wanted to kill that doctor."

Molly didn't respond. Kay kept her eyes closed but spoke again. "About being the best grandfather one day."

She opened her eyes and they immediately welled up with tears. "Can I be the best grandmother, too?"

Molly sat up. "Of course." She leaned over to hug Kay and then stayed there, lying on her chest, her head to the side. She listened to Kay's sobs and watched a person on the television creeping through a dark, scary hallway. "There is no question in my mind that you will be a legendary grandmother one day."

Kay's sobbing slowly quieted. "Thank you," she said.

Private the dog came over to the couch, his tail wagging slowly. He put his cold nose next to Molly's and Molly giggled. She scratched the top of his head.

"He's been great," Kay said. "Such a gentle companion to me."

"I think that deserves a promotion," Molly said to Private. "I'll talk to the sergeant."

[70]

WAYNE

EVEN AFTER ALL THESE years on the job, Wayne still hadn't stopped trying to win people over. He was aware of just how many people on the reservation disliked and distrusted cops. Particularly tribal police. Their history was a complicated one. Too often, tribal police had worked with the US government and against its own people. Wayne, and the rest of the force, were still seen as traitors to many. He didn't begrudge them for it. But he did continue to try to win them over. As naïve as it might be.

Which was why he stood in front of a room of young women now, faces that were clearly unamused, cynical, even angry to see a police officer at their meeting. He would try anyway.

"Good afternoon, ladies," he said to them. In the back, chewing on a pencil, he spotted Paula. She grinned, winked, and gave him a thumbs-up. He smiled back at her. He'd had no idea she would be here.

"I'm here today, first of all, to make a personal appeal." Patricia Dawes stood at the side of the room, arms crossed, leaning against the wall. Her expression was neutral but alert. She was concentrating on Wayne. He probably had a time limit before she would cut him off.

"I know many of you have a fraught relationship with law enforcement. And I understand why. I am trying to build a police force on the reservation that is unlike police forces of the past. I want tribal police to work for and with Diné to help and protect us all." He paused. Took a deep breath.

"We don't have enough officers. We need more and so I'm recruiting. What we really need are female officers."

He watched their reactions. Eyes wide, glances at one another.

"We've only ever had one female officer complete the academy. We need more. But they need to be tough. Mentally and physically. I know you ladies are tough. I know how hard you work, how much you care about our people. I've seen what you've been able to accomplish in recent years. I need that sort of grit on the force."

The room was silent, and Wayne had no idea what they were thinking. He saw Patricia check her watch.

"On an organizational level," Wayne went on, "I would love it if WARN would consider a recruitment program like you've got for other occupations here on the reservation. There are young Diné women out there who would be interested in a career in law enforcement. If WARN would be willing to partner with the Shiprock police, we could find these women. Train them. Provide them with an occupation, a decent salary. And make us all better and safer for it."

Wayne got nothing in response except one woman clearing her throat. Which was fine. He wasn't expecting applause.

"Well, that's all. Patricia here has my contact information if anyone decides they're interested."

A few seats creaked as women shifted positions.

"Thank you for your time."

It was foggy when Wayne showed up at the station the next morning at six a.m., so it took him a moment before he noticed a figure standing by the door. He walked slower. More carefully. Rested his hand on his firearm. Finally, he could see the faint outline of a young woman. It was Paula.

"You're up early," he said. "Is everything okay?"

She stood rigidly. Her expression serious.

"Lieutenant Tully, I would like to nominate myself for the next class of tribal police officers. I think I would make a pretty damn good cop, sir."

Wayne wasn't sure if he wanted to laugh or cry. This kid was something else. He pulled himself together and took a deep breath.

"I would love to have you, Paula. But I need you to graduate high school first."

"Yes, sir," Paula said.

"And I need you to get good grades these next two years."

"Yes, sir."

"And maybe in the meantime, we could train together. Get you into shape. Teach you some hand-to-hand combat."

"Shit yeah, sir."

"And you've got to cut down on the swearing."

Paula cracked a smile now. "I'll try my best, sir."

Wayne smiled too. "Enough with the 'sirs.' There will be time for that later."

"All right, *dude*."

Wayne laughed. A big, loud laugh. He stepped toward Paula and pulled her in for a hug.

"This makes me damn happy, you know that?"

"The language!" Paula lamented. "My ears! They're bleeding!"

Wayne pulled away. "Well, since you're already up, want to help me with something?"

Paula grinned. "Unpaid labor. Typical."

Wayne shook his head. Got out his keys to the front door. "Come on."

[71]

JAMES

It was the first cool evening they'd had in months. Fall was coming. Wayne and James sat on the top row at the rodeo arena. The show was long over and everyone had cleared out, but James and Wayne stuck around to chat. James pulled two beers from the inside of his jacket, racked them open. Handed one to Wayne.

"Take a load off, LT."

"Damn. That boy can ride a bull," Wayne said. "Beat his record tonight, too."

"And on top of that, he's got a lawsuit that's gonna turn out pretty well," James chuckled. They both sipped their beers.

"You holding up all right?" Wayne asked.

"Ah, I guess. Not what we had hoped for, you know?"

"I know the feeling," Wayne said.

"I know you do. I'm glad we've got you and Barb."

"I had to restrain her, you know. When she found out." Wayne smiled. "She about set that hospital on fire."

The two of them laughed at that. "Glad we didn't have to arrest your wife for arson."

The night was quiet. James heard a car backfire in the distance.

"I cannot believe Byron Cody is a federal informant," Wayne said.

"Not sure he will be for long," James said. "That information is out there now. There will be whispers. Byron won't be the asset he once was."

"You think Cecil knows?" Wayne asked.

"That's a good question, LT. A good question." James sipped again. "I think we're close, you know. We just gotta keep our ears and eyes open. The opportunity. It's comin'. They're vulnerable now."

Wayne sighed. "Lord knows I've been patient."

"I know you're disappointed that we've got nothin' but a measly vandalism charge at this point. One we're not even gonna pursue. But you just be patient a little while longer. We've got people now that are pretty damn eager to see the Codys topple."

Wayne sipped and made an "ah" sound after. "You're right." He looked sideways at James and grinned. "So, Molly's got a boyfriend."

James shook his head. "Don't even get me started, LT."

One Sunday morning, James woke before Kay and Molly. He made the coffee, the eggs, some bacon. Then he hurried outside and got the horses ready.

He woke Molly up first. "Hey. Get up." He was right near her face, shaking her shoulder. She groaned.

"We're takin' Kay on a ride."

She squinted at him. "Fine."

He smiled at her. "That's the spirit. I've got bacon and coffee."

He left Molly's room and went back into his own. Kay looked so peaceful he almost called the whole thing off, but he knew it would do her a world of good. It would do them all a world of good.

He brushed her hair away from her face, leaned down, and kissed her forehead. "Good morning, beautiful," he whispered.

"Mmmm," she said.

"I've got breakfast ready. We're takin' the horses out."

She opened her eyes. "They need to be brushed."

"Already done," he said. "And now they're eatin' their breakfasts too. Come on."

She stared at him for a moment without saying anything. There was the slightest smile on her face. "You're a good man, James Pinter."

"Even better with you."

AUTHOR'S NOTE

Between 1970 and 1976, physicians sterilized between 25 and 42 percent of Native American women of childbearing age. Concerns about overpopulation had led the United States government to embrace family planning, including tubal ligations for Native American women.

Many women wanted and welcomed the procedure, but there was enough concern about the rate at which they were being performed to warrant a federal investigation. This investigation only looked at official medical records but still found several issues with the consent process. Although hospitals were supposed to adhere to a seventy-two-hour waiting period after consent was given, this was often violated. The consent forms did not explain the risks of the procedure or offer alternative birth control methods as they were supposed to, and they did not explain that the women's decision had no bearing on their qualification for government assistance.

The official government investigation raised concerns among many Native American communities, who felt it didn't go far enough. This, along with women's claims that their procedures had been forced, led a Choctaw and Cherokee physician, Connie Pinkerton-Uri, to lead her own investigation. She found that in one Indian Health Services (IHS) hospital in Oklahoma, for every four babies born, physicians performed a tubal ligation or hysterectomy on one of the mothers. During her interviews, she discovered that many of the women had still been medicated when they gave consent, others did not understand that the procedures were not reversable, and still others had been afraid to argue with the doctor for fear of losing their benefits.

Other Native-led investigations in other parts of the country found that women were under intense pressure from medical staff to get the procedure done, did not understand the medical jargon, and in many cases, could not understand or read English and were offered no interpreters. In some instances, the procedures were entirely forced. Women attested to the fact that they had gone into the hospital for unrelated procedures and did not find out they had been sterilized for months or years later. One case in Montana involved two sixteen-year-old girls who went in for appendectomies and received tubal ligations without their knowledge.

Women of All Red Nations, or WARN, was created in 1978, and a large part of their mission was to bring these atrocities to light and to fight for reproductive rights for Native American women. WARN members testified in 1981 at the United Nations in Geneva and criticized the US government's efforts to control the population. They complained of poorly funded IHS hospitals that had high physician turnover rates and relied on inexperienced doctors learning their trade on Native women's bodies. One woman said, "They use Indians as guinea pigs."

The character Dawn Harvey was not based on any one person, but she was inspired by the hard work and persistence of real Native American women at the time, including Ursula Knoki-Wilson, whose mother was a Navajo midwife and who graduated from the University of Utah's nurse-midwifery program in 1976; she went on to work at an Indian Health Services hospital in Chinle, Arizona—one of the first Navajo to do so. For those interested in supporting the ongoing work of Navajo nurse midwives, please check out Nicolle Gonzales and the Changing Woman Initiative in Albuquerque, New Mexico, at www.cwi-health.org. Gonzales is a Navajo certified nurse midwife who plans to open the first Native American birthing center in the US.

In 1968, a book called *The Population Bomb* incited world panic about the future of an overpopulated Earth. China's one-child policy—implemented in 1979—along with India's mass compulsory sterilization of lower-class men in 1975 were among the official state-sanctioned programs to counteract what many thought was a crucial problem. Although the organization Over the Limit in this story is a product of my imagination, there were organizations in the United States at this time dedicated to controlling the population, often through questionable practices and often targeting already vulnerable members of society.

WARN was born out of the American Indian Movement, and many of AIM's leaders were, in fact, imprisoned by the time this story takes place in 1980. However, not all of these arrests occurred because of the Washington, DC, protest at the Bureau of Indian Affairs. Often called the "Trail of

Broken Treaties," nearly seven hundred Native Americans from more than two hundred tribes traveled across the country to try to reinstate the practice of making treaties on a tribal or regional basis. In that regard, the protest was unsuccessful. It did, however, raise national awareness of the various broken treaties and socioeconomic issues the tribe members were protesting. This occurred in 1972, years earlier than the timeline described in this book.

Amada Sanchez Cardenas was a real peyotera who passed away in 2005 at the age of one hundred. She was loved and cherished by many Native American Church members as well as by members of her community, and the stories told about her in this book are true. Although she is a friend to the Codys in this story, I would like to imagine it was only because she didn't know their true criminal nature. In real life, she was known to be an upstanding, law-abiding citizen and was known to win over even the most unlikely friends, including a conservative South Texas judge who made her and her husband among the first federally licensed peyote dealers in the country. Amada's husband died in 1967, leaving her to take over and run the business for the remainder of her life.

Though I researched reservation life and Diné history thoroughly, this story is not meant to be a comprehensive account of life as a Native American or life on a reservation. As a white American of European descent, I couldn't possibly provide the authenticity that a native writer can. I encourage readers to seek out these stories, as well. Some of my favorite Indigenous authors are: Louise Erdrich, Tommy Orange, Jon Hickey, Diane Wilson, Arlene L. Walker, and Morgan Talty, though there are countless others.

While researching this story, I read the following books: *Diné: A History of the Navajos* by Peter Iverson; *Dinéjí Na'Nitin: Navajo Traditional Teachings and History* by Robert S. McPherson; and *Reproduction on the Reservation: Pregnancy, Childbirth, and Colonialism in the Long Twentieth Century* by Brianna Theobald.

Thank you to my brother-in-law, Joe Boyle, who is one hell of an Army investigator. Thank you to my cousin Jess, who is an incredible nurse and who helped me comb through the medical details of this case in order to make it as believable and realistic as possible. To my readers: If you love true crime, you need to check out her hilarious podcast, *Wife of Crime*, available on your favorite listening platform. And of course, thank you to my amazing husband, who suffers through all my first drafts and whose suggestions and advice I treasure above all others.

Last but certainly not least, thank you to the Bookstagram community! You all continue to amaze me with your dedication and support. Thank you so much for your lovely reviews and shares. It means the world to me.

ABOUT THE AUTHOR

Lisa Boyle has been writing stories for as long as she can remember. Born and raised in Finksburg, Maryland, Lisa received bachelor's degrees in journalism and international affairs from Northeastern University in Boston, Massachusetts. Lisa has held many different jobs over the years from cheesemonger, to educator at the U.S.S. Constitution Museum. Lisa lives in South Carolina with her husband and daughter. The first book in this series, *In the Silence of Decay* won the 2024 IPPY Gold Medal Award for Best Regional Fiction: West Mountain and was a finalist for the New Mexico/Arizona Book Awards, crime fiction category.

Sign up for Lisa Boyle's newsletter here, and be the first to know when book four of the Pinter Series is available for preorder!

Did you love this book? Don't forget to leave a review!